NOMADS

Amid the rootless drifters drawn to the California sun stalks an ancient, restless terror. Among the hookers and bikers, junkies and losers of the hard-core fringe dwell beings of unspeakable evil who thirst for human souls. Into this twilight world of unrelenting fear come three unknowing victims: *Jean-Charles Pommier*, a French-Canadian anthropologist who has spent his life observing the world's wanderers. His lovely wife, *Veronique*, who fights to keep him from a horror she cannot understand. And *Eileen Flax*, a young doctor fleeing her past, who finds herself in a nightmare from which there is no escape.

CHELSEA QUINN YARBRO, author of *Dead and Buried* and *The Saint Germain Chronicles*, is an acknowledged master of vivid, richly woven horror. *Nomads* is a haunting, harrowing excursion into contemporary terror.

NOMADS

Novelization by
Chelsea Quinn Yarbro

From a screenplay by
John McTiernan

BANTAM BOOKS
TORONTO · NEW YORK · LONDON · SYDNEY

The characters and settings of this story are imaginary and neither represent nor are intended to represent actual persons, events, or places.

NOMADS
A Bantam Book / May 1984

ISBN 0-553- 23422-6

Published simultaneously in the United States and Canada

this is for
Suzy and Steve Charnas
with deepest thanks for the brunch

Once again the photograph caught his attention.

There on the ice a single Eskimo stood, the vast, blank emptiness around him so stark that the frigid wind seemed to come off the shiny paper. The Eskimo had been photographed at a distance, so that his isolation was almost complete.

And yet—there was a sense about him, an uneasiness that had little to do with hunting. It appeared now, as it had when Pommier had first seen the man and taken his picture, that the lone figure was—he studied the hunter intently—was *trespassing.*

ONE

When the phone rang in the dead of night, Eileen Flax came half awake, disoriented, the last shreds of her dream still in Boston with the blame and bitterness. Then there was a second ring and she reached out for it, now fully aware she was in Los Angeles, snatching a few hours of much-needed sleep on a gurney in one of the outpatient examining rooms. As she picked up the receiver, she fumbled for the switch on the wall, blinking in the shivering, fluorescent light.

"Now?" she asked the excited voice on the line, hearing the deep, unwieldy sound she made. "No, I understand. I'll be down in a minute." She started to rub her face as she put the phone down. Reluctantly she glanced at the clock on the wall. "Three-twenty," she mumbled as if saying the words would make it go away. As she moved, the gurney slid away from the wall and she struggled to keep from falling. "God, three-twenty."

In the restroom she splashed water on her face and peered at herself in the mirror. She was mildly surprised to see that her features had not altered; she had half-expected some transformation to confirm the sense of rootlessness that had possessed her since her husband had walked out. But no. She was the same. Her hair was mussed, her lab coat rumpled, her eyes slightly pink from lack of sleep, and she felt her age keenly, yet she still knew herself. With a rueful sigh and an attempt at a smile, she adjusted her name tag that identified her as a resident and headed for the corridor.

There was a wait for the elevator, even at this hour, and when she got into the cab, she found two night orderlies with the last of the food-service wagons. Idly Flax tried to imagine who would need food at this time of night. The two young men were laughing and joking with typical grisly humor, and every time one of them slapped the wagon for emphasis, the metal trays clattered and banged like badly tuned gongs, making Flax wince.

By the time she got out of the elevator at the emergency room, Flax almost welcomed the commotion and distress that awaited her.

"Hurry up!" one of the interns called to her as he caught sight of her in the fluorescent glare.

"Coffee," Flax responded, already moving with more purpose toward the only examining cubicle that was occupied. "What have we got?"

The intern, lanky, young, and so exhausted that he was being carried along on nervous energy alone, brought her a Styrofoam cup filled with a dark, silty liquid from the coffee urn. "The cops brought him in fifteen, twenty minutes ago—"

"Why'd you take so long to call me down?" she interrupted.

"Wait'll you get a look at him. They thought at first he'd been mugged. He's got lacerations and contusions up the kazoo. They wanted to get a better look at the damage, you know? Before they did anything more. He's still a mess."

"Where'd they pick him up?" The caffeine was beginning to take hold; Flax felt that first rush that passed for additional energy, like the fluttering of moth wings in her chest.

"The cops said they'd pulled him off the beach, out by the Santa Monica pier."

"A drowner?" Flax asked, and almost finished the coffee while she listened to the intern answer.

"No. They think . . . he might have fallen off the pier,

or got thrown, maybe. It's probably some kind of overdose, judging by . . . everything."

Flax sensed the young man's uncertainty. "Well? What's wrong? What *is* it?"

The intern shrugged, irritated and perplexed at once. "It's . . . well, he doesn't look the type. Son o' bitch's built like a boxer . . . not big, you know, but strong, even cut up and bruised and . . . took five of us to put him on the examination table. And he's strung *way* out. We can't even get eye contact."

Awake enough now to be intrigued, Flax frowned in concentration. "Is he violent?"

"That's one word for it. I know this, if I was the mugger who beat him up, I'd probably be in worse shape than he is now. Of course, that could be drugs, but . . . I don't know. I doubt it." He looked about uneasily. "Not all of it, anyway."

"What does the lab say it is?" She was moving again, all the while running through the various overdose cases she had seen, hoping to find an edge in dealing with this emergency case. She reached out to move aside two of the orderlies who stood in the entrance to the cubicle.

"They're working on it. Be careful, Flax. He's in bad, bad shape. It's like he doesn't even see us." He pressed after her. "We got saliva and blood, so far, but nothing more. He looks a bit dehydrated, but we don't know for sure. . . ."

Flax heard little of this last because a sound erupted from the cubicle, a terrible cry that was compounded of terror and rage.

"He's been going on like that since—" the intern said more loudly.

"But . . ." Flax objected, trying to make out what she was hearing.

"Yeah. We don't know what it is. It's too fast." The intern made a face as they came up to the examination table and looked at the man being held down.

One of the two policemen, a large, somber-faced Mexican, was bending low over the struggling, howling figure. "Alto, alto! Cómo se llama? A dónde vive? Cómo se llama?" It was as persistent and mindless as a waiter's smirk, and made no impact on the patient.

The other cop, a burly young man, stood off to one side with an icepack pressed to his face.

"That's another problem," the intern went on as he followed Flax's glance. "You should've seen him. His clothes were soaked with blood. I mean *soaked*. He looked like he'd been swimming in a vat of it. We cleaned him up, as much as we could. There were a couple lacerations, nothing important. Where the rest of it came from, who knows, and . . ."

Flax had been listening to the patient as his voice rose and fell and the incomprehensible words tumbled out of him. "Is that French?"

The intern stopped, his head on one side. "It could be. I don't know the accent. And it's so fast. . . ."

By now Flax had been able to pick out a few more words. "Yeah, it's French. Not what I learned in school." She put her hand to her head, a frown forming between her eyes. "Who do we have around here who speaks French, that kind of French?"

The intern gave a hopeless gesture and tried to continue over the sounds. "The lab said it would be another fifteen minutes before they can get an analysis on what's in him. Taking care of him until then is not going to be easy, but if we can calm him down enough to start detoxifi—"

One of the nurses who had kept watch over the patient pulled away the last of several bloody towels and started toward the door, almost bumping into Flax.

"Sorry, nurse," she said, stepping out of the way. She wished she could get a clear look at the man, but there were so many people standing around him that only an occasional thrashing knee or elbow was visible.

"It's okay. I'm just finishing up." She gave that weary twitch of her mouth that was intended as a smile, then moved out of the cubicle, going quickly down the hall; there were corrugated, faintly rust-colored stains where her shoes pressed the floor.

"Look . . . Keenan," Flax said, reading the name on the intern's tag, "I want a chance to—"

Keenan was on a rush, and would not be interrupted just yet. "His pupils are constricted. The skin is clammy. Pressure's up. The motor responses look like PCP, but I'm not sure. I don't know, and we haven't got enough out of him to check, and until the lab gives us the report, you don't want to try to sedate him, just in case it's counterindicated."

Flax noticed the *you* in Keenan's warning, and shook her head, asking, "What did the cops say? Anything we can use?"

The younger officer handed his icepack over to a nurse who had just arrived at the cubicle.

"That's a bad bruise, officer," the nurse said to him in a determined tone, her eyes challenging him to object.

"I don't need anything," the young cop muttered, shoving the nurse aside and going to the examination table.

Flax saw one of the patient's arms strain and was appalled to see he had been handcuffed. She turned around to face Keenan, barely able to keep her words calm. "Who ordered him handcuffed?"

"Something had to be done. He slugged two of the orderlies and you saw what that cop's face is like." His protest had just enough petulance in it that Flax knew Keenan recognized he was in the wrong. "Look, doctor, we didn't have time to bring in proper restraints. The cops had the cuffs on him already, and I thought it was better to stop him—"

"But you've sent for restraints, haven't you?" Flax demanded, and was not surprised when the question met with silence. "I think you'd better do it right away, Keenan. Don't you?"

"Yeah..." he mumbled. Then he straightened up and defended himself. "This is emergency service, and we don't always have the chance to do things by the book. The cuffs had to be used."

"But not anymore," Flax persisted.

"And I know you're new. I didn't mean to put you on the spot like this. But hell! If I sedate him without an okay from Neurology, my ass is in the sling." It was as much of an explanation as he would give her.

"Your ass is secure," Flax told him. "Get those restraints, set up an emergency scan so we can find out where all that blood is coming from, and see if you can find someone who speaks good French. Maybe a priest, too." She took one last sip of the coffee and found that it was cold. "Yikk. A priest. He's probably Catholic, if he's French."

"A priest? You don't think that... is he that bad?... You know..." Keenan burst out, his protest dwindling away in his distress.

"I don't know what to think. I haven't had the chance to examine my patient yet, remember?" This last pointed comment struck home.

"I'll see about the scan. I'll arrange it," Keenan said, grateful for something to take him away from the emergency room. He hurried off.

Flax tapped the nearest nurse on the shoulder and stepped up beside the examination table as the other woman moved away. At last Flax looked down; for all her experience she had to stifle her dismay.

The man on the table screamed, the sound ragged and becoming hoarse.

"He's in pretty bad shape," the younger policeman declared with pride, as if there had been a contest and he, having only a bruise to show for it, was the winner.

"I can see that," Flax answered, and felt the fear that

had been wriggling its cold tentacles down her spine fade under a mixture of anger and sympathy. "And he needs help." Saying those few, mundane words steadied her and she was able to look at her patient with more detachment. Swallowing hard, she put her hand on his arm and felt the muscles tighten into knots in response. Assuming a confidence that she did not feel, she kept her hand on his arm, speaking quietly and sensibly over the shouts and whispers in that unfamiliar, rapid French. "Well, what happened to you, then? Hum? Do you want to tell me about it?" She reached for her stethoscope, though she already knew what she would hear; his pulse showed clearly in the distended veins on his neck and face. She went through the motions methodically, needing the reassurance of that ordinary, habitual, rational act to keep her mind on her work.

The younger cop looked at the patient with a mixture of repugnance and triumph in his face. "Whatever happened to him, it must've been some party." He turned toward his partner for support. "We got the call less'n an hour ago. Somebody saw him stagger across Ocean Avenue toward the park. They said he was limping, but I ask you."

"With bruises like this, he might very well limp," Flax said, giving the officer no encouragement. "I thought he was on the pier."

"Under it," the policeman answered with a tinge of resentment in his voice. "By the time we caught up with him, he was almost at the water." As if to justify this delay, he added, "We must've wasted a good ten minutes looking around the boardwalk for him. That's where most of the junkies go."

"What made you think he was a junkie?" Flax asked, more to keep the policeman talking than to gather real information.

"Aw, come on, lady, look at him!" He made an emphatic gesture with his hands, almost touching the patient's forehead.

"Hey . . ." Flax cautioned him just as the man let out a long, desolate wail and wrenched himself as close to sitting upright as his cuffed hands would allow. The metal clanged against the metal of the table legs.

The policeman yelled and reached for his nightstick, his face turning from confident to alarmed. Only the restraining touch of his partner kept him from lashing out at the patient. An orderly who had just come to the entrance of the cubicle was even more upset; the tray of slides and vials he carried went flying, the glass splintering where it struck.

On the examination table, the patient writhed, his wrists starting to bleed where the force of his movements dug the cuffs into his skin. One of his legs kicked free and his foot slammed into the nurse's shoulder. He was screaming without words, like a cornered animal.

"*Stop it!* Damn it, *stop it!*" Flax shouted, almost unheard above the chaos. "All of you!" She pushed nearer the man on the table. "He's tearing his wrists! Stay *away* from him! *Get back!*"

The younger cop had recovered enough to feel embarrassed, and as if to make up for it, he lunged at the patient as his partner shouted in protest.

"No!" Flax cried out, and for the first time in her life used aikido outside of class. As she moved the policeman away from the table, she felt oddly pleased with herself that she had remembered this from a course she had taken two years ago. When she had gotten the policeman out of the cubicle, she let go of him and smoothed the front of her lab coat. "Officer, you've got to excuse us. All these people are . . . making it worse for that man. I'm sure you won't mind waiting outside." She gave him no time to respond. "Please. Thank you." Then she caught sight of the orderly who was scrambling about in a half-crouched posture, searching for more splinters of glass. "You, too, orderly."

"Larry," he offered.

"Larry. Out." She was relieved to see the Mexican policeman leave voluntarily.

"But the glass," Larry was saying, waving his hands toward the floor. "Somebody's got to clean . . ."

Flax brought her hand up for silence and forced herself to be patient. "Go," she said quietly.

Larry squared his shoulders and gave an uneasy glance back into the cubicle where the unknown man had stopped screaming and was instead growling what sounded like curses. "I'll be right out here. I know some karate, if . . ." He looked once at the policemen, as if he was not sure they would be able to deal adequately with the patient should he become violent again.

"Thank you," Flax said in a low voice that was intended to calm the cops as well—she had noticed the way Larry regarded them—and motioned to the nurses in the cubicle. "I think it would be best if there's only one person around him." Her voice was as reasonable as she could make it. "He's too frightened."

"If you want, doctor," the oldest nurse said doubtfully. "But it cuts both ways. He's likely to get active without warning."

"I'll call," she promised the plump woman, and stood aside to permit the nurses to leave.

And then she was alone with the patient. He lay half on his side now, trying to draw himself up into a fetal position, though he could not because of the way the handcuffs held him down, arms extended to the sides and back, a perverted crucifixion. He was clammy with sweat, his eyes moved in febrile starts, the tendons stood out on his hands, and when Flax came closer, he kicked out at her with his one free foot, giving an anguished yelp.

"Easy," Flax whispered. "Easy. There's nothing to be afraid of. I'm here to help you. I'm a doctor. Eileen Flax . . ." She came around the table to his head, out of range of his legs and feet. Very carefully she touched his forehead, making sure that her hand was steady and firm without being hard, just as if he were a captive or wounded animal, incapable of understanding anything she said. To her relief, the patient tolerated her touch. "That's better," she said aloud, talking to herself. "That's good."

Under her hand, the man trembled and made a whimpering sound that was somehow worse than his shouts and thrashings had been.

At another time, Flax thought, she might have found him attractive, if he had been groomed and sociable, untouched by terror. He had large, smoke-colored eyes, short-trimmed fine brown hair fading to gray, a square face and well-defined features, a thin-lipped mouth set in a grimace but might have a humorous smile. His body was sturdy; his hands were torn now, but had the look of good care. Bruises and lacerations marked him like primitive ritual tattoos.

"Boy, you've been in quite a scrap, haven't you? . . . a regular brawl. What happened to you? . . . humm? . . . Who did this to you?" She paid little attention to her own words, wanting only to keep up a steady stream of soothing, human sound. Carefully she slipped her otoscope out of her lab-coat pocket and positioned it to check his pupils. "Now, I'm going to shine light on your face, but it won't be for very long . . . you don't have to be afraid of it . . . this is just to find out if your eyes respond . . . if you can see at all." She leaned over him with care, moving without hurry or abrupt movements. "I sure hope you aren't blind . . . we're going to have a hell of a job if you are."

As she turned on the pencil-fine beam, she noticed that he had gone quiet at last, and that there was a new feel to him, as if he was *waiting*. . . . The light struck his pupil, his head shuddered, and his eyes closed convulsively; a spasm went through him as if he had been struck.

Then his eyes opened again, and stared up at her.

"Hey . . ." Flax murmured, drawing back a bit.

Bloodshot, dark as storm clouds, he caught and held her in his stare, and without thinking, she leaned closer to him, hardly daring to breathe.

He is seeing me, she thought. He is *really* seeing me.

"Perfide!" he shouted. "C'est la *chasse!*"

Flax reached to restrain him, determined to calm him without intervention. As she touched his chest, she felt renewed strength in him, and alarm spread through her.

But before she could move away from him, he thrust outward with an enormous, inhuman scream, and tore one of his hands free of the handcuff that held him. With a burst of adrenaline-fed power, he lurched upward, reaching wildly outward for balance.

As the examination table started to topple, he flung his bloody arm around her shoulder and neck, and carried her and the table to the floor with him, his open mouth pressed close to her ear, the crash of their fall drowning out the tortured cries he made as they fell.

Not until Flax struck the last bits of shattered glass on the seamless vinyl did she scream, as much from shock as pain. She felt the weight of the patient on her, and the examination table across her thighs, but neither made sense to her for an instant as she stifled a second scream.

The first had been enough. Four nurses, two orderlies, and the older policeman all strove to get into the cubicle, all of them trying to get the others to leave as insistently as they struggled to remain.

"Jesus *Christ!*" Larry shouted. "He's attacked Dr. Flax."

Flax tried to speak, to protest this accusation, but there was too much confusion around her, and her own thoughts were still ringing with the sound of the patient's voice in her ear. She made a vague, swimming motion with her one free hand, unaware that it was already slick with blood.

"Help!" the oldest nurse insisted as she bent down toward Flax. "She needs help. Move that table, can't you, someone?"

The policeman bent to lift the table, and grunted at the weight of it. "Madre Maria," he muttered, trying to get a better grip on it.

"Wait!" Larry shouted, grabbing the Mexican's arm. "The . . . guy's still . . . uh . . . attached to it."

"What?"

"Oh, God!"

"But how . . ."

"Shit!"

The babble gew louder, more confused. Flax felt hands under her arms and heard the scrape of metal against the floor. She wanted to protest this handling, to say something for the defense and protection of her patient, but she could not get the attention of those around her. At last, she was dragged to her feet, a bit unsteadily, and she met the worried, troubled, unhappy expressions of those who crowded around her.

"Dr. Flax . . ." one of the nurses said, not quite pointing to her ear.

Flax gave a shaky laugh as she tried to touch it. "I think he bit me."

One of the younger nurses exclaimed at this, but the oldest merely clicked her tongue in exasperation. "You have that looked at."

Flax nodded absently as she tried to see what had become of her patient. "I must check him . . ." she said to those around her, trying to get near him.

The intern, Keenan, had come back into the cubicle, restraints draped over his arm. He had gone down on one knee beside the unknown man, and Flax could see that his fingers rested against the patient's neck.

"What is . . ." she began, and the rest fell silent.

Keenan frowned, ignoring Flax. Only the arm of the

patient was visible, the wrist torn, the rest of the flesh bruised.

Flax took two restless steps forward, then stopped still as Keenan looked up at her, his face ashen.

"I . . . Jesus, he's dead."

TWO

Half an hour later the emergency room was quiet once again; only Ted Oldsman was busy, and he was stitching up the tear in Eileen Flax's ear. The interns and nurses and orderlies had gone off to other duties, much to Flax's relief, and she was able to regain her composure under Oldsman's lighthearted banter.

"So," he was saying, making the word an outrageous pun as he made another stitch in her ear, "you made up your mind what you're going to call it yet?"

"You mean this?" she asked, not quite daring to touch anywhere near her head yet. "For the first week, I think I'll call it *swell*."

Oldsman leered at her over her shoulder. He liked Flax and he knew how difficult it was for her to maintain her lighthearted attitude. "Wait. Just wait'll you see the *weekend*."

Flax pretended dismay. "Oh, no. Not that. I'm *off* on the—"

"Aaah, my pretty, then they'll get you next week." He fell silent as he set the last of his stiches. "You know that my ex-wife had the gall to do needlepoint?"

"Look, Oldsman . . ." Flax began, somewhat more seriously.

"Weekends here, they make tonight look like nursery school. This was nothing but rambunctious kids, compared to those knife fights and surfer war casualties that come in from mid-afternoon until after dawn. And there's always the freeways. They have their own brand of carnage—no pun intended—to contribute. Last month, there was that six-car pile-up on the Ventura Freeway. That was quite a show."

"I know," Flax said somberly. "We've got two of the victims in intensive care still, for what little good it does." She started to sit up, then winced.

"Take it easy, Eileen," Oldsman advised.

"You know, sometimes on the freeway," Flax said, trying to keep her mind off the pain that reached from the back of her neck to the bridge of her nose, "I get the impression that it's all a foxhunt and I'm the fox." She clenched her teeth and went on, moving her jaw as little as possible. "Driving out here, I thought it was fun, starting out to someplace new, before I got too old to do it. But I don't know. Sometimes I think that I went too far. Los Angeles is like a foreign country, compared to Boston."

"I know the feeling." He reached out and helped her to come upright on the table. "Don't try to move just yet. Keep your head still. It's not easy, but try, will you?"

Flax made the mistake of starting to nod, then murmured "Yes," through her aching jaw.

Oldsman leaned back and looked at her. "Seriously, Eileen, what are you doing on the weekend? I think it might be best if you weren't alone. Is there anyone you can call, or stay with?"

"This weekend I have a date with my apartment." She meant it to sound unemotional, but there was a lingering sadness in her voice.

"You hurt?"

"No. Not really. I've been wanting something to happen in my life—you know, something other than the job and moving—something exciting. But that poor man... Not that way." Her smile was more on her mouth than in her eyes. "It's a new place. You know how it is. Don't ever try to move and work at the same time. Nothing gets done."

"Let it ride for a while." He suggested this without thinking and saw the resignation in Flax's face.

"It'll just be so much worse, if I do. Got to take care of it sometime and it might as well be now." She decided the tension in her throat came from the ache of the stitches.

"Isn't there someone in your building who—"

Flax cut him short. "I don't know anyone but the managers. They charge for changing a light bulb. I'll handle it. I need something to do, anyway." Saying the words gave her a greater sense of resolution than she had felt before. "I wouldn't mind hiring a good butler," she said after an instant's hesitation, chuckling a little at her own feeble joke.

"Butler?" Oldsman laughed, going along with her, adding unthinkingly. "That's what wives are for."

"Yeah." Flax fixed her gaze on the middle distance. "I guess."

Now that it was too late, Oldsman realized his mistake, and did his best to lessen its impact. "Do you think you'll miss the East, once you're settled?"

Flax shrugged, grateful for the shift in subject. "Hard to say. There're people in Boston and Cambridge who . . . Most of them are university colleagues. . . ." She shook her head, once, and regretted it.

"But?" Oldsman prompted her, setting his tools aside.

"Oh, I don't know. I suppose they were more Eric's friends than mine. He's gunning for the chairmanship of his department. All the politics and partying and jockeying. And after a while . . . I . . . got in the way . . . or I felt out of place. . . . Nothing major, but enough to make for resentment."

"You or him?" Oldsman asked, knowing that he should not press her for an answer, but curious about her nonetheless.

"Both of us eventually, but him first, I think. I'd have to stay away from department social functions because I was interning. At first, that gave him a distinction

among the rest—none of their wives were in medicine—
but after a while, it was awkward to show up alone,
time after time, or have to leave early because I had to
go on duty and he didn't want to appear nonsupportive."
She sighed. "You going to irrigate the stitches?"

"In a minute." He knew that she would not confide
any more, and so he said, "LA's a long way from
Boston."

"Cambridge. It sure is," she agreed, resisting the
urge to nod. "At some level, I think this going west
business appeals to me. It's like an adventure."

One of the nurses came through the door with a tray.
"You wanted this, Dr. Oldsman?" She kept glancing
covertly in Flax's direction, curious to see how she was
doing.

"An adventure? Put the tray right here, Kranz." He
looked over the vials and other supplies.

"Better than a retreat," she admitted.

Oldsman picked up a bulb-shaped plastic syringe,
taking the time to read what was on the label. "There're
some places where that's a euphemism for dying."

"What? Retreating?"

"You know, they say that so-and-so's gone west." He
motioned the nurse away. "Lean back a bit, Eileen."

"Want me to hold the basin?" she offered, anticipating the unnerving sting of the antiseptic solution.

"Not necessary. I can manage." He pressed the bulg-
ing side of the syringe and a stream of chill liquid
flowed over the newly set stitches.

Flax gritted her teeth. "Why the hell do they keep
that stuff in refrigerators? I feel like an Eskimo."

"Swab," he said to the nurse without taking his
attention from the work he was doing. "There's a
shaving of skin, Eileen, but I think it's yours."

"Goody." To take her mind off what was going on, she
said, "I'll tell you what I do miss from Cambridge—
trees. It's so barren out here. God, you get the feeling

that every last, pathetic bush is cataloged and numbered as an endangered species."

"People don't realize . . ." Oldsman said in a remote tone as he moved to permit the nurse to bring fresh sterile dressings to him, "that this is a city built on a desert. We're as far south as Algeria."

"But it's . . ." Flax began, then broke off with a hissed intake of breath as Ted Oldsman commenced bandaging the side of her head.

"Think of it as extended parking for the beach," he said, leaning far enough forward that she could see him wink.

She started to laugh aloud, but the movement made her dizzy and opening her mouth caused the pain from her ear to flare. "Don't," she protested.

"Hold still, there. I'm almost finished." He was pleased to see her more responsive, but did not want to add to her discomfort.

Flax tried to talk without moving her jaw, needing another distraction. "Hey, not so tight. I may have to answer the phone." She was silent, then picked up where he had left off. "What beach? You mean there's a beach? On a resident's hours, who goes to the beach?"

"Almost finished," Oldsman said again, this time meaning it. "How long have you been on duty?"

"Uh . . . thirty . . ." She lifted her wrist to read her watch—"two hours, twenty minutes, give or take. Four more to go."

"Those bandages will have to be checked in the afternoon, and we'll take them off then. I'll give you some ointment, and with any luck you can leave it uncovered. I just don't want anything more getting in there for a day or so. Just in case."

"Thanks," Flax said, knowing that he was still worried that she might develop an infection because of the bite.

"That does it, all finished." He helped her get down off the table. "Well, you've had enough excitement for one night. Never mind the four hours; go home and get some sleep. Surgeon's orders." Then, because he had something of a reputation to maintain, he added, "Besides, you're not like the rest of these whippersnappers. You need a little extra sleep at your age."

"You mean like my contemporaries who are up to their asses in ten-year-olds, dogs, and other delights?" She made a halfhearted kick in the general direction of his groin. "I'm not in my dotage yet."

"See! See? They get to thirty and all they can think about is sex! Sex, sex, sex."

Flax had heard far worse teasing through medical school, and no longer rose to the bait, either in jest or in earnest. She sighed once, and could tell by Oldsman's suddenly sheepish expression that she had made her point.

"Hey, Eileen, you need a tetanus booster?"

"Nope. I had one last summer." She tested her legs for a few steps, and though they were wobbly, she knew she could manage.

"You need some help getting home?" Oldsman asked, noticing how she moved.

"No, not at this hour. I can make it." She gave a bit of a smile to the nurse who was clearing up the last of the sterile dressing Oldsman had discarded.

"Is there someone in your apartment building you can call if—" Oldsman began only to have Flax cut him short.

"I can take care of myself, Ted. I'm a big girl now." She shrugged. "If I get into trouble, I'll let you know."

It was plain from the skeptical expression on Oldsman's face that he doubted she would be so sensible, but he took her proffered hand. "Then goodnight."

"Goodnight. And thanks. Will you tell the others I said thanks?"

"Of course." Oldsman stepped back and watched her stifle a yawn as she started to leave. "What did he say?"

Flax frowned and turned back toward Oldsman. "Who?"

"When he jumped on you, what did he say?" He had been curious about this since he heard about the attack.

"Oh . . ." Flax shook her head, trying to recall the moment, but all it did was make her face sore. "I don't remember; nothing."

"Pity. Identifying him is going to be difficult." He folded his arms. "They say that a man's last words are supposed to be . . . significant."

"I can't help you out—sorry." She was sincere, for she knew what it was to be alone and among strangers.

"If you think of anything . . ." Oldsman hinted broadly.

"Yeah, yeah, I'll call. And *you* call if the autopsy turns up anything interesting. Thanks again, Ted."

He ignored this last, and said in his most bantering way, "Suppose it was spooks?"

"You mean, woo-oo-oo-oo-ee-ee-eeee?" Flax asked, attempting to hum and whistle at once. "It's as good a cause as any." She waved, making her departure final.

The hospital was almost deserted, and the parking lot across the street was even more so. What would future archeologists make of it, she asked herself as she started from the elevator toward her old Volkswagen bug, four or five thousand years from now when they picked their way through the ruins of Los Angeles? Would they know cars for what they were, or would they relegate them to that great catch-all of the archeologist to be labeled "ritual items of unknown significance"? As she drove away from the hospital, she took extra care; lack of sleep and the remnants of shock did not make for the safest driving. She stared at the rest of the traffic on the road at—she checked her watch—4:51. Who were these people? Who in his right mind was on the freeway at this hour?

Yet there were cars, some of them less certainly driven than others. A fifteen-year-old battered Buick went by, blaring rock, the teenaged passengers screaming to each other to be heard over it. Big semis roared along, massive dinosaurs, at speeds that made them terrifying. A station wagon cut in ahead of Flax, and she saw that it was covered with the call letters of a local television station: a reporter or morning-show host rushing to work. There were two Winnebagos trundling along, top-heavy and awkward. Vans, some of them fantastically painted, cruised the night like smugglers' ships. Here and there, the highway patrol slipped through traffic, squad cars sliding up behind other vehicles, then pulling away or signaling an offender to the side of the road.

Flax had never quite mastered the rhythm of LA. She was still too much a part of Cambridge and Boston. She could not get used to the vast, single-story sprawl of houses, the eternal warmth, the movement of it all. Rationally, she knew that it was foolish to build brick houses in earthquake country, but her eyes longed for the sight of those formidable, familiar buildings where she had lived most of her life. She took her exit and headed for her apartment complex.

In the center of the courtyard formed by the three four-story units, the swimming pool steamed, its eerie blue underwater lights making it appear vital, alive, like an eye or a new form of life spawned in a laboratory. She skirted it, paused long enough to retrieve her mail from the rank of boxes at the entrance to her building, then, looking through the gaudy, uninteresting flyers, she pressed the button for the elevator instead of using the stairs as she usually did.

What she wanted most, she thought as she opened the door, was a shower, but with bandages on her head, it had to be a bath. She let herself into the apartment and turned on the light.

It was a one-bedroom place, with a short hall leading from the front door to the living room on the left and the kitchen on the right. The walls were off-white, the closed draperies were off-white, the carpet was a color somewhere between toast and curry. All of it neat, all of it utilitarian, all of it without character. Flax paid it little attention. She dropped the flyers onto the coffee table in the living room—it was one of three pieces of furniture in the room; the other two were a recliner chair and a sofa upholstered in a garish shade of plum—then went into the kitchen to the refrigerator.

The interior was unpromising, but at last Flax chose one of two cans of V-8, and closed the door on the half-dozen eggs, two cubes of margarine, last three slices of bread, and a jar of orange marmalade that made up the rest of her supplies. Taking the can with her, she went into the bedroom.

This was even more disheartening. Her unmade bed was a thick foam mattress on the floor, and though there was a small chest of drawers in one corner, her open suitcase was mute testimony to her transitory existence here. On the floor beside her bed, a telephone—off-white like the walls—and an answering machine waited. Slowly Flax sat down and checked the messages.

"Eileen, this is Mary Wyler, the manager's wife. If you want us to let the men in with your furniture, I need your signature on the authorization to let them in. You can call me tomorrow morning."

"Dr. Flax, my name is Jerry Hardy and I represent the Proctor Insurance Fund, and we specialize in professional insurance. If you haven't purchased malpractice insurance yet, I'd like to make an appointment to call on you and outline the advantages of our plan. We also have an investment counseling service. My number is 555-3731."

"Eileen, this is Jenny in Boston. Harold and I just wanted to know how you are."

"Miss Flax, this is Norman at Ken's Service. We've got that part for your bug in. It'll cost about seventy-five dollars."

"Does Lou Turner live here? If he does will you have him call Terry?"

Flax rewound the tape and considered calling Jenny. It would be almost eight in the morning in Boston, and

Jenny would be getting the kids ready for school. No, Flax decided, she would call later, when Jenny didn't have her hands so full. Slowly she got out of her clothes and pulled on a terry-cloth robe. What would she tell Jenny, after all? That she had treated an emergency patient who had bitten her ear and then died? All that would bring would be Jenny's worry and predictions of disaster in crazy California.

In the bathroom—white with a blue vinyl floor that was flecked with something that was supposed to look like mother-of-pearl and didn't—she drew a bath and settled back into it. She had to admit that the warm water felt good. Occasionally she took sips from the V-8 can that she had balanced on the rim of the tub. Gradually the tensions of the night drained away from her, her thoughts softened, running and fusing with the bathwater. She kept thinking about that poor man who had died, who was so badly hurt and so terrified. She wished she knew what it was that had caused him to suffer so. The warm water gave a degree of remoteness to her concern, as if it had happened long ago, not just a few hours since. His face floated in her vision, and she tried to imagine what he had looked like before she saw him. Nothing suggested itself except the attraction of those gray eyes that might have been humorous or acute or perhaps even dreamy. Flax settled back in the water, her head canted to one side so that she would not get her bandages wet. The water was soothing, just hot enough to turn her skin rosy and begin to float away the fatigue. It was luxury to lie back and surrender to the lassitude, to let go. She stared in fascination at the shine of the bathroom lights on the chrome fixtures, as if she had never noticed them before, while her thoughts drifted.

Strange, what triggers the mind.

The light bobbed and moved, then became the beam of a flashlight on a wall, and in the light, a hand moved, leaving markings in its wake. There were words, disgusting words, obscene drawings—it was impossible to tell which in that inadequate circle of light, but the intent was blindingly clear. The hand continued to scrawl, huge and terrible on what must have been the side of a house. One or two persons, young or old, male or female, there was no way to tell, whispered to each other as they worked. It had to be two, or . . .

And then the first two were gone and there was another hand, this one with what might have been a brush, working frantically to obliterate the markings.

"What are you doing?" A woman, fairly young, distinctly pretty, was caught in the beam of the flashlight as she came around the house. She was not quite frightened, but definitely anxious and a little vexed; her voice was sharp when she spoke.

Flax came awake with a start; her flailing hand struck the V-8 can and set the last of its contents spattering across the floor.

The bath was cold and the room was bright in the advancing morning.

Only gradually did Flax come back to herself. I was tired, she said as she got out of the bath, shivering now, the comfort of the water lost with its heat, or so she told herself. I was upset, she thought. And good reason. Nothing unusual in getting a case of bad nerves after someone tries to bite your ear off. It's normal. It would be odd if I didn't have some sort of reaction. The man got to me. All beat up, and so frightened. Dying like that. She steadied herself on the rim of the tub. It'll pass. Give it time, it will pass. I was worn out, jumpy, I'd had a hard night. After a case like his, bite or no bite, there's nothing peculiar in overreacting a little. I got in the tub, that let-down and depression made me groggy. I saw the light on the chrome and it . . . triggered some kind of dream. Or autohypnosis. These things happen. You can't let it throw you, Eileen Flax.

As she wrapped herself in her old terry-cloth robe, she reminded herself that she had been through a rough experience. It takes time to get over it. It's like everything else—if it leaves an impression, you can't shut it out entirely, not all at once. It's perfectly normal to be apprehensive and troubled after stress. It was what she always told her patients, and there was no reason to think that she was any different from them. If this had happened to anyone else under the same circumstances, would I be alarmed? she questioned herself inwardly as she stared into the mirror at the discolorations forming under her eyes. Only if the symptoms continued, she answered her own inquiry. If the symptoms continue for too long, then there might be reason to check further. But for the time being, don't let it worry you. It's a natural response; nothing to get uptight—was that still the right slang expression?—about. Give yourself time. It'll work out. If you're upset, it'll just take longer.

With great care she brushed her teeth, opening her mouth as little as possible. It was shock, she said silently to her reflection. You know what shock can do. And it doesn't go away just like that. There's nothing to be frightened of. That frisson is just a residual effect of the shock. It's not unexpected. Or so she tried to tell herself as she made her way into the bedroom. Really, there was no reason to be so upset by what had happened. She was suffering from mild shock. And it served her right, that dream, for falling asleep in the bathtub. This last made just enough sense to her that she was able to stop worrying as she got into bed and pulled the covers around her.

Before she fell asleep, she thought vaguely that she really ought to call Jenny, just in case.

In case what?

She had no answer, and the impulse was quickly gone.

THREE

With the bandages off, Flax felt much less conspicuous sitting in the cafeteria. Patients were expected to have bandages, not doctors. She had intercepted one or two curious glances, but nothing more, and she assumed that the excitement over the dead man had calmed down.

"And so, I didn't want to try the freeway, not with that kind of a pile-up slowing everything to a crawl," Cassie Maybeck declared, leaning toward Flax. She was patting her hair for emphasis, making it look even more like a scouring pad than it usually did.

"Makes sense," Flax said carefully, not wanting to admit that she had not been listening closely.

"I thought so. But then, this kid in a yellow Datsun pickup cuts me off for a left turn, and *you* know what it's like trying to turn left on Sunset! Well, so, I gave him the finger, and that crazy son of a bitch hits the brakes and jumps right out of his truck, smack in the middle of Sunset Boulevard. And you should've seen him!"

"Attractive?" Flax ventured, knowing how eclectic Cassie's tastes were.

"Hell, no! He's got long hair, all of it stringy, looks about fourteen, and has a belly already. He starts walking toward me with a goddamn *tire iron!*"

"Oh, shit!" Caught between laughter and dismay, Flax almost dropped her sandwich. As she retrieved the bacon, she asked, "What did you do?"

"I got the hell out of there, what else? Let me tell you, that creep didn't want to tango. Flax, I'm telling you, there are more crazy motherfuckers out there than you . . ."

Ted Oldsman had come up behind them, and he spoke now. "What'd you major in at Barnard, Cassie—sailors?"

"No," Cassie said with complete aplomb, "no; rhesus monkeys from Columbia."

Oldsman accepted her answer with a chuckle. "Mind if I join you?" he asked, and before either had a chance to say yes or no, he took the seat beside Cassie, facing Flax. As he stirred an anemic bowl of tomato soup, he gave Flax a thoughtful stare. "You know that nut case of yours from last night? The mystery man?"

Flax did not want to seem too curious, so she nodded and busied herself with eating her sandwich.

"Yeah," Oldsman said, taking this for interest. "We finally got the lab reports back on him. That intern, Keenan, you remember? He said that the lab ran the series on the specimens three times. Believe it or not, there's not a trace of drugs. Adrenal residue, muscle toxins enough to frizz a racehorse, but *no dope*."

"But . . ." Flax began, then fell silent.

"This is the guy that went for Eileen's ear?" Cassie asked. "Everyone I talked to said that he had to be on something. But if he wasn't . . ."

"No traces? Not even alcohol?" Flax wondered.

"Jeez, then what happened to him?" Cassie inquired of the air.

But Oldsman was not to be hurried. He traded arch looks with Cassie as he went on. "And he looked like some creep off the beach, didn't he?"

"I didn't see him," Cassie reminded him sweetly.

"Eileen? Wouldn't you say that he looked like a rough character?" Oldsman asked, not to be deterred.

"He's dead, that's enough. Anyone who'd been through whatever he . . ." Flax bit her lip.

"Okay, okay, if not a beach type, at least not a pillar of

the community," Oldsman persisted. "A strong type, rugged. Wouldn't you say that?"

"You're talking pretty loudly," Flax said in an undertone, feeling an embarrassment she could not explain. "Unless you want the entire hospital to be—"

"Yeah, okay," Oldsman said, lowering his voice. "He *did* look more like a beach crazy than a bank president; you'll give me that, won't you?"

"In some ways," Flax said cautiously.

"In some ways," he echoed her. "Well, believe it or not, our mystery man is a cultural anthropologist from good old UCLA itself."

"He *was* an anthropol—" Flax started to correct him testily, then the information sank in. "A cultural anthropologist?" The face she had seen last night went through her mind again, and after an instant's disbelief, she did not find this announcement as preposterous as it seemed at first.

"His name . . . was Jean-Charles Pommier. He's lived all over the world, one of those wandering types; he's supposed to be the top man in the field—no pun intended."

"Jee-zuss!" Cassie exclaimed, delighted to have so much rich material for gossip as well as the attention of Ted Oldsman. There would be a week of enlivened coffee breaks on this story, and perhaps an excuse to spend more time with the man who was providing it. "What kind of people did he study, if he lived all over the world?"

"I didn't ask. Whatever cultural anthropologists study, I'd imagine," Oldsman answered, not caring very much. "Most of them are interested in primitive societies, you know, like Margaret Mead, or they become sociologists instead." He smiled at Cassie, thinking that his response wasn't bad for off-the-cuff.

"Sounds like the wild man from Borneo didn't like his reviews and decided to get even." Cassie had a hooting laugh, one that seemed out of place with the rest of her, and it filled most of the cafeteria so that heads turned toward them again. "God, aren't we ghoulish?"

"Comes with the territory," Oldsman said seriously. "If we stop joking, we crack up. You ever noticed how that happens?"

"Sometimes." Cassie nodded, looking older suddenly, and tired.

Flax was fiddling with her watchband, more disturbed than she cared to admit. The man had not been one of those homeless, rootless people who wandered the oceanfront looking for the last landfall or the end of the world. The gray eyes burned in her mind. "Pommier," she said quietly. "French."

"French-Canadian," Oldsman corrected her smugly, a little of his jauntiness coming back. "His wife was in this morning to . . . uh . . . claim the body and take care of the paperwork. You know." He was suddenly and intensely embarrassed, and he determined to cover it up. "I saw her in Richter's office! She's gorgeous; this lean, elegant redhead. You could've tossed me through a window."

"A redhead," Flax repeated, the image of her dream coming again.

"It was crazy, seeing that lovely French charmer, so incongruous. The way he looked, and then her . . ." He pushed his chair back.

"Well?" Cassie demanded, wanting more than these tidbits.

"Enough. I've got a minute flat to get to seven." He stood up, no longer much interested in the two women.

"Walk in backward," Cassie suggested, her head tilted flirtatiously to the side.

Oldsman chuckled. "I tried that Tuesday. Today I promised I'd actually be there, and on time. Eileen . . ." He tapped her on the shoulder by way of farewell, and then hurried off at a fast, stiff-legged walk.

Flax was hardly aware he had left. She continued to stare down at her watchband.

"Stop it," Cassie said after a moment.

"Pardon?" Flax asked, looking up sharply. She had almost stilled the tremor in her hands.

"Your lip. It'll look like your ear if you keep biting it." She reached over and rattled the ice cubes in her glass. "Something the matter?"

"Oh, not really," Flax said evasively. "Just . . . hearing that the man was French and all . . ." I have to stop thinking of him as *the patient*, she told herself. He had a name: Jean-Charles Pommier.

"French-*Canadian*," Cassie reminded her. "Free Quebec and all that."

"Um." Flax picked up the last of her sandwich and did her best to eat it, though for her it had the taste and texture of moldy straw. She had forced down the last of it when she got up enough nerve to ask something more of Cassie. "You speak French, don't you?"

"Enough to handle simple foreign films," Cassie said, then her eyes narrowed. "Does this have anything to do with that French-Canadian anthropologist? Hum?"

Flax did not answer the question. "What does 'n'y sont pas, sont des innois' mean, do you know?"

"What?" She cocked her head to the side. "Run that by me again?"

"N'y sont pas, sont des innois." She said it with more confidence, hoping that she had got the words right.

Cassie frowned at her. "N'y sont pas, sont des innois? Lord!" She patted her frizzy hair. "Well, that first part is simple enough. That 'n'y sont pas,' that's 'they are not there.'"

"They are not there?" Flax was more baffled than ever.

"Look, it's your phrase, not mine, Eileen." She screwed up her face, concentrating. "They are not there. Are you sure those are the correct words? Could it be something else?"

"I'm pretty sure," Flax said, a trifle defensively. "Forget it if you like."

"No, no, I'm curious." Cassie shrugged impatiently.

"Well, give me the rest. I might as well have a try at it."

"'Sont des innois.'" Flax quoted, her own voice sounding odd to her ears.

"Sont des innois. They are not there, they are... ah... well, des innois. Of the innois. Maybe it's a... place. You know, people wanting to find someone. A guy asks you if you have a certain patient here and you say, no, that patient is a Christian Scientist. Something like that. Could be."

"I guess." Flax shook her head in bafflement.

"Well, fuck a duck," Cassie said, exasperated.

"Cassie, why do you..." Flax began, then stopped.

"Swear? Use obscenities?" Cassie asked impishly.

"Yeah," Flax admitted, thinking that she must seem very old-fashioned to Cassie.

"Well, *someone* has to liven the place up. Everyone goes around shocked at me and they don't have time to get tired or depressed. It performs a public service, talking like a sailor. I don't do it around the patients, not most of them. Some of them like it—helps them handle their own anger. You ought to try it sometime."

"I'll think about it," Flax said without much conviction.

"Besides, if I don't swear, Ted pays no attention to me at all. If I do, then he gets to be all scandalized. Everyone has their own way of flirting." She cast a roguish eye around the cafeteria. "Most of these guys can stand to be taken down a notch or two. They're too full of themselves. This way, a couple of shits and a screw you and they calm right down." She wadded up her paper napkin and threw it, accurately, across the table into the open trash bin. "Why'd you ask about the French?"

"You're not going to let that alone, are you?" Flax said with a resigned shrug.

"Well, I wouldn't mind a little reward for my effort," Cassie declared.

Flax considered briefly. "I heard it somewhere. I

don't remember. All this talk about French . . . French-Canadians brought it back, I guess. It's probably not important. Just one of those things that sticks in the mind, like some songs do. Thanks for your help." She started to get up, but Cassie detained her.

"Hey, is that all? I mean, aren't you going to tell me what this is all about? Really?" She was almost angry, but her disappointment at losing out on inside information was worse than the hunch she had that Flax was deliberately withholding something from her. "Eileen, do you mean to tell me that there's nothing more to this?"

"I don't know, Cassie. If I remember, I'll let you know." She did not want to be evasive but she could think of no other acceptable explanation. "Maybe it does have something to do with the patient . . . Pommier . . . but I don't know what. That's the truth."

"You know, you're still rocky, Eileen," Cassie told her. "All kinds of crap get dredged up out of the mind when you go through a bad spot."

Flax thought of the desolate months after her divorce, while she tried to get enough of a grip on herself to make the necessary changes. "I know. But thanks for reminding me."

"And if it turns out that it *is* . . ." Cassie persisted, her face perking her interest.

"You're incorrigible." Flax laughed. "It was just one of those memory triggers, that's all." Then she added, almost without thinking, "It's strange, what triggers the mind."

Cassie rolled her eyes upward as Flax got up from the table. "You can say that again."

Most of the day went by in a busy blur, and secretly Flax was grateful for the distraction. That moment in the cafeteria, when the French phrase had come back into her mind had unnerved her more than she cared to admit. It was not until she was finishing her rounds that "des innois" began to ring in her thoughts again. She decided, three times over, that the word was French-Canadian slang for something, or a place, an obscure village far away from the rest of the world. The man was an anthropologist, he must have known dozens of such places.

"What?" asked the floor nurse on rounds with her, pausing in making a recently vacated bed in a semiprivate room.

"Yes?" Flax asked, surprised to hear the other woman speak to her.

"You said something," Sally Bell said.

"Oh. It's nothing. Just trying to think of a way to handle Mrs. McInnis." She indicated the other bed that would soon be occupied by an elderly and difficult patient.

"She should be finished with her hip bath in a few minutes," Sally agreed. "Maybe it would be best just to send her home to her family."

"Her husband's in a walker. He can't take care of her by himself," Flax said, thinking that it must have been the similarity between the name McInnis and the sound of the words "des innois" that brought it back to her mind.

"Lucky for him," Sally said, and turned toward the door to see the old woman herself, leaning on two canes, come into the room. "You've got a nice clean bed again, Mrs. McInnis," she told the woman, speaking loudly enough to compensate for the poor hearing of the patient.

"High time," Mrs. McInnis snapped back, and hobbled to the bed. "You should have been here half an hour ago," she accused Flax.

"We had some difficulties," Flax soothed her.

"Well, what do you think I've been having. That creature who calls herself a physical therapist ought to be taken into court for what she does."

Flax had had this conversation with Mrs. McInnis before. "Now you know that you need to have your leg exercised. If you don't get those muscles working, you'll be needing canes all the time, and you don't want that, do you?" She argued pleasantly but with an inner weariness.

"O' course not. But that woman is such a grouch. She is always telling me that I'm not trying hard enough, and that I'm impeding my own progress. She says that having a stroke is no excuse for being lazy."

That afternoon Flax had had to listen to the therapist's version of the conflict, and she knew that Mrs. McInnis was not above taking advantage of her semi-invalid status. "Well, you grouch right back at her, then. That's expected. But you do what she says, okay? Walking practice right now is the best thing for you. We're all doing everything we can to get you into full mobility. And tomorrow, I want to hear that you've been able to get all the way across the room without your canes, or ... with ... out the assis ..." Her words straggled to a halt and she stood, her eyes focused on nothing, while Mrs. McInnis tried to make herself comfortable in the bed.

Sally Bell, unaware that there was anything amiss, came up to Flax. "I'm finished in here for now. Dr. Stafford's on first thing in the morning. Do you want to leave instructions for checking her OVR level again, or ... "

"No ..." Flax said as if from a great distance, "the carpet's fine. I *like* the color."

"What?" Sally stared down at the gray linoleum floor. "The carpet?"

The words penetrated the silence that held Flax. "I ... sorry. Moving into a new place, you know ... I was woolgathering."

"Oh. Sure," Sally said, anything but reassured. She knew, as did most of the rest of the nurses, that Dr. Flax had been assaulted by a patient, and she assumed that she had not yet recovered from the shock. "The OVR levels?"

"Oh, yes. The usual checks." She smiled at Mrs. McInnis, too brightly. "We'll get you out of here in no time. Keep up your exercises and don't ask your husband to bring you any more candy bars."

The old woman sputtered at this treatment, but Flax headed out of the room, the aluminum-covered clipboard still held close to her chest.

Sally watched her, then rushed after her. "Dr. Flax?" she called out, keeping her voice low, but imbuing it with urgency. "Dr. Flax?"

Flax stopped outside a supply room. God in heaven, what is happening to me? She rested her forehead against the cool, enamel-painted metal, and tried to clear the impressions from her mind. She looked up, hoping to see the long, sterile corridor with the nurses' station at the end of it, and instead she had the feeling that she was looking into a room.

There was nothing in the room; two closets, standing empty, and a door to a tiled bathroom gave the appearance of a bedroom. It was spacious, the ceiling high, all suggesting that the house was an old one, built back before the Second World War when labor was cheap and materials were readily available. Three tall windows glowed with sunlight.

Flax pressed her free hand to her mouth and suppressed a shriek. She blinked once, twice, and shook her head, forcing herself to recognize her surroundings. She was on the fourth floor of a hospital. It was night. She was a physician on rounds. There was no house.

"Dr. Flax?" Sally asked, coming up beside her. "Are you all right?"

It was foolish to pretend nothing was the matter, and for once Flax did not bother. "I guess—" she attempted a quivery smile—"I'm tired out. Last night was harder than I . . ."

Sally gave her shoulder a concerned pat. "You're not

in the best shape ever. I know what it can be like, losing a patient. And in your case, getting bitten, well . . . We have support groups for dealing with ambivalence and guilt. Maybe something like that would be helpful." She pointed to another door a little farther along the hallway. "Why don't you go into the nurses' lounge and lie down for a bit, say twenty minutes or half an hour? No one's going to bother you at this time of the evening. I'll call you in half an hour, and if you're still not up to doing the rest of the rounds, I'll ask Carstairs or Nakamura to take over for you. Deal?" She gently propelled Flax along the hall toward the lounge door as she spoke, noting that Flax was pale and her breathing was not as regular as she knew it should be. "You've been through a bad time, doctor."

"Yeah," Flax said, afraid that if she let herself speak, she would cry. Her head felt stuffy and swollen. This is ridiculous, she ordered herself firmly. Get hold again— she trembled. How she welcomed the firm handling Sally Bell gave her, with a quiet way of speaking that sounded so dependable, so sensible in a world that had been invaded by chaos. You've got to stop thinking that way, Flax's inner voice admonished her. You've seen patients die before and you will see it again and it will never be easy. That's the rule. Don't let it get to you.

"Now, you sure you'll be all right?" Sally held the door to the lounge open. "I can call Dr. Giffith or—"

"No, Sally. Don't bother. I . . . a few minutes and I'll be okay again." She hoped devoutly that it was true.

"Well, you can lie down on the chaise and put your feet up." With a nod, she indicated the Naugahyde-upholstered furniture, and with a start Flax realized she had not noticed the door closing behind them. "I'll call you in thirty minutes. Do you want the light off?"

"Uh . . . no," Flax said, suddenly dreading the darkness. "That won't be necessary. I just want to rest, not sleep." She sat on the chaise gingerly, as if she expected it to explode under her weight.

"Do you want an aspirin?"

"No, I'll be fine." She swung her legs up. "It feels more like sinus trouble than a regular headache. Could be an allergy, couldn't it, triggered by stress?" She wanted to believe that explained the peculiar numbing, stuffy, buzzy feeling she had in her face.

"Whatever you say," Sally told her, and with a touch of a frown, she let herself out of the lounge.

Flax lay back, ordering herself to relax; she felt all her muscles grow taut. She gave an exhausted yawn that provided no relief to her tension. Quickly she blinked, terrified that she might be weeping, and sighed her satisfaction when she knew her eyes were dry.

" . . . it was such a mess, the old one, and yellow. It didn't clean well—what do you expect?—so they put in all new upstairs." The voice was professionally cheery, and for a moment Flax thought it was another nurse, but then she looked around, and discovered she was once again in that house she did not know, the sun streaming in the windows over the new carpeting. Her teeth clenched. It's a nightmare, a leftover incident of shock, that's all, she insisted, but could not break the images that had got possession of her.

A woman came into the room, a tall, leggy redhead in very smart clothes. She looked over her shoulder, gesturing for someone to follow her.

The syrupy voice went on, puffing a little. "Of course, you'll find there's plenty of storage. These older homes, you know, are marvelous for closets."

Flax could see the speaker now, a middle-aged woman in a polyester pantsuit with earlobes and fingers glittering with jewelry. Her hair was a shiny, unlikely blond and she walked with mincing little steps. "Now the owners live out of the area. When they moved, well, obviously I tried to convince them to stay long enough to sell the house instead of rent, but apparently his transfer was pretty sudden and they did not want to get all caught up in the sales negotiations. Well, with

interest rates the way they are, it might have taken a
fair amount of time to sell, but . . ."

"What do you think, chéri?" the redhead asked over
her shoulder, the words softened by her French accent.
"It is charmant, yes?"

There was a low chuckle, a man's laugh, warm with
his fondness for the redheaded woman. "As you say."
His English was tinged with a faint foreignness but was
no stranger than a Texan's or a Maine fisherman's to
unaccustomed ears.

There was a bend in the hall, leading to a stairwell. A
mirror hung at the top of it. There Flax saw, as if
through her own eyes, the reflection of a man's face.
Though it was clean-shaven and calm, she had no
trouble recognizing him.

"*Pommier!*" she cried out, and at the sound of this,
Sally Bell left the nurses' station and ran for the lounge.

"Call Dr. Giffith!" she called out. "Something's wrong
with Dr. Flax." In the next instant, she was through the
door and into the lounge, where she found Flax on the
floor where she had fallen, eyes enormously open and
unseeing, fixed on the light in the ceiling. Her breathing was rapid and shallow, and when Sally felt her
pulse, she was doubly alarmed.

"Pommier," Flax whispered, the name barely audible. "It was Pommier. Pommier. Pommier."

FOUR

It was clear to the real estate agent that the foreign couple would rent the house. She followed them out into the garden, explaining that there was a local gardening service employed to keep up the yard. "Unless you care to take over the job yourself?"

Pommier laughed. "You speak as if this is a certain thing," he said, indicating the house.

"Well, your wife seems to like it," Dorothy Praeger protested, her shiny mouth turning down at the corners.

"Yes, she does," he agreed, looking after the stunning redhead. "But," he went on, his rationalism reasserting itself, "we've seen so little, it would be premature to suggest that this is the best place."

"But this is so convenient to UCLA. I haven't got anything listed that is half this nice and so close." She did not want to sound desperate, but Dorothy wanted her commission, and she did believe that this was the best house for the couple. "I know that three bedrooms is a little large, but—"

"Oh, no, no. That's not the trouble. I need extra room for my work. One of the rooms will be a study, the other a place for guests." He knew that he, too, was speaking as if the whole matter were closed.

"What is it you *do* at the university, professor?" Dorothy asked, buying more time for Pommier's wife to convince him to take the house.

"I'm an anthropologist," he answered a bit absently as he watched Veronique bend over to smell the blooms on a low-growing shrub.

"An *anthropologist?*" Dorothy exclaimed brightly.

"Science isn't my strong point, but isn't that like with bones and tombs and things?"

"No, you're thinking of archaeologists. I do nothing so dramatic." He was able to conceal his amusement with a disarming smile that made Dorothy Praeger understand why a woman as beautiful as Veronique would marry a man almost twice her age. "My work has to do with living cultures, mostly agrarian and nomadic populations, such as . . ."

Veronique dashed into the driveway, her arms lifted. "Je l'adore!" she announced at the top of her voice. "Ah, tell me I may have it!"

Pommier shook his head. "You do not know what it costs. Where is your French shrewdness, ma belle?"

"But I love it!" she protested. "It is large and warm."

"Yes, it is." He looked back at Dorothy, who was rummaging in her purse to extract a formidable ring of keys. "You see, in my work, I *watch* people."

"Oh," she answered blankly. "I see. And that's what you'll be teaching this fall? How to watch people?"

Once more Pommier smiled. "Yes, I'm afraid that's so."

"Afraid?" Dorothy repeated, baffled.

Veronique had overheard, and she responded with a friendly growl. "Listen to him. You heard him!" She came back toward Pommier, her hand out to shove him affectionately. "This is the first time in *years* that we have lived in a civilized place, and already he is bored. What am I going to do with you, Jean-Charles?" She put her hand out. "Look; we have a house, not a tent here. It has no vermin in the walls. The walls—look at them!" She slapped the side of the house gruffly, almost as if she were a proud parent.

"Mrs. Pommier . . ." Dorothy warned her, but it was too late.

White paint covered Veronique's hand, and she held it out, staring in disgust. "What? What is this?"

Behind them a black surfer van heavily ornamented

with chrome and swirling designs roared past, punk rock blaring so loudly that for a few seconds that was all Pommier could hear.

"They go to the beach," Dorothy explained when she could be heard. "Here in Santa Monica, it *is* an occasional problem. Though," she added, pursing her mouth fussily, "most of the time they keep to Venice."

"Venice?" Pommier asked. "Oh, yes, the next town—is that right?"

"What am I to do with this *paint?*" Veronique demanded. She had opened her handbag and was trying, with her clean hand, to find something to wipe it away.

Dorothy plunged her hand into her large purse and came up with two wadded tissues. "Here. I am so sorry about this. It's those . . . freaks."

"Freaks?" Veronique said as she took the tissues and began to wipe the worst of the paint from her hand.

"You know how it is, when a house is empty for a while . . ." Dorothy explained evasively. "There are always a rowdy few who like to . . ."

"Graffiti?" Pommier suggested.

"Yes," Dorothy admitted. "We've done our best to discourage it, but inevitably, there are difficulties, so close to the beach." She pointed to the side of the house. "It's gone. You see how well it was covered. And with residents, the house . . ." She did not finish what she was going to say.

"Well," Veronique said with a smile that was not quite natural as she gave the used tissues back to Dorothy, "then we almost owe it to the house to take it."

Dorothy took the tissues but held them away from her as if they were contaminated with more than paint.

Flax reached up and caught the wrist above her forehead as water from the cold compress dripped onto her face. "Hey . . ."

Sally yelped. "Doctor!"

David Griffith, his tie askew and his hair not quite combed, barged through the door of the nurses' lounge. "Let me have a look at her!"

Two other nurses who had come in at Sally's first alarm looked about in confusion, uncertain what they should do now.

"I'm all right," Flax said, attempting to sit up. "Really."

"You're pale. And your pulse was terrible," Sally accused her, not at all sure that she should permit Flax to rise, but trained to follow the instructions of physicians.

"What's going on here?" Griffith demanded, standing squarely in front of Flax. "Are you all right, Eileen?"

"I'm fine. I'm all right. Just fine." She tried to get to her feet again, and was pressed back on the chaise by Sally.

"Let Dr. Griffith check you, so long as he's here," Sally insisted in her most soothing tone.

"Yes, you'd better," Griffith agreed at once. "From what I hear, you've been through a lot these last couple days."

Instead of being pleased with this care, Flax was becoming annoyed. "I'm *fine!*" she told them, a bit louder. "I just . . . got overtired."

"It wasn't that," Sally said to Dr. Griffith. "Her pulse was thready and her color, well, it's pretty good now, but she was pasty a couple of minutes ago."

"Okay," Griffith said, and assumed a more forceful attitude. "Lie back down there and let me have a look at you, Eileen."

Rationally, Flax knew that if she were David Giffith, she would do the same thing he was doing, but she could not bring herself to accept his aid. For some reason that she could not understand, she felt trapped and in danger, and she thrust out with her arms. "I said I'm *fine!* Now get out of the way."

"But . . ." Griffith protested, disliking her tone. "For God's sake, Eileen, hold still."

"No," she said, but it was more to the cold she felt

touching her again, the feeling that she was out of control of her mind. "No!" She staggered to her feet in a desperate attempt to escape the images that formed in front of her eyes. She had to get away immediately.

"This is what I mean, doctor," Sally said, and it seemed to Flax that the nurse was whispering at the far end of a long corridor. "Check her pulse."

"Holy shit," Griffith said, and Flax heard him as if they had a very poor phone connection.

"Strange, what triggers the mind," Jean-Charles Pommier said to himself as he sat at a cardtable sorting photographs. The room was lined with bookcases, empty now but several stacks of large boxes gave mute promise of filling them. Three file cabinets, drawers stuck out like black tongues, were set up by the door. Only the stereo had been unpacked and had just begun to fill the air with the orderly, sensual music of Monteverdi's *Orfeo*.

The photographs had been taken on his last Arctic expedition, more than three years ago. There were photographs of artifacts made of bone and wood and ivory, of Eskimos with sled dogs and dead seals. And there were the personal photos, photos of Veronique unloading sleeping bags from their Land Rover, of Veronique at the door to their primitive cabin.

There was one other. Once again the photograph caught his attention.

There on the ice a single Eskimo stood, the vast, blank emptiness around him so stark that the frigid wind seemed to come off the shiny paper. The Eskimo had been photographed at a distance, so that his isolation was almost complete.

And yet—there was a sense about him, an uneasiness that had little to do with hunting. It appeared now, as it had when Pommier had first seen the man and taken his picture, that the lone figure was—he studied the hunter intently—was *trespassing*.

"Oh, God!" Flax cried out, and clapped her hand to her mouth. "What's happening?" she whispered around her fingers.

"Get her lying down," Griffith said tersely. "I don't want her going all the way into shock. Bell, I want blood samples right away. That drug addict..."

"No, no," Flax murmured, trying to correct them about Pommier.

"...bit her, didn't he? God alone knows what he had. Move!"

"Yes, doctor," Sally Bell assured him. "Come on, Cynthia. Do you want me to call Oldsman?"

Griffith peered down into Flax's face. "I think you better. He treated her last night, didn't he?"

"But..." Flax objected, and was astonished that she hardly made enough sound to be heard.

"She's trying to talk," Sally said.

"Get moving, Bell!" Griffith shouted, but he could not make himself heard over the sinuous melodies of Monteverdi. Orfeo was lamenting the loss of his Eurydice, and though Flax knew she had never heard the music before, she found herself humming along with it, as if it were as familiar as "Yesterday" or "Sweet Betsy from Pike."

Pommier had about half his books on the shelves; the files had all been tucked away and the cabinets were closed. A massive rolltop desk had been put in the alcove by the western windows, and that was where he sat, going over a list of titles. He looked up at the sound of a firm tap on the half-closed door.

"Yes?"

"I'm looking at the draperies. I've narrowed it down

to five," Veronique said from the hallway. "I must have your opinion."

"Fine," Pommier said, the smile in his voice as much as on his face. He rose to open the door wide for her, and had not got halfway across the room when Veronique came twirling into the study, five lengths of fabric draped over her shoulders.

"Ah!" Veronique said as she came to a stop in front of him. "What do you think, you? Heh?" She beamed at him, pleased that she had surprised him with her entrance. "We must have one of these." Then for convenience, she lapsed into French. "It is always so difficult to choose, but this one is best, isn't it?"

"The persimmon?" Pommier said uncertainly. "And in English, Niki. You will not learn if you do not practice."

"Pah! English. Do you like this color?" She held up the fabric she preferred. "Is it too bright? A little is wonderful, but across the whole of the window, it may be that it is too..."

"Overwhelming?" he supplied. "I don't think so, not with the paneling in the living room."

She nodded. "Then it is decided. If it is too... effrayant..."

"Dreadful," he translated. "If it is, I'll take the blame." He had reached out to stroke her cheek with the back of his hand. "Do as you wish, ma belle. I will love it if you do."

"You say that now," she responded, "but later, what then? It will be too late and you will hate it." She folded her arms. "I have the material, then. But you will have to help me more. I need the ah... ah..." She held up her hand, fingers folded into tubes, and stretched them out in the direction of the window. "Comment dit-on 'tringle de rideau'?"

"Curtain rod."

"The curtain rod. That's silly." She tried not to giggle. "Curtain rod, curtain rod, curtain rod. I forget faster than I learn. English! What am I to do with it?"

"English or the curtain rods?" Pommier asked, a glint of mischief at the back of his eyes.

"English, you!" she protested, slapping at him with the end of one of the drapery samples.

"It will come, Niki, it will come." He leaned toward her and kissed her cheek, thinking as he often did that she was lovely. He did not know why she had been willing to marry him after she had been his graduate assistant, but he was still grateful, whatever the reason.

Veronique held out the persimmon fabric. "Are you *sure*, Jean-Charles? Wouldn't you rather have this one?"—she offered a dusty-rose length to him—"or this?"—a burnt-orange—"ou bien, this one?" The last was almost peach.

"On you or the living room?" He reached back for the lists on the desk. "I still haven't found that one box of photos from Lapland. I hope they haven't been lost."

"Cochon!" Veronique said, her chin coming up sharply.

Pommier shook his head playfully. "For the living room, I think you are right. For when we lived in the Land Rover, this." He touched the burnt-orange. "That's hot enough to keep us warm all night."

"Oh!" she roared softly, using her feigned disgust to lunge into his arms.

He held her close against him, roused by her. He never tired of the joy she gave him; moments like this, when he could touch her, were as close to magical as anything in his life had ever been. "That orange," he said softly, "would keep away evil spirits. Oh, Niki."

"You don't believe in evil spirits," she reminded him, but snuggled closer as she spoke. Until this man had come into her life, she had felt intolerably vulnerable. He had breached her defenses within a month of knowing her and she had learned not only to love him—that had been easy—but to trust him as well, which was vastly more difficult. "You're not really bored, are you? You don't want to go back on an expedition?"

"Not now, no," he answered.

"But which?" she persisted.

"Pas du tout, pas du tout. I am looking forward to being here, in this place, in this house. I am looking forward to teaching for a change. I am looking forward to water we do not have to carry and heat in kettles. Uhn? I'm looking forward to working five-hour days for a change. I'm going to enjoy getting food at a supermarket, all wrapped up in plastic and labeled for weight and price. I'm going to eat hamburger... comme les Américains! Alors, maintenant, je suis Américain, hein?"

"French-Canadian," she said.

"French-Canadians are Americans," he reminded her.

"Oui, and Mexicans and Chileans."

"But you mean Americans," he said, trading his Montreal accent for something closer to St. Louis. "Amairicaaan. Ou là! Amuricun." Encouraged by Veronique's giggle, he imitated a broad Texas drawl. "Murkun."

"You're ridiculous." She laughed, then reached into the pocket of her skirt. "And tell me, my fine American, which one of these splendid boys is you?" Cautiously she held up a faded photograph. "You and your photographs..." she began.

"Where did you get th—" he shouted, grinning and embarrassed at what he had glimpsed before she tucked the photograph back into her skirt pocket again.

Veronique shrieked and giggled and then broke away from him, scampering out the door just ahead of him, losing only one of the drapery samples in her escape.

Pommier caught up the fabric and, brandishing it like a lasso, chased after her down the hall. "Come back here."

"Catch me!" she taunted back, bouncing down the stairs to the front hall.

He almost reached her there, but she was a shade too fast for him, and raced into the living room, coming to a halt at the fireplace. She managed to gasp out a few amused words there as she held up the little photograph once more. "We'll mount it... over the mantle! Commes les Américains!"

"You do and I'll . . ." Grinning, he caught her up in his arms, ignoring her giggling pleas. "You started this, ma belle, and I will finish it," he promised her with triumph as he at last seized the offending picture. Then, knowing how easily injured she was, he kissed her and slowly lowered her feet to the floor. It was some little time before they broke apart and each was a bit breathless.

"Jean-Charles . . ."

Belatedly he stared down at the photograph; it showed a grade-school class of awkward little boys flanked by four stern old nuns in elaborate old-fashioned coifs. "Where the devil did you find this?"

Her smile was shy. "Your mother . . ."

"I should have known," he muttered.

" . . . gave it to me, a long time ago, before we married. It's been in storage."

"It should have been buried," he said, glaring at it.

Veronique ran her finger down his nose. "We have never before had a mantel to put it on." He covered her hand with his and brought her fingers to his lips. "Stop that; I'm being serious."

"So am I," he told her between kisses.

"I love it here, Jean-Charles," she said in a little voice, suddenly self-effacing. "I love it that we have settled down in a proper house, even if it is only for a little while."

He looked into her eyes, knowing how her shyness often masked fear. "Were you getting tired of expeditions, ma belle?"

"A little," she admitted, her slow nod revealing more than her words.

"You should have told me," he chided her gently. "You must not be afraid to tell me these things, Niki." He pulled her close again, one hand tangled in her red hair, the other across her back.

She returned his embrace silently, not knowing how to tell him that she would endure far worse than exhaustion to be with him. Her head rested against his shoulder and she felt that there was no better place to be than in his arms.

This time their kiss was deeper, awakening desire and need. Pommier knelt, his hands traveling down Veronique's body. "Come," he murmured, drawing her down beside him on the carpet. He kissed her ear, her neck, her mouth as he unbuttoned her blouse and unfastened the front clasp of her bra.

She closed her eyes and let the sensations of his touch engulf her. She flung out one arm to the side and her hand reached a packing box. This mundane intrusion brought her back to her surroundings, and her obligations. Reluctantly she started to move away from him. "No. Non, non. Nope, not now. There is still too much to do. We will be unpacking until October."

His hand slid from her breast to her hip. "I don't want to wait until October."

"You won't. But it is only eight o'clock." Her protest sounded feeble to her own ears and she could see that he was not at all convinced.

"We have a new house, ma belle, which you love. It is as if we are just married." His tongue touched her nipple. "Ah, Niki, je t'adore."

She shook her head, pretending she did not know how provocative the movement was. "Do not make me presents, you. When we first married, you were following seal hunters. You would disappear for days going after them, and when you would come back, you smelled like them!" She touched his hair and pulled at it in teasing reprimand.

"I don't smell like them now. Do I?" His mouth met hers, undeniable.

"Tu es impossible! Impossible!" she said when she could speak once more. "Very well. You have undone me," she informed him haughtily while her hands unfastened his shirt. "But upstairs. In our bed. And..." she added primly, "we will each carry up boxes."

"Ah, well," he sighed, bracing himself on his elbow and permitting her to rise.

"The linens," she said, pointing to two boxes.

"Tout de suite."

"I will get the other," she said.

"It's not necessary," he said as he hefted the larger of the two boxes. "Lead on, Niki."

She made no attempt to restore order to her clothes. She flung up her head and started toward the stairs, pausing to blow him a kiss. "Perhaps, Jean-Charles, we will not be unpacked until November," she suggested innocently.

Pommier followed her, chuckling. "It would be my pleasure, ma belle."

FIVE

Flax shoved outward with all her strength and heard David Griffith grunt in surprise as she struck him. Immediately she flushed a dark red, the—was it a memory? a fantasy? what?—presence of what she had witnessed still impressing her. She felt like an eavesdropper, a voyeur. That kind of intimacy should not be intruded upon, and certainly not in the way she had done.

"Eileen!" Griffith burst out. "God, *now* what?"

Sally Bell shook her head. "I don't know, doctor. I told you she wasn't feeling well, and after that shock . . . Should I get a sedative?"

"Not until I know for sure she's not in shock. I don't want to compound the problem," Griffith said decisively. "You two," he added over his shoulder to the other nurses, "get out of here and see if we can arrange to get a CT scan on Dr. Flax. Quickly. I think we might be dealing with a hairline skull fracture here."

This was too much for Flax. "No!" she said firmly. "I don't need a scan. I haven't got a fracture or a concussion or anything of that nature. It's not anything . . . like . . . that." She wanted to sound sensible, in control of herself, but she knew that those around her would not be convinced; she would not be, were she the examining physician. "Really, Dave. I know it sounds crazy. But believe me, I'll be all right."

"I doubt it."

"It's just delayed shock," Flax said.

"My ass," Griffith countered. "I want to get you checked. You were the color of a brick when you woke up, and now you're like chalk. How do you account for that, doctor? Give me a halfway reasonable diagnosis and I'll buy it."

"I don't know what's happening," she admitted. "It's not . . . physiological." She flushed again. Under her embarrassment there was an envy. Never in all the seven years of her marriage had Eric looked at her as Pommier had stared at Niki. She had read of a look that had all the heart in the eyes and until that moment she had thought it was mere poetic allusion. Now she had seen for herself, had felt it in some obscure way, and her own life seemed to her immeasurably empty and . . . poor for lack of such love.

"Have you got a fever?" Sally asked, her hand going to Flax's forehead.

"Not that kind," Flax answered with a shaky laugh. There had been sensations, too, physical responses that she had never felt, that were physically impossible for her to feel, and yet because Pommier had experienced them, she had, too. She could not help but be fascinated. "I'm . . . kind of disoriented," she said, pushing Sally back, determined to put a stop to these disturbing episodes. "No, please, don't get in a fuss about me."

"You're more than disoriented . . ." Griffith began.

"It's just some kind of delayed reaction from yesterday," Flax insisted. "Ted Oldsman warned me I might have a couple of episodes like this, but I didn't think they'd be so . . . severe."

"Well," Griffith said dubiously, "if you're not in good shape . . ."

"I'll be okay," Flax insisted, her tone sharp.

"I think you'd better let us check you over, just in case," Griffith said, intercepting a warning lift of the eyebrow from Sally. "You can't go on rounds like this. What would happen if you collapsed in front of a patient?"

"Bad press?" Flax suggested, making an attempt at humor to cover the dread that fluttered in her chest.

Griffith made an amused sound to show he appreciated her attempt, but there was little real enjoyment in him. "Eileen, if you don't have the scan, I'll have to recommend that you be taken off active status until you do. You could be concussed from that fall. You said that you didn't have much of a blow to the head, but it doesn't take much, sometimes. You could have a hairline fracture and that could cause all sorts of problems. You're in Neurology: I don't have to tell you about skull fractures."

Flax had gotten to her feet and was able to stand without swaying, but she was inwardly aghast at how weak she had become. "It shouldn't be . . ." she began, then sighed. Perhaps all the strange things that had happened in the last twenty-four hours were nothing more than hallucinations brought about by stress and pressure on her brain. It would be reassuring to think so, she told herself. If it turned out that she was suffering from a mild concussion or other trauma, she would not have to worry about the images in her mind.

"Hey, Dr. Flax," Sally said, putting a hand on her shoulder, "we know that you doctors aren't infallible. Let them do the scan, and I guarantee that if anything has to be done, you'll get the best treatment the nursing staff can give."

"What?" Oh, dear God, Flax thought, what if they have to operate. For all her years of neurological studies, she had dreaded surgery, and to have a surgeon probe her own brain terrified her as nothing else could.

"Hey, Flax, don't look that way," Griffith said, trying to calm her. "It doesn't have to be anything bad. We shouldn't take chances; you know that."

"Sure," Flax said quietly. "It makes sense." Her pulse started to race, and she found that her hands were trembling. "I'm sorry," she said, as she tried to smooth her skirt to hide how badly she was shaking, "I don't . . . I've got overtired, that's part of it."

"Residents are always tired," Griffith said, attempting

to make a joke of the remark. "You know what it's like better than I do." He nodded to Sally. "Bell, why don't you go down with Flax, and . . ."

"Shit!" Flax burst out. "Don't you think I can make it on my own?"

Griffith winked at her. "I'm not worried about that. But I know you, and you're likely to decide to finish your rounds, complete your records, have a cup of coffee, read your mail, and *then* go for a scan. Right?"

His description was so close to what she had planned to do that she blinked at him. "I wouldn't," she said.

"Why not? I would." He shrugged. "I think it would be better if you got this over with. It'll take a load of worry off your mind and you'll do your job better if you aren't thinking every minute that you're about to collapse." There was more determination in his tone now than he had had at first, as if he was beginning to think of Flax more as a patient and less as a colleague. "Ted and I'll go over the scans ourselves, if you'd like, Eileen."

"Do whatever you think is best, Dave," she said with insincere heartiness. "You're probably right."

"Now you're being a sensible girl." He patted her on the arm, unaware that she was growing furious at his cavalier treatment. "Bell, you'll see that she's taken care of, won't you?"

"Of course, doctor," Sally said grimly.

As soon as Griffith was gone, Flax turned to Sally. "Where does that bastard get off talking to me like that? And to you?"

"They're all like that," Sally said, pointing to the door. "He's right, though. You should get a scan series done and right away."

Flax felt her shoulders droop in defeat. "I know. But I don't want to."

"Who does?" Sally asked, her manner becoming more sympathetic. "You ready to go down?"

"Sure. Why not?" Flax answered, permitting Sally to

hold the door open for her. As she stepped out into the hall, she was grateful it was empty. There were enough curious people on the staff that she had been half afraid that there would be a dozen orderlies and nurses lingering around the door to the lounge waiting for the chance to have a look at her. Nevertheless, she took great care to walk straight, moving at a good pace toward the elevator.

"I don't think you have anything really wrong," Sally said, making the effort to keep pace with Flax. "I've been a nurse a long time, and you get a feel about these things. I think you've got a mild concussion and a delayed shock reaction."

"Thanks," Flax responded with a wooden smile.

"Any time," Sally said as they reached the elevators and began what seemed an interminable wait.

The big doors whisked open and Flax stared into the dark, shiny interior. Her eyes swam and it was all she could do to force herself to take the step into it.

"Something wrong, doctor?" Sally asked, pressing the button for the third floor.

Flax shook her head, but more to try to rid herself of the fresh images that flickered in her vision than to deny Sally's concern.

At night the driveway in front of Pommier's house was largely in shadow, the street light shining on the front porch on the west side of the building instead of the south. Perhaps two figures scurried in the dark, their furtive movements accompanied by the faint strains of a punk rock band.

"Hurry up, fuckhead," one voice whispered.

"Jerk off," said the other.

There was the distinct sound of the front door opening and Pommier's voice calling, "I think I left it in the car, Niki."

Her comment was too indistinct to hear clearly.

"Hurry up!" the second voice hissed.

Pommier had reached the corner of the house, and he paused, his head cocked to one side to listen. His years of living in the remote parts of the world had taught him a sort of caution that was not often found in those more accustomed to urban sprawl than enormous empty plains.

"Move!" the second voice whispered, and there was a rapid and quiet scramble as the two figures fled.

In the next yard, a small dog yapped, the sound one of greeting instead of warning. Hearing it, Pommier smiled to himself. "I'm being foolish," he muttered as he made his way to the blue Rabbit parked in the driveway. He unlocked the door and leaned over the front seat to pick up the three packages in the back. The continuing ruckus of the dog caught his attention once more and he looked toward the neighbor's house, thinking absently that a noisy dog might be a pest. Out of the corner of his eye he noticed that there was something not quite right about the garage door.

At first he did not move; then he turned slowly to stare at it. In the dark he could not make out what was there. He reached into the glove compartment and pulled out a flashlight. Stepping out of the car so that the beam would not be reflected on the windshield, Pommier turned the light on the door.

In the bobbing, uneven circle of brightness, the words were hard to read, scrawled in haste as they had been, the red letters still dribbling wetly down the wall.

SEX DEATH PIGS KILL

Beneath the words was a crudely drawn cruciform dagger with a phallus instead of a blade.

Pommier stared at the wall in disbelief, as if the words were in a wholly unknown language, and the drawing was of something he had never seen before. Then apprehension and disgust took hold of him, and

he reached back into the glove compartment for the rag
he kept there to wipe off the windshield. Now he used
it on the wall, working in swift, desperate swipes to
take the words and the picture away before morning
could reveal them to the world, to Veronique.

There was a sound behind him, and Pommier swung
around, the flashlight moving with him, finding Veronique's troubled face.

"What are you doing?" she demanded, vexed.

As the elevator doors opened, Sally shouted for help,
supporting Flax's lolling head against her shoulder.
"Hey! We've got a hemorrhage here!"

Cassie Maybeck, an open paperback romance in one
hand and a can of cola in the other, looked up at Sally's
cry. "Jesus!" The book dropped from her hand and the
can was set on the counter before she pressed the
emergency button by her hand.

Sally got Flax out of the elevator, but hesitated to
move her any more than necessary. "Hurry! I think it
might be a detached retina."

By the time Cassie reached her, there were two
orderlies and an intern rushing toward them. Cassie
checked Flax quickly and rapped out orders. "Hem-
morrhage at the eyes and nose. Possible skull fracture,
possible stroke. Get Neurology at once. Set up for
emergency scan. Blood work-up at once. Move it!"

"But that's Dr. Flax," one of the orderlies said,
distressed.

"That's right, stud," Cassie said. "Now, move!"

One of the orderlies had already found a gurney and
was bringing it along the corridor. "Just a sec. I'm
coming!" he called to Cassie.

"Good for you," Cassie shot back, turning to Sally
Bell. "What happened?"

"I don't know," Sally said helplessly. "She had something go wrong about twenty minutes ago. She almost

passed out, but not quite. Or I don't think she was all the way out. David Griffith wanted her to come down for scans. She said no. And it looked like she was okay." Her hands fluttered, the only sign of her turmoil. "She didn't want to have scans. She . . ."

"Damned stubborn broad," Cassie muttered, biting her lower lip. "I swear that doctors are the worst patients that ever were."

Sally nodded her agreement as she went on. "She was a little shaky, that's all. She said she'd take a little more time off, have a cup of coffee. I got into the elevator with her, to keep an eye on her in case—"

"Good for you," Cassie interjected.

"We started down, and then, out of nowhere, she turned pale, says 'No, not again,' then her nose starts to bleed, and before I could do anything about it, her eyes . . ."

Cassie helped the orderly get Flax onto a gurney. "I don't like the look of her. She's too limp. She's got the muscle tone of a baked lasagna." She beckoned to the intern. "Check all the vitals; I want a nurse doing blood pressure every five minutes until she's stable. You got that?"

Another intern had joined them in time to hear these orders. "Shit, look at her."

"Don't waste your time looking," Cassie snapped. "Get her into intensive care and put a guard on her, if necessary. I don't want to hear any more of this crap about her being fine. She's not fine. If she says any different, ignore her."

The first intern was about to object to this rough treatment, but the second one complied without protest.

Cassie had already started back toward her counter. "Get Ted Oldsman on the phone right now. I want him down here."

"But David Griffith . . ." Sally started before Cassie shot a dark look at her.

"Oldsman worked on her last night, and he's the one

who should see her now. If she was showing any symptoms whatever, he'll know about it. David's good at his job, but Eileen is Ted's patient, not David's. Ted should be informed of what's happened and he should be down here. Got that?"

As Cassie followed the gurney, she saw Flax's hands move. "Hold it!" she shouted to the interns, and ran after them. "She's coming out of it."

Flax's eyes fluttered open, unseeing, and she made an ineffective attempt to clear the blood away from them. "The door," she whispered. "Oh, God, the door."

Pommier had turned off the flashlight, but not before Veronique had recognized the last word. "Kill? Is that what it says?" she asked.

Pommier tried to block the sight with his body; even the faint shine of the streetlight revealed too much. He could not bear to think that Veronique might be frightened by this senseless vandalism. "Go inside, ma belle. It is nothing, nothing. Children making mischief."

"Children?" she said in rising horror. "What kind of children? It says kill."

"It's nothing, I tell you. Let me wipe if off before it dries, so we won't have to look at it anymore," he insisted gently, still trying to pull her back into the light from the porch, away from the hatred that ran red on the garage door.

"Dieu! Qu-est-ce qu'il y a?"

"I don't know, Niki. I don't know what is going on or who is doing it. Please go inside. Please!" He wanted to take her in his arms and hold her, but not now, not here with those words and the drawing behind him.

"Qui l'a fait?" she demanded more loudly.

"I tell you, I don't know. Niki, I beg you, go upstairs." He was determined not to become irrational about this episode. "These things happen, sometimes."

"It is not enough, Jean-Charles," she warned him.

"Niki..." All he could think of now was the red paint. He had to get it off the door.

"Qui..." she shouted.

"I don't know!" he yelled at her, and once he had her attention, dropped his voice to a lower level than usual. "Niki, don't argue with me. Go inside. Please!"

She folded her arms, prepared to resist him, but something of his determination broke through her resolution. "What are you going to do?"

"First I am going to clean the door. Then I am going to see if I can find who did this. If nothing else, I will report this to the police." He thought that perhaps he ought to leave the words for the police to photograph, but was not willing to permit them to remain on his house any longer, contaminating the building with their obscenity.

"Very well. But you must not do..." she began as she started toward the stairs.

"I will not take risks. And you must not take risks, either. Lock all the doors and do not open them to anyone. I have my keys. I'll let myself in. But don't open the door to anyone, do you understand?" He gave his instructions in a steady tone in the hope that Veronique would be less troubled, but he could tell from the stiffness of her shoulders that he had not succeeded.

"As you wish, Jean-Charles," she said in a chastened voice, and turned away to obey him.

Had he been less concerned for her, he would have detained her to ease her mind, soothe her worries with a joke or a promise, but he was too uneasy for that. He watched the front door close and heard the deadbolt turn, then went to finish wiping off the red paint, leaving wide smears where the letters had started to dry.

Toward the end of the block, a surfers' van drew up at the curb, lights still on; punk rock and derisive laughter came from the open windows.

Pommier glanced once at the van as he got into his blue Rabbit, disliking the intrusion. "You're being foolish," he said to himself as he slammed the door and started the engine. As he turned on the headlights, he averted his eyes from his garage door, backing down the driveway more quickly than was wise, so that his tires squealed as he swung backward onto the street.

And braked to a stop. Along the wall between his house and the next were more letters, these spray-painted in electric blue:

GUTTERMAN IS A HERO!

He pulled on the emergency brake and started out of his car. From the van he heard more laughter, sly and insinuating. Trying to convince himself that the van's presence was a coincidence, unrelated to the ugly words he had discovered, he forced himself to move slowly, as if among nomadic tribesmen instead of on a suburban street in Santa Monica. Who, he asked himself, is Gutterman? Any why is he a hero? He reached the fence, his shadow cutting starkly across the *RO!* The spray paint was tacky to his fingers.

The punk rock from the van grew suddenly louder and Pommier spun around, thinking that it had moved closer. But no. It was still near the end of the block, caught in the glare of a streetlight. All Pommier could see was the long light-colored hair of the driver as he tipped his head back to pour beer down his throat.

Pommier took another step and caught the toe of his shoe on something that had been dumped against the fence. He looked down carefully, knowing that his discovery might be unpleasant or hazardous.

There was a roll of carpeting; as Pommier moved his foot, he saw that the color was a splotchy yellow. The carpet unrolled slowly, to reveal newspaper clippings stapled to it, and the word "WELCOME" in electric blue paint.

Another, louder burst of laughter came from the van and there was the sound of splintering glass as bottles were thrown from the open windows.

Carefully Pommier bent down to inspect the scraps of newsprint, pulling the first from the thick pile.

POLICE SEIZE BURGLAR IN BRUTAL SLAYING
School Children Surprise Thief

The bodies of two children, ages 7 and 10, were discovered yesterday when their parents returned from work. Police investigators were called to the scene at once and speculated that the children were the victims of a burglar who had been in the house when the two children returned from school at about 3:45 that afternoon.

Captain Arthur Coglan, in charge of the investigation, has requested that anyone in the vicinity of . . .

The rest of the article had been torn away, and below it was a second clipping, this one with a photograph of a man handcuffed and flanked by police. Pommier studied the picture, but could see little in the man to suggest the violence that had brought about the slaughter of two children: the man was little more than medium height, casually dressed, his hair a bit long but adequately trimmed; he appeared to be no more than thirty.

MUSICIAN ARRAIGNED
Parents Find Mutilated Bodies of Children

said the *Los Angeles Times*, reporting the same horror described in the previous article. There was a second, more blurred photograph, of two covered stretchers with pathetically small burdens on each being loaded into a police ambulance. A number of people crowded around the stretchers, a few curious, but most of them

showing that blank avidity that spectators at a disaster
always have about them.

The next four clippings covered the trial of Patrick
Gutterman, sometime musician, for the murder of Thomas
and Joanne Kimball, culminating in a final interview
with Robert and Sandra Kimball, the bereft parents.

GUTTERMAN GUILTY
Grief-Stricken Parents Returning to Midwest

Pommier had become so engrossed that he caught
himself reading aloud: " . . . who had moved here to
begin a new life, away from the crowding and crime of
Chicago, found that it had pursued them. That dream
came to an end with the first sight of the blood-soaked
carpet which . . ." He stopped, aware for the first time
of the carpet in his hands. Until that instant he had
assumed it was a scrap, something handy to attach the
clippings to. But now he saw that the mottling he had
thought at first was dirt was too rusty for that. Involun-
tarily he let out a cry, dropping the thing.

At his back, the van roared into life, leaving patches
of rubber as it sped away toward the ocean.

Dorothy Praeger came back to Pommier's mind, and
her glib explanations of transfers and new carpeting. He
had to fight the urge to phone her now and demand the
truth. If it was the truth. He had seen enough in his
travels and studies to know that newcomers and for-
eigners were convenient targets for malice, and this
could be more of that familiar pattern.

He went back to his Rabbit and moved it back into
the driveway, turning off the engine and headlights.
Then he sat, thinking that he must be rid of those
articles before Veronique could see them. He did not
want her to feel distressed when she had only just
achieved the comfort and security she had longed for.
He hoped the neighbors would understand if he put the
section of carpet in their trash. Reluctantly he got out of

the car, taking care to lock the doors before going slowly back to the house. In the morning, he decided, he would call Dorothy Praeger. And perhaps he would call that Captain Arthur Coglan as well. His steps sounded hollow as he climbed to the front door and turned his key in the deadbolt lock.

SIX

"It's the house," Flax muttered, and everyone around the gurney stared down at her. "The house."

"What?" Ted Oldsman demanded, not sure he had understood her, for the words were slurred.

"She said, 'It's the house,'" Cassie said, and finished wiping the blood off Flax's cheek. "Want me to write it down?"

"You better. The house. What the hell?" He leaned over Flax, lifting the lid of her left eye. "No noticeable change. Damn it, anyway."

Two nurses also worked with Cassie and Oldsman, and both of them hesitated before going on with their tasks. One of them, an older nurse and one not easily distressed, shrugged. "When someone's gone out like this, they can say all kinds of things. Doesn't mean much."

In the next partition, two physicians looked over the first results of Flax's scans; one of them had a pen to make notations.

"When do you think they'll be through in there?" Cassie asked, looking over her shoulder toward the partition.

"Don't rush them, Cassie," Oldsman reprimanded her. "They're doing the best they can."

"Yeah, well, so am I, and I don't like the way Eileen looks." Cassie shook her head, growing more nervous as she watched Flax, pale and still, on the gurney. "Shouldn't we get her into intensive care?"

"Not quite yet," Oldsman said. "We don't know what we're dealing with, remember?" He paused, then patted her arm. "You must be upset. You haven't said shit or fuck since we brought Eileen in here."

Cassie managed a wan smile. "Sure. Well, that's the way it goes. Goddamn it, I wish she had someone, anyone who..." She folded her arms as if to protect herself from hurt. "It's bad enough, going through shit with someone who... cares. Doing it alone, well..."

"You're her friend," Oldsman pointed out, looking steadily at Cassie. "You care about her; you care about everyone."

"It's not the same thing, and you know it," she snapped, though there was the shine of tears in her eyes. "Who's she got to come home to? Not even fish."

"She just moved out here less than a year ago," Oldsman reminded her, but his expression was troubled.

"Big fucking deal—"

"Cassie, for heaven's sake," Oldsman interjected and was ignored.

"That only makes it worse. What's she got to hold onto? Right now, that dead anthropologist is more real to her than most of us, and that's a... a terrible thought. People *die* of loneliness; you know that as well as I do."

Oldsman reached out and touched Cassie's arm, very lightly. "Cassie, don't take it so much to heart. We do what we can, and that's all we can do."

"That's great." She pinched the bridge of her nose between her thumb and index finger, then glared toward the partition. "Tell them to hurry it up, will you, Ted? What's taking them so long?"

He sighed. "Oh, Cassie, Cassie. It's not any easier for me than it is for you. I keep thinking that if I'd been more careful when I sewed up her ear, made her get a couple of X-rays or..."

"Unhunh," Cassie said, shrugging. "Do you think it would have shown anything?"

"Probably not," Oldsman murmured, and gave his attention back to Flax.

In the next partition, Bradley Cort ripped off another

length of graph paper. He studied it carefully, as he did everything carefully; he clasped his big, black hands together after handing the graph to his associate. "Well? That's the latest."

Paul Schacter was fifteen years younger than Cort and his ambition was going strong, not yet having encountered the experience that would teach him to doubt. He read the graph and shook his head. "What a mess."

"It is. And it's worse than the first," Cort said heavily. He had a headache starting behind his eyes, the gnawing kind that took a long time to fade. "What do you think, Paul?"

"It's fakacht," Schacter declared, tapping the graph with the end of his pencil. "Can't be anything else. It's gotta be... Let's get the techies in here and pull the thing apart. We can't turn in a good diagnosis with a screwed-up computer."

"It's after six," Cort reminded him.

"So we call the night number," Schacter said, hitching up his shoulders.

"You're right: call 'em." He leaned back and knocked on the clouded glass partition. "I'll have a talk with Ted and Cassie while you take care of the machines."

That was the way Schacter preferred it. "Sure," he promised as he reached for the phone and dialed for an outside line.

Ted Oldsman stepped around the partition, anticipating Cort. "What have you got, Brad?"

Cort shook his head and rubbed his eyes. "The machine isn't doing too well, but it's a pretty good guess that there's no trauma. The bleeding has stopped and we can't find any evidence of an aneurysm."

"Thank God for that," Oldsman said.

"But I think we ought to run another series in the morning, when we've had a little better chance to observe her."

Oldsman shook his head, feeling guilty. "Christ, I

examined her myself, and I thought she was okay. What did I miss? I feel . . . sick about this. I should have been more careful, but she kept saying she was fine. . . . There was blood in the ear passage. I saw it, and I thought that it came from, you know, outside, from the bite."

Cort leaned back in his chair. "Relax Ted. You didn't miss a thing."

"Then what's going on?"

On the phone, Schacter had drawn one blank and was trying another approach. "Hey, Judy, this is Paul Schacter. Will you see if you can get me a night service number for Data General . . . ?"

"We're as baffled as you are," Cort said to Oldsman. "We're getting some screwy numbers. Have a look for yourself," he offered, handing the graph over. "The first time through it was faint—see that?—and only showed on the automatic functions."

Schacter reached over to pluck Cort's sleeve. "Data General is the one we want? It *is* who we're looking for, isn't it?" He saw Cort nod and gave his attention back to the phone. "That's got to be the one, Judy."

Cort leaned forward, using his pen to point out significant tracings. "Then we started getting cortical propagation, like this. Those lines are coming from something real deep, primitive. Whatever's causing it, it goes right through to the roots of her brain. And now—"

"Wait a minute," Oldsman interrupted him. "I don't understand what's going on here."

"Neither do we. That's the trouble. Flax is out cold, but have a look—that's the brain function of somebody who's wide-awake."

"But . . ." Oldsman stared at the tracings as if he could make them change. "You sure this isn't a mistake?"

"We're going to get the machine checked before we run the scan again. But looking at it, I'd say we were dealing with an active person. I mean active. Seeing, hearing, moving around, talking to people." He broke off to give a suggestion to Schacter. "Tell her to check with Mrs. Lockman. She'll know how to find it."

"She *did* say something," Oldsman remarked to the wall.

"When?" Cort asked.

"Just now, a couple minutes ago, something about a house, or that's what Cassie thinks she said." He frowned. "And earlier, she said something in French."

"So?" Cort asked, not following Oldsman's thought.

"It's just . . . that wacko professor who jumped her, he kept swearing in French." Now that he had said it, he thought it was foolish, but he shrugged. "For what it's worth."

Schacter had finally got off the phone. "They say they'll be out here before midnight."

"Wonderful," Cort said sarcastically.

"It was the best I could do." He sat on the edge of the desk. "What's this about French?"

Oldsman was starting to be embarrassed, so he did his best to make light of it. "That crazy talked a lot in French, that's all."

"So she had a run-in with a crazy, you don't think that did this to her, do you?" Schacter inquired restlessly. "Hey, this place is full of crazies, French or no French. Read the papers, or come into emergency service."

"I work emergency, remember?" Oldsman said sharply.

"Then you know," Schacter declared, refusing to end his diatribe. "They find four bodies a day on the freeways, nobody knows who they are or where they're going, they're just out there on the freeway." He cleared his throat. "We better put her in a room for the night and make sure she gets hourly checks. She's stable now, but who knows what will happen next. We have a technical problem here, and we'll have to let the computer boys straighten it out for us. . . ." He turned his head sharply at a sudden sound from the other room.

Oldsman stared at Cort. "We better get moving. It's starting again."

"Ted!" Cassie shouted over Flax's calm, reasonable voice that did not sound like herself at all, saying, "Good afternoon, Captain Coglan."

Oldsman burst into the examination room, Cort close behind him.

"Hey, Schacter, put a monitor on her! Fast!" he bellowed to his associate as he rushed up to the gurney.

"What's happened?" Oldsman demanded of Cassie as he bent over Flax.

"I don't know," Cassie answered helplessly. "One second she was lying there, well, you know what she looked like. The next thing I know, *this* happens."

Schacter burst into the room, shoving one of the nurses out of the way. "Jesus, look at the eyes!" he cried as he began to fasten electrodes to Flax's head and neck. "You'd think, with her respiration and . . . she might as well be climbing a flight of stairs!"

"It's eerie," Cassie said softly. "It's weird."

Police Captain Arthur Coglan was a well-mannered man, as suited the city he worked in. Not for him the rough treatment and brusque talk some officers affected. He was polite and pleasant as he ushered Pommier into his office.

"What can I do for you, Dr. Pommier?" he asked, hardly pausing to add, "Would you like some coffee?"

"No, thank you," Pommier answered. "I am here on a curious matter." Now that he was actually in the police station, he was not at all certain he should be taking the captain's time, but he had come this far. "There was . . . an unpleasant episode at my home last night, and . . ."

"I don't usually handle domestic disturbances," Coglan said, forgoing the coffee because Pommier had not accepted any.

"It was not quite that," Pommier said, thinking of the carpet he had in the plastic trash bag he carried. "In fact, I do not know precisely what it is, which is why I have come to you."

Coglan would have loved to ask why he had been chosen, but knew it was not wise to push; in time he would learn what it was the man wanted.

"You see," Pommier explained diffidently, "my wife and I have only just moved here. I am teaching at UCLA and we wished to find a house instead of an apartment. Santa Monica is convenient to the campus, and the community is very pleasant." He shifted the bag against his knees. "We have only been in the house a week."

"Getting some hazing from the neighborhood kids?" Coglan asked.

"I . . . I don't know." He folded his arms. "Captain, I am a rational man, an educated man, and I pride myself on my good sense."

Coglan grew more apprehensive at what was to follow. "And?"

"I do not wish to alarm anyone unduly." He caught his lower lip between his teeth, more in thought than worry. "Last night, someone painted some . . . ugly words on my garage door and my fence. I have removed most of what was on the garage door. It might not have been wise, but I did not want my wife troubled." He exhaled sharply. "The words were not all. I was going to dispose of this and forget the whole thing, but it has been preying on my mind, so I've brought it to you." He handed the plastic bag across the desk and sat down in the visitor's chair.

"What's this?" Coglan said, hesitating to open the bag.

"Do not worry, there is nothing alive in it," Pommier said, permitting himself to smile a bit. "It was part of the whole . . . demonstration."

"I see." Reluctantly Coglan opened the bag and stared into it. "What the devil?"

"It is, as you can see," Pommier told him, "a section of yellow carpet. It is badly stained. There are newspaper clippings—they were stapled to the carpet when I found it, but I removed them to read them."

Coglan winced at the headlines, recalling vividly the terrible murders. "The Gutterman case," he said disdainfully.

"Your name was mentioned in the stories, so I brought the thing to you. One of the phrases on the fence called Gutterman a hero." Pommier could see that Coglan was more concerned now than when he first came into the office. "You were in charge of the investigation. I was hoping you might tell me the best way to deal with . . . this."

Holding the section of carpet in his hands, Coglan was not able to answer at once. He knew where the thing came from, what the stains were. He could not imagine who had taken such a souvenir, but did not doubt that someone had picked it up as a trophy. "There . . . uh . . . there was some difficulty for the Kimballs during the trial. They had . . . problems."

"I'm sorry," Pommier said earnestly. "They had enough to contend with, I would think."

"Yes." Coglan pinched the bridge of his nose. "That's why they left. The story about the transfer was just that, a story." He sighed. "Look, let me show you some pictures. If you're getting some of the same thing, maybe I can finally get a lead on these creeps." With that, he stood up and went to the files at the back of his office. "I don't know. Out here, we get all types. They come out to the end of the world, sunshine, beaches, and they have no place else to go. Some of them are nut cases, not sick enough to be in an institution"—he closed one drawer and opened another—"not well enough to do much of anything but bum around. There are surfers and sun bunnies and bikers and street freaks. . . ."

He pulled out two thick files. "Here it is. Have a look at the photos, will you?" As he sat down, he handed the files across the plastic bag to Pommier.

The first three were nothing more than disgusting words and offensive pictures in spray paint on a blank wall. Pommier looked at them carefully. "I couldn't say if these are by the same hand. I was not able to learn much about the handwriting." He tried to smile in order to take the sting out of what he said, as he often did when correcting a student in class, but this time he could not pull it off. The next two photos showed abandoned cans of spray paint on the sidewalk, and he shook his head as he stared at them. "Nothing so far."

Then he picked up the sixth photo and stared at it. There were words and drawings scrawled all over two sides of a house, some proclaiming the heroism of Gutterman, some of them depicting the murdered children, but that did not hold Pommier's attention. "Captain," he said lightly, "what house is this?"

Coglan half-rose to look at the photo Pommier held out to him. "The Kimball place. That's what I mean about difficulties. For three months that kind of thing went on almost every night. Why?"

Pommier gave a little laugh. "Really? Because that's where my wife and I live."

"*Now* what?" Oldsman shouted in exasperation.

"Why'd she stop?" came the call from Schacter from behind the partition. "Is she all right?"

Cassie stepped back, her face going strangely pale. "She's not—"

"She's alive," Oldsman snapped. "But she's . . . out again."

"What is going *on* with her?" Schacter asked the machines as he watched the tracings return to those expected of deep, nearly hypnotic sleep.

"Something has got to be doing it," Oldsman said through his teeth. "But what? What?"

"She looks so . . ." Cassie shook her head, not wanting to finish. She had seen patients in coma with that same, waxen calm. "What can we do?"

"For the moment, we watch her," Cort said grimly. "And nothing else unless she goes into cardiac or respiratory failure. I don't want to mess with whatever it is she's got until we know damn well what's going on."

"And what then?" Cassie asked softly.

"Then we'll decide. I guess," Cort answered with a careful look at Oldsman.

"Great," Oldsman muttered. "And how long do you think it's going to take?"

Cort shook his head. "It can't take too long. She can't stand much more of this." He waited while Cassie and Oldsman digested this. "You've seen the tracings and you know how much of a strain she's under." He narrowed his eyes, giving Flax a careful scrutiny. "You think this was started because of that attack?"

"I do," Oldsman said.

"And you, Maybeck?" Cort tapped his fingers together impatiently.

"I can't think of anything else." Cassie resisted the urge to take her anxiety out on Cort.

"Suppose there was something else," Cort mused. "Suppose there was something that happened to her before she came into work, something that might have been working on her before the emergency."

"Such as what?" Cassie demanded, hands on her hips. "Don't start that crap about the lady needing a good fucking. I don't know about anyone in her life, but I do know when a woman is going up the walls, and let me tell you, Bradley Cort, Eileen Flax isn't one of those women. Got that?"

"If you say so," Cort responded, wholly uncritically.

"Wait a minute," Oldsman cut in. "You're not seriously suggesting that what Flax has got is psychosomatic?"

"It's a possibility. We have to consider it."

"Just a minute." Oldsman said, motioning to Cassie to contain her outburst until he had got more out of Cort. "I *know* Eileen. She hasn't been here long, and she's not settled in, but she's a good, dependable, steady, competent doctor."

"That's not in question," Cort said mildly. "But put yourself in my position for a minute. I have a patient here who has symptoms that make no physiological sense, but who clearly is suffering from some major dysfunction. All right?"

"Okay," Cassie admitted grudgingly.

"Look at her," Cort said, moving closer to the gurney. "You'd never know that a couple of minutes ago her respiration was up, her brain activity was that of someone in a fully awake state, that the tracings were like those of a person taking part in a conversation, one that was stimulating or exciting or . . . disturbing. If I hadn't seen it for myself, I would have doubted it. If there is no sound physiological reason for her condition, then there must be a psychological reason. *Something* is going on here." He put his hand on Flax's forehead. "Her temperature is down, her pulse is down, her color is terrible, there's no eye movement. You figure it out, you two. If you can come up with a better explanation for her condition, I'd welcome it, believe me."

Cassie swallowed against a tightness in her throat. "You said yourself that your machines aren't working quite right, that you want to do the scans and monitoring over again. Well, it could be that a lot of what you're seeing is due to that machine and not to any . . . looniness on Eileen's part." She could hear the defensive tone of her voice and she wished she could find a way to sound more confident.

"Cassie's got a point," Oldsman said, unexpectedly

coming to her assistance. "When you've got the new
readings, then we can consider..."

"You're probably right," Cort said, his expression
perplexed. "Poor lady, going through something like
this." He started toward the door. "I'll make sure she
gets into a room at once. I think we should keep
monitors on her all night. That way, if she has another
episode, we'll know at once. If we watch her, we might
learn something."

"Such as what?" Cassie asked, making no attempt to
disguise her anger now. "You have any idea, Brad?"

"I wish I did," he said as he went into the hallway.
He was baffled by the case, which troubled him. It was
one thing if a physician was wrong about a sprained
ankle, but quite another if he messed up on a neurological case.

"Well?" Oldsman turned to Cassie once Cort was
gone.

Cassie tilted her chin up. "Well what?"

"Do you think he's right?" Oldsman was staring down
at his hands, flexing his fingers nervously, not willing to
look at her for too long.

"You mean, is it psychosomatic?" She would like to
have shaken him for asking, but she was able to speak
without shouting. "No. Nothing so simple. I think that
she's... out of control. Like one of those cars on the
freeway with a stoned kid behind the wheel. You can't
say that the car has a psychosomatic disease, can you?"

"Eileen's not a car, she's a woman, and a good
doctor." Oldsman wanted to get more heat and conviction into his argument, but it rang false in his ears.

"I think that something has happened to her, and that
she's got something of that anthropologist... stuck in
her, like a bacterium with a virus stuck in it, and...
changing it." Cassie had begun emphatically, but her
voice faded as her thoughts turned inward. "Eileen's
not just obsessed with a patient she lost, Ted. There's
more to it than that."

"You're really stretching," Oldsman said, heading toward the door. "You on call tonight?"

"I'm supposed to be," Cassie informed him, still feeling defensive.

"Good. So'm I. Maybe we could split breaks, so that we can check on her. Just to be sure. Are you willing?" He waited for Cassie to reply. "I keep thinking that this is partly my fault. Logically I know that it probably isn't, but still . . ."

With an overly casual lift to her shoulders, Cassie agreed. "Okay. We can split breaks and compare notes when we finish checking. I take my first break at ten-thirty. What about you?"

"I don't come on until midnight. I was going out to dinner, but . . . strictly speaking this time is time off right now." He patted Flax's unmoving arm as if this gesture would express his concern in a way she could understand. "I think I might try to find out more about who that guy was. What name did she say?"

Cassie frowned. "I don't know. Coogan, I think, or maybe Cadman."

"Well, come on, which is it?" Oldsman persisted.

"I think it was Captain Coogan. I don't know what kind of captain. It could be a headwaiter or an army officer or the skipper of a fishing boat."

"Thanks for the encouragement," he said wearily. "I've got to do something, Cassie."

"I don't want to stop you," she said, and there was only affection in her manner. "But it's such a long shot. After all, there's no saying he's anywhere around here— she's from Boston, remember."

Oldsman shook his head.

"Good luck with your wild goose," Cassie said, giving Oldsman the friendliest smile she could. "I wish there was something I could do."

"Don't we all?" asked Oldsman.

SEVEN

Around ten-thirty, shortly after Cassie entered Flax's room, there was a change. The heart monitor showed more frequent beats, and then her breathing grew deeper. Cassie checked her over, then hit the intercom toggle to the nurses' station. "You better get someone down here into Flax's room," she warned. "There's another episode beginning."

At that, Flax began to laugh.

Veronique stood in the open door to the study, her face almost rigid. "Why are you laughing, Jean-Charles?" She could not keep from shouting. "What is funny?"

Pommier sat at his desk with a number of photocopies laid out on it. Captain Coglan had been obliging enough to give him all the information the police had gathered on the various defacings and vandalism at the house since the Gutterman crimes. The cumulative effect on these records dismayed him, but left him so puzzled that his only release was in laughter. "These . . ." he managed to say on the second try.

"But what?" she insisted, coming to stand beside him. "Jean-Charles?"

His laughter was less wild now, and he wiped his eyes. "Oh . . . c'est rien, ma belle. It has been a difficult day." He put his arm across the photocopies, not wishing to show her what some of them contained.

"And for that you laugh?" She was more concerned now, but he was not behaving as he usually did. "You're not yourself."

"Perhaps not." He rubbed his face with both hands and at last began to hope that his irrational mirth had passed. "I caught myself thinking, as I looked at these, that there are some... strange people in this world."

She nodded. "You are the one to know that, Jean-Charles."

"Um." Abruptly he swept the photocopies into one of the drawers.

"What is that?" she asked, no longer worried but cautious just the same.

"Nothing. The police gave me some papers. It is nothing at all." He cleared his throat and got out of the chair. "I'm sorry, Niki. I didn't expect we should have to cope with anything like this." Gently he put his hands on her shoulders. "I stopped at the hardware store on the way home. Don't worry about the door. I will repaint it in the morning."

"You have a faculty meeting in the morning," she reminded him, suddenly petulant.

"Then I will paint it before we go to dinner." He tried to soften his curtness by kissing her forehead. "Niki, I will take care of it."

"And the police?" She was resisting his warmth and they both knew it. "What about them?"

He dared not tell her everything he had learned. "I have told them as much as I could, but what was that? What should they do, if I call them and say that children have painted disgusting words on my garage door, come quickly? I have been assured that the cars that patrol the neighborhood will come down this street more often for the next two weeks. That is a sensible offer, Niki."

"Oui. C'est satisfaisant."

Pommier wrapped his arms around her and for once he did not sense her response to his nearness. They stood together, unmoving, for some little time, then he stepped back. "I'm going to bed. Would you care to join me?"

"I do not think it was children," she said softly.

So that was part of it. He took her hands. "Niki . . .
children come in many sizes. You said that the old men
in the desert were like children, remember?"

She would not be put off. "But those old men would
not do . . . that. What kind of people write such things?
And why do they write it here?" She sniffed once, then
shot him a look that challenged him to notice her
moment of weakness.

"They probably won't come back," Pommier said, not
at all sure he believed that.

"And if they do?" Before he could answer, she put her
fingers to his mouth. "No. Do not tell me anything. I
think you would lie to make me feel better, but it would
not, and if you tell me bad things, I will be worried
again."

He kissed the fingers. "Then what am I to say, ma
belle?" He pulled her close again and draped one arm
over her shoulders. "I don't know what kind of people
do such things. I don't know." With his free hand he
smoothed her hair off her brow. "Come, let's go to bed,
mmm?"

Veronique hesitated, looking at him gravely. "You do
not have to protect me, Jean-Charles. I have been over
half the world with you, and we managed well enough
then; we will do so now."

"But this isn't the arctic or the Sahara," he reminded
her, saddened by what he said. "Here we live in a
house and watch TV in the evening. We're not out
following the nomads of the world. We have time to
rest, and . . ." He was at a loss to know how to finish.

This time she kissed him. "It will be well, Jean-
Charles."

They made their way out of the study and down the
hall toward the bedroom, occasionally exchanging light,
teasing kisses. She was able to unfasten the top three
buttons of his shirt and he opened the zipper at the
back of her dress. When they reached the door of the
bedroom, she paused.

"You did lock the doors." She did not want to ask, but she feared she would never give her whole attention to him if she was unsure.

"Yes." He outlined her lip with one finger. "Yes. The door is locked in front, the deadbolt is on; the door is locked in back and the latch is in place. The windows are locked. The drawbridge is raised," he added with a trace of a smile, hoping that her anxiety would fade. "I would not endanger you, Niki, not for anything in this world or out of it." The phrase was one he had learned from Eskimos and he had always liked it. "We're not in any danger."

"No, Jean-Charles," she said.

"Of course, if you want to worry, you can do it in the morning. Tonight, there are other things to do." He pushed the bedroom door open.

"Because it is October so soon?" A little of her playfulness was coming back.

"Oui. It is nearly November. Les feuilles tombent." He led her into the bedroom and did not trouble to turn on the lights.

"The leafs . . . leaves?" she translated obediently as he lifted her dress off her.

"Yes, leaves." He kissed the nape of her neck before going to the closet to find a hanger for the dress.

"The leaves are falling."

Pommier opened the closet door, saying in a rather abstracted tone, "Et des vents froids soufflent."

She giggled. "Your French-Canadian always sounds so funny. And cold winds blow . . ."

"Are blowing," he corrected her as he put the dress away. "Et bientôt, de grandes hampes de glace se leveront."

"And soon great shafts of ice will . . ." She grinned at him as she felt him unfasten her bra from behind. "I like that ice, for then we will have to stay indoors for days and days and days."

"Sorcière," he whispered. Then he moved away to

undress himself. Standing by the window, he glanced down into the street.

And under the streetlight, there was a black surfers' van, idling. Faint, brutal bursts of punk rock came from the vehicle.

"It is like something by Brecht and Weill," Pommier said, standing very still, his gray eyes hardening as he looked down.

As Veronique pulled on her lace-trimmed gown, she went on, unaware that he had been distracted. "Mais non. Je n'suis pas une sorcière. Je serais une bourgeoise. I will be Madame . . . no, *Mrs*. Pommier now, wife of the famous professor, with le suntan and le barbeque. And you should take care, Jean-Charles. I might come to like it, this new settled life."

"You are always a sorceress to me, bourgeoise or not." He meant it, but he did not pay much attention as he spoke.

"I will do everything I can to be . . . Californian. It is a change." She lifted her arms over her head and shook out her hair, wanting to recapture him.

"C'est bien," he said distantly, turning back to her from the window. "You are lovely, Niki."

"And you're still dressed . . ." she protested as she stared at him, apprehension taking the pleasure from the moment.

"Yes." He looked swiftly back at the van. "Get into bed. I will . . . I'll be back in a minute. No more than a minute."

Veronique stared at him, her anxiety increasing. "But where are you going, Jean-Charles? Tell me?"

"I . . . ah . . . I want a glass of wine." It was the best excuse he could find, and was glad that she did not hear the deception in his tone.

"Bring me one, too."

"Of course," he said as he hurried out of the bedroom, starting to rebutton his shirt. "Of course. Red wine."

Veronique's voice stopped him. "Jeany?"

"Yes?" He hesitated on the stair, knowing that she would not now accept glib explanations from him, but he had nothing more that he could say to her.

"Tout va bien?" She knew that his mind was not entirely on her any longer, that his curiosity had got hold of him once more, and it rankled a bit. She thought that he wanted to test the doors again, to be sure, and to stare out into the street at the vehicles that went by; it was the sort of thing he would not tell her.

"Yes. Yes, yes. Everything is fine, quite fine. I'll be . . . right back." He hurried down the stairs, almost running. In the darkened living room, he went to the window nearest the fireplace and pulled back the edge of the persimmon-colored drapery, carefully, very carefully.

The van had not moved. It waited there, the engine muttering to itself while the figures inside moved and contorted in ways that Pommier could not see clearly enough to understand.

"Who are you?" Pommier whispered to the van, and wished that one of the passengers would get out long enough for him to have a look. Moving back from the window, Pommier dropped into a chair, leaning forward, his elbows propped on his knees, his chin held in his hands. He was perplexed; he was intrigued. He could not understand what was going on, and that alone held his interest. After a while, he found that he was staring at the small, lumpy statue of an Armenian fertility goddess. "What do you think, little one?" he asked the statue softly. He got out of the chair and picked up the statue, patting it affectionately as if it was excused from answering his question. Without being aware of it, he had begun to pace, not rapidly, but with steady, determined strides. As he often did when confronted with a new problem, he talked to himself. "Why do they come? And why *here*? What is this place to them? Is it the murder? What kind of people . . . want . . ." He went back to the window and gazed out at the van, heard the faint, jarring notes from the speakers. "So . . . yes . . . it is possible."

"What is happening to her?" Cassie wailed. "What's doing this?"

Cort shook his head. "It's . . ." He lifted his hands in helpless despair. "It's taking quite a toll on her," he said softly. "She can't keep on this way indefinitely."

Cassie started to cry. "Her temperature is over one hundred-three. That's too high."

"Any temperature is too high," Cort answered. "I wish to God Ted would get here." He glowered at the monitors. "If I knew where to *begin*. If there were a history of this, or a family-connected . . ."

"I don't know about her family," Cassie said. "She's never said anything about them."

"Well, most doctors don't go around discussing the peculiarities in their own families. Not most that I know. Still, she's in Neurology for a reason." He rubbed his jaw thoughtfully. "If we don't get any hard information on her soon, I think we might start making some phone calls."

"That sounds awful," Cassie accused him. "Listen to you."

Cort turned to her. "Hey, Maybeck, we're not talking about party gossip, we're talking about a woman with what appears to be a major brain dysfunction. It could kill her. It could keep her out of work for the rest of her life. If getting the answers causes a little embarrassment, well, to use your phrase, tough shit." He looked at Flax again. "It might be easier if she had someone out here, but from what you say, she's entirely on her own. No family. No kids. No husband. No boyfriend. Nothing. Poor lady."

"Cort, don't," Cassie whispered.

As Flax thrashed once on the bed, Cort stared at her as if willing her body to give up its secrets to him.

"Look at her. You'd think she was about to . . . go somewhere."

The light of the study glared on as Pommier flung into the room. He rifled two of the file drawers, pulled open the rolltop desk until he found his camera and four rolls of film intended for low-light photography. It took him less than two minutes to pack his camera case and gather together his tape recorder and three cassettes. He paused in the center of the room, running a swift mental check on what he would need, added a notebook to his supplies, then reached for his jacket hanging over the back of the chair. It was of good quality leather but was old enough to show it had been much used. He tugged it on like familiar armor, gathered up his camera and other supplies, then turned to leave.

Veronique stood in the door, her robe tied loosely over her nightgown. There was a resigned look to her; she had seen him this way many times before but never in a city. "Jean-Charles?"

"I'm going out," he said, trying not to make an issue of it.

"Oui. I can see that." Her hands hung at her sides and she shook her head slowly.

"I won't be long." He said it automatically. "I'm going for a walk down the street."

"With a camera and three rolls of film and a tape recorder," Veronique agreed sarcastically. "You are going off on one of your hunts, Jean-Charles. That is what this is all about."

"Perhaps." It was an honest answer, for he was not sure he knew what it was he sought. "There is something about all this. If I can't figure it out, I'm a poor excuse for an anthropologist."

"And what are you after?" She looked tired, far more tired than the hour would dictate.

"Something. Nothing. I don't know." He paused,

then slung the shoulder strap of his camera case over his arm. "Probably nothing, but . . . we'll talk about it later, Niki, ma belle." He bent to kiss her, not expecting her to return his kiss and was pleasantly startled when she did. "I really won't be long." His smile was sheepish, but he did not hesitate any longer. He was almost at the back door when he heard her call to him.

"Jean-Charles!"

"Niki?" He looked back at her.

She made a complicated gesture. "Oh, it is nothing. I have never been able to convince you to remain when you wished to go, and I doubt I could do it now. Do whatever it is you must do."

He was grateful to her for this, and he tried to show her in how he blew a last kiss to her. As he pulled the door open, he said over his shoulder, "Keep the doors locked."

"Oui," she sighed. "Allez! Allez! The sooner you are done, the sooner you will come back. Vite!"

Pommier nodded once, knowing that he had disappointed his wife, and knowing that there was no way to undo the harm he had done. He closed the door quietly before running to his car, which he used for cover as he stared into the street, eyes narrowed in concentration.

The van was there, motor idling, the passengers moving about in the dark interior. The blond driver rested one arm on the open window and Pommier thought—though in this light and at this distance he could not be sure—that the arm was tattooed. There was laughter again, loud, taunting, more abandoned than cruel. One of the passengers, a young woman in a skimpy tank top, leaned over the driver and kissed him.

Carefully Pommier tried to reach for his camera case, hoping to take at least one photograph before the people in it noticed his presence, but he mistimed his attempt; with a sudden snarl from the engine, the van lunged off down the road, no lights turned on, making it appear to be a ghost on the dark street.

Pommier pulled out his keys and twisted the lock open angrily. Now he would have to follow them, to learn who they were and what they wanted. During his expeditions he had developed a sense of the hunt that both stimulated and calmed him, and now he felt it course through him again, heightening his senses and lending a curious serenity to his mind. This he knew how to do, and he did it well. He was no longer a man trapped within walls, but a scientist on the trail of new knowledge. Few things in his life thrilled him more.

The Rabbit roared out of the driveway and took off in the direction of the beach, where the van had gone.

The nursing station was the one haven of light in the dark halls. It was late in their day, almost three in the morning, when the only things that happened were sudden and desperate. One of the orderlies had brought a Frisbee and was engaged in an impromptu game with the youngest nurse and a Japanese intern. As the disk went flying close to the ceiling, causing strange, sailing shadows to course down the walls, Cassie Maybeck stepped out of the elevator, her tired eyes trained on the door to Flax's room.

"Oh!" said the Frisbee-playing nurse with a swift, guilty look in Cassie's direction. "Hi, Dr. Maybeck." She gave an underhand toss to the intern.

"Hello, Samuels," Cassie answered, paying no notice to their game, which was strictly against the rules. "Ted Oldsman ready to be relieved, do you know?"

"Him? He left more than an hour ago. There was an emergency in CCU. Half the staff turned out for it. Massive infarct."

"Um," Cassie said, a bit nonplussed. "Did he leave a message for me?"

"I don't think so," Samuels said, then called over her shoulder to the senior duty nurse who sat at the desk reading a paperback thriller. "Hey Louise, is there anything there for Dr. Maybeck?"

"Wait a sec," Louise Jansen protested, "I'm just getting to the good part." She read quickly, turned the page, sighed, then placed the book down on the desk while she checked her message records. "No, nothing here for Maybeck. Nothing from Oldsman, period." She swiveled in her chair and looked at Cassie. "You back for another stint?"

"I've got a thirty-minute break and I thought I'd look in on Eileen." She made it sound as if it were an ordinary occurrence. "If that's okay."

"Yeah, it's fine," Jansen said, returning to her paperback. "It's a real quiet night up here, thank God."

"Amen," Cassie agreed, and went down the hall. She was trying to gather her thoughts so that she would not appear to be upset if Flax were awake or groggy, so she paid little attention to the dark room as she came through the door. The monitoring equipment was not on, but Cassie was not disturbed by that; Ted had suggested that they take off the electronics for a little while since nothing useful had been learned from them. "Hi, Eileen," she said quietly, on the odd chance that she would be heard. "It's Cassie." She walked softly toward the bed. "How're you doing." She had not expected a response and was not surprised that there was none, but the unearthly quiet of the room bothered her, and she reached for the low-level nightlight. She hesitated to turn it on, afraid of what she would find, but she knew that if Flax were worse again every minute she delayed would only make her friend's condition more precarious.

Light glowed from the concealed bulb and Cassie turned apprehensively toward the bed. "Oh, God! Oh, shit," she whispered as she saw the empty bed. "Eileen . . ." She raised her voice. "Eileen?"

There was no answer to her call; Cassie went into the

bathroom, hoping against all logic that she would find Flax there. Nothing.

"Jansen!" Cassie said sharply as she came out of Flax's room. "Where's Dr. Flax?" There was always the chance that Cort had ordered her downstairs for another scan series, but she was not convinced this had happened.

"In bed," she answered, putting her book aside.

"No, she's not," Cassie corrected her. At this announcement the Frisbee game stopped and the other three came closer to listen. "I want a check made of this floor. And fast. If Eileen's wandered off and had another one of those attacks, I don't know what could..."

"We'll get right on it," Jansen vowed with a significant look to the other three.

"I checked her closet," Cassie added. "Her clothes are gone. You're looking for someone carrying clothes or wearing them—probably wearing them." She put a hand to her hair. "Get me Dr. Oldsman, Louise. I have to tell him..."

"Of course," Jansen said. "Samuels, you take 321 through 349. Go into all the rooms: that includes patients' rooms, lounges, bathrooms, restrooms, storage rooms, conference rooms, the works. Di Lucci, you take 350 through 370. Same instructions. Bering, do the same for 371 through 398. Be fast, but don't be sloppy." She turned to her phone bank. "I have two nurses on a coffee break. I'm going to page them back from the cafeteria, and then they can start checking out the other floors. Is there anyone in Neurology we should contact?"

"Oldsman. I'll give Cort a ring; he's at home." Cassie felt as if her thoughts were moving far too slowly, but she could not break out of her dazed state. What was she going to do if Flax had got out of the hospital? It made no sense, and in Flax's condition, anything might happen to her.

"Dr. Maybeck?" Jansen cut into her thoughts. "Dr. Oldsman would like to speak to you."

Cassie sighed. "All right." She took the receiver and braced herself for the onslaught. "Hi, Ted."

"What's this crap about Eileen being missing?" he demanded, not disappointing her.

"Just that. We've been looking for her, but . . . well, I think she's gone." Cassie heard the tremor in her voice and tried to bring it under control. "We're checking this floor now, but I've got a feeling that—"

"Have you tried the guard at the parking lot?" Ted cut in, sounding much less abrupt; he had heard the quaver as well.

"What?" Cassie asked.

"The guy at the parking lot. That's where Eileen leaves her car. If it's gone, we can be pretty damn sure she's gone with it." He paused. "Look, you give Brad a call, never mind about waking him up, and then get back to me. I'll call the parking lot and find out what goes with her car. She drives a VW bug, doesn't she?"

"That's right. There's a dent on the right front fender, if that helps." She remembered that Flax had told her the car needed some minor repairs. "I think . . ."

"What?" Ted asked when Cassie's voice trailed off.

"Oh, nothing," she said in a helpless way. I'll talk to Cort."

"Great. Get back to you in five minutes." He hung up.

Cassie buzzed the physician's switchboard. "This is Dr. Maybeck. Please get Dr. Cort on the phone for me. It's an emergency." She could not think what to tell Cort, but that did not matter to her now; what mattered was that Flax was missing.

EIGHT

Insistent, malevolent music brayed from the open door of the sleazy storefront that advertised itself as a nightclub. The black surfers' van pulled up in front of the place and came at last to a stop.

Half a block behind them, Pommier slid his Rabbit into a parking place and began to set up his camera. He found the punk rock intrusive and distracting, a constant invitation to destruction. As he slung his camera around his neck, he watched the occupants of the van pile out of it.

The first was the girl, looking little more than fifteen or sixteen, a skinny, blond kid in Day-Glo pink running shorts and minimal tank top; her erect nipples were made more evident by an outrageous pair of glasses drawn inexpertly on the fabric to give her breasts the appearance of enormous pop eyes. She laughed low in her throat at something one of the others said, tossing her hair for emphasis. There was a sulky, spoiled prettiness about her.

Second was an older woman, perhaps in her mid-thirties, very tall and cadaver-thin, with slicked dark hair in short, spiky disarray. There was a streak of color through it that appeared green in the dim streetlights. Her makeup was heavy and obvious, adding to the look of dissipation she so clearly sought. Her slacks were very narrow, of a black, shiny fabric, and above them she wore a tight blouse open to the waist in a sharp V. She was smoking an obviously hand-rolled cigarette.

Next a man emerged, with thinning shoulder-length hair and long mustaches. He wore ancient jeans and a

vest that might have belonged to a gang member once;
there was a large rose on the back out of which crawled
worms and spiders under the elaborate lettering *Satan's
Angels*. He could not be much older than thirty, but
there was a world-weariness and cynicism in his face
that made him appear ancient.

A tall, broad-chested black man emerged, his hair in
elaborate Rastafarian locks. He moved nervously, looking
around every few seconds. His clothes were all dark
and tended to shapelessness so that Pommier would not
have been able to describe him at all but for color and
hair. He looked back toward the van, signaling to the
driver to step out.

The driver came out of his own door, stretching as if
tired. There were indeed tattoos on his arms. He was
tall, lanky, his blond hair caught back in a pony tail. He
wore a striped T-shirt with the sleeves hacked off, and
very tight, dark red jeans tucked into calf-high heeled
boots. He swaggered when he walked. Just before he
entered the nightclub, he turned and looked, tauntingly,
back at Pommier. His lantern-jawed face split in a
hostile grin.

Pommier watched them, trying to place them all as
types, but nothing came to mind. He had not been in
Los Angeles long enough to know what these clothes
and behavior meant. He chided himself for being
unobservant, a primary error for a man of his profession. He began to take pictures. Two of the van, in the
hope that there might be an identifying mark on it,
since from where he was, he could not see the license
plate. Three of the door to the nightclub, where figures
moved in glaring red and amber light as if in the flames
of hell. Pommier sat back against his seat, thinking that
this was apt to be a long night, and knowing from his
long experience that it was necessary to prepare for it
carefully. Think of it, he told himself, like an expedition, like all the times before, following Eskimos and
Bedouins and Lapps and Afghan shepherds. Do not

alarm them. Do not get too close. Study them; but carefully, carefully. He propped his camera on the edge of the window and waited.

"I don't *know* how the fuck she walked out of here, and no one noticed!" Cassie shouted to Cort for the third time. "I came up here, Ted wasn't here, and Eileen was gone. That's *it*. Got the picture?"

On the other end of the line, Cort sounded half asleep, which he was. "But didn't the nurses . . . I know. You told me. And you say that there's about forty-five minutes that are unaccounted for. What about the nurses?"

"They put Flax in the first room down from the station. You'd think that if anything was happening, they'd notice," Cassie said. "At least, they say they'd notice, and I'm standing at the station right now. You can see the door clearly. It's so . . . weird that no one saw her."

Samuels, looking shamefaced, added her own protest. "There's no way she could have gotten out of here without one of us seeing her."

"I heard that," Cort said. "What about the windows?"

"Hey, Brad, this is the third floor, that means four floors up. Even if she could get the windows open and the screens down, that's a long drop." Cassie sighed once more. "What do we do now? Got any suggestions worth more than a pint of shit?"

"No," Cort said. "What about Ted? Does he have any suggestions?"

"I haven't talked to him yet since . . ." Cassie said with a gesture that Cort could not see. "We're supposed to have coffee together. Compare what we know, which ain't much. Think we should call the police, or what?"

"Not yet," Cort answered. "Alert the emergency room, though, and the security people, in case she's found somewhere or turns herself in." He yawned. "I'll

be in around four. I've got to get another hour of sleep,
Cassie. I'm too worn out to think clearly right now. It's
not like I was twenty-five anymore."

"I'll be looking for you," Cassie promised him. "I'm
off duty at six A.M. After that, I've got a full day. I'm not
going to lie around on my arse for that time."

"Good," Cort said, and hung up.

Pommier was fascinated and bemused by the various
habitués of the nightclub, and he hardly noticed that
over two hours went past as he watched, waiting for the
people from the van to reemerge. When they did, he
was not prepared for the suddenness of their return.

One moment they were not in sight, and the next
they seemed to erupt out of the noise and movement.
They were laughing still, and Pommier was struck by
the thought that though he had often heard them laugh,
he had never heard them speak. They piled into the
van and rushed away into the night.

It took the better part of a minute for Pommier to set
his camera aside, then start the Rabbit, and so he was
afraid that he might miss the van. He sped down the
dark street, his eyes flicking quickly to the sides at each
intersection in the hope of discovering the van if it had
turned.

Then he saw them drawn up to the curb two blocks
ahead. One of the passengers was leaning out the
window laughing with three young men dressed in tight
denim cutoffs and little else. Two of the men had a
strange manner about them and Pommier, watching
them from where he hovered half a block away, wondered if it were possible that the men were on drugs.
Was he following a dope dealer, was that it? It made
some sense, but not enough to explain why the van had
come to his house repeatedly. Pommier raised his camera and took a few more pictures.

A few blocks farther on the van slowed down for a

small group of male prostitutes who posed and strutted on the street corner. Even at a distance, Pommier saw that one of the prostitutes was wearing makeup, though he was dressed in slacks and a cotton sweater. He reached for the tape recorder and thumbed it on. "So far the van has gone more than"—he checked his odometer—"fifteen miles, has stopped four times. Each stop has been with the apparent purpose of seeing other people. From the way these various groups behave, it seems that each group has a carefully defined territory, and the people in the van are allowed or expected to cross territories." He flicked the recorder off, and not an instant too soon, for the van was pulling away from the male prostitutes, heading toward the central part of Los Angeles with increasing speed.

Hollywood Boulevard was frenetically alive, though the hour was growing late and many of the stores, though open in the evening for business, had closed. The van cruised up to a transient hotel and a huddled figure in the doorway shambled up to the window, reaching for something extended in a dark hand.

Pommier reached for his camera and photographed as much of the curious transaction as he could. He checked the number of exposures and was relieved that he would not have to change film for a while yet. As he followed the van, he determined to get as much of the actions of its occupants on film as he could without being discovered. The air of violence that hung around that black van warned him that he would be in great danger if he actively opposed the five people inside it.

The next time the van stopped, a group of long-haired bikers came up to it and were received with what passed for friendliness with these people. The punk rock was very loud, advertising the van's presence and covering anything that might be said near it.

On the third photograph, one of the bikers noticed Pommier, and he poked the beefy man next to him. This biker gave Pommier a sinister nod, then dropped

his hands to his crotch, indicating he had a gigantic
prick. Pommier photographed it all, and at that two
more of the bikers grew threatening, starting across the
busy street toward the Rabbit. As they walked, one of
them unwrapped a heavy chain from around his waist
and began to swing it suggestively.

For an instant all movement except that chain stopped
on the block and there was a silence beyond the punk
rock that was more ominous, a holding of breath before
the fall of the ax.

Pommier did not bother to put his camera aside or
put his tape recorder safely on the floor; he pulled away
from the curb and gunned the engine in his hurry to
get away from the bikers. The air fizzed with anger and
resentment. As Pommier drove, he imagined he heard
angry laughter all around him.

He caught up with the van again in a roller-disco
parking lot where the Rastafarian was half out of the van
on the passenger's side, gesturing emphatically at the
parking lot attendant. From his vantage point in front of
the 7-Eleven across the street, Pommier watched closely as the Rastafarian reached for the front of the short
red jacket the attendant wore. The driver of the van
opened the door on his side, too, and started to get out.

With a bleating sound, the attendant broke away
from the men in the van and scuttled away to the haven
of his kiosk, reaching for a telephone as he closed the
door. His face was pale and beaded with sweat, and as
he raised one arm as if to ward off another attack,
Pommier saw that his hands were shaking.

The Rastafarian and the driver got back into the van,
then headed off down the sidewalk before finding a
convenient place to return to the street.

Pommier was fascinated at how casual the whole
thing had been for the passengers of the van, and how
distressed the parking lot attendant was. Another time,
he might have taken the time to interview the shaken
young man to find out if any special threat had been

offered him, or if the men themselves were the source
of his fear. There was no chance to do that now, with
the van rolling away and disappearing into the traffic.

The next stop was an all-night restaurant not far from
Sunset. This time Pommier was able to photograph
each of the van's riders as they left the vehicle. After
considering his position briefly, Pommier parked the
Rabbit, locked his camera and other equipment in the
trunk, and hurried into the restaurant. Not only was he
curious, he was hungry.

It was crowded and noisy and much busier now than
during the daylight hours. Pommier found a place at the
counter that gave him a view of the whole place.

Three seats down the counter, two drag queens were
having an argument, each one affecting swooping hand
gestures and high, fluttery voices. "It was not proper at
all," the taller was saying as he tweaked the curls on his
platinum-blond wig.

"Oh, stuff it, darling," said the other. He lowered his
eyelids and they glittered from the sequins he had
pasted there. "If Miss Violet thinks she can get away
with it, that's her lookout."

The first ran a hand over the deep cleavage of his
cocktail dress. "What happens to the rest of us if she
gets caught at it?"

Pommier did not hear the answer; punk rock spewed
out of the jukebox speakers. The blonde in the shorts
and tank top ambled back to the table where the other
four from the van sat waiting for service.

The door opened and a hooker strode into the restaurant. She had dark circles under her eyes and an
enormous marabou wrap flung around her shoulders.
Her high spike heels were loud enough to cut through
the music as she made her way to a booth at the back of
the restaurant. "Hey!" she shouted as she got nearer. "I
told you I don't do kinky sex. That john had a whip he
wanted to use. Something like that'd keep me out of
business for more'n a week!"

Someone at the counter tittered.

Three young men, dressed like members of the early Nazi movement, shoved their way to a booth and sat there with hard, contemptuous expressions in their blue eyes.

The waitress, chewing gum and staring blankly at a spot about a foot above Pommier's head, brought him a cup of coffee without having him order it. "That's seventy-five cents," she announced in an automaton's voice. "We got blueberry cheesecake and apple pie."

"No, thanks," Pommier said, grateful for the coffee.

"Suit yourself." She turned away to take another order.

Pommier drank the coffee while covertly keeping an eye on the five from the van. No one approached them aside from a young waiter. It was almost as if they were invisible, Pommier thought. Perhaps in these surroundings they were. He finished his coffee and signaled for a refill. Now that he was not actually moving, he could feel his exhaustion settling into him. His responses were a smallest shade slower than they had been an hour ago; his attention was marginally less acute. At least the caffeine would remedy that for a time. Wryly he thought of the boundless energy of his students and wished that there was a way for him to borrow some of it. The coffee, which was the taste and color of ink, would have to be a substitute. He glanced at his watch and was startled to see that it was almost four in the morning. This strange, nocturnal world piqued his curiosity. He had feared a year of teaching, without the stimulation of research and expedition, would bore him, but now Pommier knew that he had found something that would sustain his interest.

As the five from the van left the restaurant, the older woman in the shiny black clothes turned to him and waved.

Flax held her hands to her eyes until the worst of the headache was over, then she started the bug again. She

had been parked in the remote section of a lot attached
to a shopping mall, where she was convinced she would
go unnoticed. Now that she was out of the hospital,
there were things she had to know. She put her car in
gear and drove through the predawn stillness, looking
for a phone booth. It was 5:00 A.M., more or less, which
would mean she could reach someone in Boston and
Cambridge without disturbing the day's routine.

At last she pulled into a large all-night service station
and headed for the blue-light of the phone booth. She
reached for her purse and pulled out her wallet, getting
change and her telephone credit card.

"Hello, is Richard Holder there yet?" Flax asked
when she was connected.

"Yes. Whom shall I say is calling?" inquired the
meticulously polite voice on the other end of the line,
the flattened New England vowels sounding strange to
Flax for the first time in her life.

"Please tell him Dr. Flax in Los Angeles wants to
speak with him. It's fairly urgent," she said, and was
pleased to hear a slight gasp from the receptionist. She
had to wait for almost two minutes before she heard
that familiar bass growl wish her good morning. "Hello,
Dick," Flax said in response.

"Eileen, good to hear from you. Christ, what hour is
it out there, anyway? It *is* earlier, isn't it? I get that
mixed up."

"It's early. I'm coming off night shift," she improvised. Now that she had Holder on the phone, she did
not quite know how to approach him. "Look,
Dick . . . uh . . . I was wondering . . . would you be willing
to do me a favor? Nothing big, or I don't think it is."

"You name it," was his immediate reaction. "You
know I've always felt badly about the way things turned
out with you and Eric. This might help."

"I know you . . . were troubled," Flax said, not wanting to go over that old ground now. "It's over, though.
What's more important to me right now are some

questions that have come up about a patient I . . . treated.
He . . . keeps talking about something called des innois,
or something that sounds like that. It isn't any word I
recognize, not that my French is so great. I was hoping
you might have an idea about it."

Holder hesitated. "Des innois. Doesn't sound familiar to me."

"Well," Flax said, a bit more emphatically, "the
patient . . . is French-Canadian, and I thought, with the
ethnography studies you did in Montreal three years
ago, you might have run across a place or a phrase or a
slang word or—"

"Would it help your patient?" Holder interrupted.

"I hope so," Flax answered fervently, dreading the
next time she lapsed under the influence of Jean-Charles
Pommier.

"All right then; I'll get to work on it this morning. Is
that number you gave me three weeks ago okay?" He
was all business now; Flax could see him in her imagination, a big man with large hands spread out on the
desk in front of him, thumbs touching, his head lowered
as if he were about to go into battle with one of the big
predators.

"Yes, the number's fine. If I'm not there, please leave
the message on the machine. I'm on call, so . . ."

"I understand."

"The machine's set up to take messages up to five
minutes. If there's any difficulty, just let me know and
I'll see if I can find another approach." Flax took a deep
breath to stop the tumble of words that poured out of
her. "I . . . I'm afraid I do need the information pretty
quickly, Dick. The patient . . . is in a pretty bad way. I
couldn't think . . . of anyone else to call. I hope you
don't mind." Now that she had asked, she felt chagrin at
her actions.

"I'm glad you did. I've been hoping to hear from
you," Dick said at once, soothing her. "Don't you
worry, Eileen. I'll get one of my hotshot grad students

on this this morning and with any luck I should have
something for you by tomorrow at the latest. I'll try for
this afternoon. Is that good enough?" He laughed at the
suggestion. "Hey," he said in another, more serious
tone, "I want you to know I was shocked about Eric and
Diane. I mean it. I never thought he'd actually marry
her."

"Diane?" Flax repeated, saying the name as if it had
a peculiar taste. This was the first she had heard of her
ex-husband's remarriage, and it was an effort for her to
preserve a degree of indifference. "Well, I guess it had
to happen."

There was an awkward silence. "I'm...sorry. I thought
you knew," Holder said at last.

"I've been expecting it," Flax lied. Why did it hurt
her so much, this news? It was nothing like the paralyz-
ing anguish of the end of her marriage, but still the pain
was there, not as intense, not as numbing, but real
enough. She cleared her throat. "Well, they'd been
sleeping together for two years, hadn't they?"

"Eileen, I'm truly sorry," Holder persisted.

"Don't, please don't," Flax said, swallowing hard
against unexpected tears.

"I guess I shouldn't have brought it up," Holder said,
coughing once. "I've got the tact of a four-year-old.
Well." He did his best to recover his earlier, more
friendly manner. "You'll be hearing from me, soon,
Eileen. Just as soon as I can get the information for
you." He paused again, continuing more shyly. "I hope,
when you're back this way, if you ever do come back,
that you'll let me take you out to dinner."

"Sure," Eileen said readily enough, knowing she had
no intention of returning to Cambridge, especially not
now.

"Well, good. And it was a pleasure to hear from you,
Eileen." This was a last attempt to keep her talking,
and they both knew it.

"It was good to talk to you, Dick. Thanks for your

help. Later." She hung up before she broke down and asked more about Eric. She could not bear to demean herself with questions about her former husband. She had promised herself when she moved west that she would not allow herself to become involved, even tangentially, in his life again and she intended to keep that promise. It was strange, she thought as she walked back to her car. Even two months ago she would have been in tears learning that Eric had remarried. Now, thinking of the passion that Jean-Charles Pommier shared with his Veronique, the ache she felt was for the love she had never known rather than the end of her marriage. She drove back toward her apartment slowly, planning to change before she took to the road again.

NINE

At dawn the van reached the ocean again, pulling into a parking lot not far from the Santa Monica pier. It was a bright morning and the water glistened in rosy tints. The five from the van got out for a walk along the pathways. They did not romp or play the way many others might have, but walked along in a steady manner, as if looking for something.

Fairly soon, they found it. A tattered figure sleeping on the grass, all wrapped up in filthy blankets, caught their attention. The man with the pony tail gestured to the others and they laughed that low, sinister laugh that Pommier had come to dread. The ragged man clutched an old navy duffel bag, and this he held to his chest as if it were the only thing of worth in his world. The Rastafarian reached out and grabbed the duffel bag, waking the ragged man with his theft.

The ragged man moaned and crawled after the five, finally getting to his feet as he saw the blond man with them start to open the bag.

From his parking place a hundred yards away, Pommier saw the cruel sport. He photographed it, and then debated coming to the disturbed man's assistance. While he hesitated, the bearded man flung the duffel bag back at its owner, knocking the man down and throwing much of the contents over the grass and the sand beyond. The victim shrieked and began to scrabble about, trying to recover his treasures while the five continued on their way toward the pier.

At an old delivery truck now painted with fanciful beasts and symbols the five stopped, knocking on the side of the truck in a strange and persistent rhythm very like the beat of the punk rock they listened to. Angry voices came from inside which made the blond man caper with pleasure. The woman in the shiny black clothes made obscene gestures with her hands while moving her body in obvious sexual invitation. Pommier photographed it all, puzzling over the pattern he felt was just out of reach.

Within thirty minutes the van was back on the road, racing up the freeway toward the hills. Pommier followed after, beginning to worry about gasoline. He could follow another forty miles at the most, and then he would need gas. With luck, so would the van, he thought.

His opportunity came when the van stopped at a hot-dog stand. While the five were eating, Pommier drove to the Texaco station at the other end of the block and had the tank filled. He also changed film for the second time and wished he could get another roll of film. He knew he was taking a chance, but he decided to find a camera store. If he lost the van, he would find it again, he thought—parked in front of his house in the middle of the night.

"Is that all?" the clerk asked when Pommier had purchased four rolls of low-light film and three of standard fast-action film. "We got a good sale on lenses."

"Thanks, I have what I need," Pommier said as he loaded the film into his camera bag. "Is there a telephone here? A pay phone?"

"There's one at the corner," the clerk said, pointing toward the door.

"Okay," Pommier said with a wave as he left the shop. At the corner he fumbled for a dime, and then for the quarter to call Santa Monica. He heard the ringing on the other end, but there was no answer. He was about to call Captain Coglan when he saw out of the corner of his eye the five returning to the van. Swearing, he hung up and hurried back to his Rabbit.

Through the afternoon he followed the van going from Van Nuys to Pasadena to Anaheim, then back toward the coast. Traffic round him grew thick as the day wound down toward evening, then started to thin once more. He was waiting for a light to change when Pommier noticed his vision was fuzzy and he knew he needed sleep. But the van was still rolling. "I will follow them until they are near my house," Pommier vowed, speaking to his windshield and reassured by the sound of his voice. "Then I'll develop the pictures and get some sleep." As the light changed, he took off after the van.

They passed within three blocks of his house, but the van did not deviate this time, keeping on a straight track for the park along the Palisades, that well-groomed stretch of grass and trees at the edge of the bluff over the beach. There the van turned south, back toward Venice where they had begun that morning.

Pommier thumbed on the tape recorder. "It is a territorial patrol, perhaps," he said excitedly. "They have a region that is theirs, and they must cover it. They are similar to the tribes in the Northwest Territories that always move in specific areas at specific times. They are maintaining their claim." It pleased him to have found an explanation at last, or what could prove to be an explanation. He would have to test it. The worry nagged him that this did not answer the question about his house. "But they mark their territories," he suggested to the air. If that were the case, why had they not selected other houses to mark in the same way? He picked up his camera and prepared to take more pictures.

This time when the five stopped for food, they took their hamburgers and strolled to the picnic tables beside the beach. In the warm afternoon sun they looked much like many of the other denizens of the Venice beachfront. At the table beyond the one where the five sat, two ragged men in old bathing trunks and unkempt cotton shirts played chess; after a few minutes the

Rastafarian went to watch them, studying their moves
with intelligent attention.

After ordering food, Pommier moved to a spot only
two tables away. Now he was able to see the faces of the
five clearly for the first time, and he positioned his
camera on the table so that he could take shots of them
without appearing to do so. He had become expert at
the technique sometime ago, with Afghani tribesmen
who regarded photographs as evidence of the evil eye.
He chided himself for what he decided was ridiculous
caution, but he did not change what he was doing. As
he wiped his chin, he felt the scratchings of his beard
on his hand. No doubt, he would have to return home
soon.

At some unseen signal, the five rose and set off down
the boardwalk in an exaggerated saunter that radiated
contempt for everything around them.

Hurriedly Pommier tossed the last of his food into
the trash and went after them, bringing his camera up
as he went.

The hazy dazzle of the afternoon sun combined with
lack of sleep so that Pommier had trouble seeing the
five; he rubbed his eyes, hoping to sharpen his vision.
When he looked again, the five were gone. He stood
still, then broke into a jog through the crowd. There
were hard-faced kids on roller skates; old men drinking
beer from paper cups; young women, some with pleading and some with predatory eyes; a large-bodied young
woman with a madonna's face riding a bicycle with
expert ease; shoals of children, some pleasantly excited,
some prowling; vacant-faced men aware only of their
inner worlds; strutting boys with thumbs hooked into
thick leather belts; derelicts seeking others of their
kind; a handful of misplaced and bewildered tourists;
slick and saucy dealers waiting confidently for those
who needed them; cops with features like granite and
eyes flat as pebbles; young men and women in swim-
suits of colors and cuts that begged for attention; uncaring,

cynical drifters; frenetic men and women, no longer
quite young but as yet untouched by the age that
pursued them; a few with a faded negligent glamour
who had given up on the dream and were indifferent to
reality; one or two who, like Pommier, were watching
the world around them, with tolerant or condemning
demeanors; a scraggle-bearded man with a fire-scarred
body sitting on the sand, all his attention given to
making a sandcastle—Pommier saw them all, but not
the five from the black van. He made sure that the
vehicle was still where they had left it, then went in
search of them.

After half an hour, he called his house; the line was
busy. "I'm tired, Niki," he told the persistent buzz. "I'll
be home soon. I miss you. Don't worry about me." As
he hung up the receiver, he added, "It's important,
Niki."

Flax deliberately chose a table a fair distance from
the reference desk in the main UCLA library. She had
avoided the office of the anthropology department and
using the school directory. If anyone from the hospital
was looking for her—and she was fairly certain that was
the case—the first place to be checked would be the
haunts of Pommier. There were two books in front of
her and she decided to tackle the larger one first,
knowing that it would be the more succinct. There was
a disquieting feeling in her when, looking for Pommier's
name in the index, she ran across Eric's among the
sociologists. Her breath caught in her throat, and though
she knew it was as much from fatigue as regret, her
confidence diminished briefly. It was foolish to spend all
this time hunting a dead man. That was what Eric
would have told her. But Eric was out of her life. He
was Diane's husband now, not hers. And Jean-Charles
Pommier, dead or alive, was more real to her than Eric

had ever been. At last she found the entry and turned
to the page.

Pommier, Jean-Charles Ewing. Born 1 Jan. 1936,
Roberval, Lac St.-Jean, Quebec, Canada. Father Claude
Louis Pommier, MD 1921 Ontario; mother Lisette
Ewing, BA, MA, secondary credential 1926 Toronto.
No siblings. BA linguistics 1958 Montreal, MA, MS
anthropology 1960 Paris, PhD cultural anthropology
1968 Oxford. Military service, Royal Navy 1961-65,
NATO and submarine duty, rank attained, Lt. Com-
mander. Married Veronique Celeste Segre 23 Aug.
1977 at Repulse Bay, District of Keewatin, Northwest
Territories, Canada. Publications—

The list that followed was long, and Flax despaired of
ever finding the one thing she was looking for in all his
work that would give a clue to his terrible warning.
Roughly half the titles were in French, which Flax had
studied for two years in high school but had not used
beyond menu reading since that time. A scholarly
article was far beyond anything she was prepared to
tackle. She read over the titles of the publications,
hoping to find the word "innois," but without luck.
Perhaps, she thought as she put her hand to her aching
head, she had misunderstood the word. Pommier had
been badly hurt, his mouth had been cut and bruised,
he was barely conscious, and he was verging on massive
shock, both emotional and physical. It might not mean
anything. What was there about that one word that
gave it significance? Or was it part of a word? Had he
been trying to say something more when he collapsed?
Was it only a fraction of a word, or a memory? Was it
something he had seen recently, or was it from his
childhood, a goblin his three-year-old self had feared
lurked under the bed? Certainly those goblins were not
there. Or was an innois a thing at all? Was it a misproven
theory or some other bungle—it could also apply. She
gave a long sigh and put the book aside. She was almost

ready to go driving through Santa Monica until she found the house. If the house existed at all.

And what then? she asked herself. Did she simply go up to the door and tell the newly widowed woman that her dead husband had been ... possessing her?

Resolutely she picked up the other book. *Field Techniques in Anthropological Studies.* The second article was "Determining Territoriality in Nomadic Populations"; the author was Jean-Charles Pommier.

At the end of an hour, Flax was still no closer to knowing what "innois" was, but she was beginning to understand what Pommier had been doing as he chased the black surfers' van through greater Los Angeles. He was behaving as if he were on a field expedition, studying a nomadic tribe. Flax stifled an exhausted chuckle. It was so absurd that she found it hard to believe he would take the time for such an exercise. LA *moved*. The whole place was on wheels: cars, trucks, buses, motorcycles, bicycles, skateboards, roller skates, wagons, shopping carts, tricycles. She had not gotten used to it herself. Coming from Canada, the constant motion must have been even more unsettling to Pommier, who had spent the greater part of twenty years following nomads in the most remote parts of the world. The speed of Los Angeles alone would be strange. And so he had decided to look for a pattern in all that movement? Was it as simple as that? She skimmed the article a second time, hoping she could anticipate what Pommier might do—had done—next, so that her next encounter with him—and she was certain there would be a next encounter—would not be so alarming. Her head swam. What was he doing to her, this rational scientist? And how? And why?

There were no clues in the writing. The article presented concise and orderly instructions for appropriate ways to deal with nomads, how to track them without violating territorial rights, how to observe them without breaking social taboos. He gave a number of sensible precautions, a few warnings; for the most part he avoided the tone of academic superiority Flax had too often found in Eric's writings. By the time she was through rereading, her eyes ached and her concentration was failing. She forced herself to get up and took the books back to the reference desk. "Thank you," she said to the faded woman who accepted them. "They were very useful."

"You're welcome," was the toneless answer.

Flax almost decided to visit the anthropology department, then decided against it. Inquiries about Pommier now would probably not be welcome and might bring about more trouble than she wanted to handle. Instead, she left the campus and looked for a place to eat where she could spend half an hour gathering her thoughts and assuaging her hunger at the same time.

She was halfway through a chicken sandwich when the next visions seized her.

Pommier was haggard, his body ached, his clothes were rumpled and smelly, he was almost out of film again, he needed a shave, a bath, a meal, sleep: he *loved* it. He no longer had the faint malaise of boredom oppressing him. He felt alive, useful. He dropped the last roll of low-light film into his camera. There were more than a dozen exposed rolls in the pockets of the camera case now, and he had five cassettes filled with his remarks.

Not far away, the black van stood where the five had left it several hours ago. It was night now, and the occasional glare of streetlights marked the paved walk of the beachfront park. There were figures huddled in doorways or under the few trees. A hundred yards north, a beer bar spilled amber light and boisterous singing into the night, but for the most part, the world was quiet. For the first time that day, Pommier could hear the surf over the noise of the people who came to it.

Then there was another sound; a sliding step, a whispered protest, and a single, sharp cry.

Pommier turned, peering down the narrow alley that paralleled the oceanfront park. In the dark he could just make out a group of figures. With a start, he recognized the five from the van, with one other huddled shape in their midst.

The man in the *Satan's Angels* vest reached down to the figure and struck it once, twice with his fists. The figure whimpered, trying to draw into a ball for protection.

Both girls laughed and the older one kicked their victim with her long spike heel, smiling hugely at the sound of the impact and the way the figure gave a thin, anguished shriek.

The driver, his tattooed arms akimbo on his hips, had hung back, but now he swaggered in, lashing furiously with his feet.

After the fourth kick, the figure on the ground uncurled, back arching in response to the pain of his beating. In the indistinct light, Pommier could see that it was a boy, no more than fifteen, with the thin, waif-look of a runaway.

Pommier edged closer, suddenly concerned for the youth as much as for his own safety. It was one thing to watch the casual brutality of the five's manners, but he had not seen what they could do when they gave free rein to those furious impulses. Now the evidence was in front of him, and he was sickened by it.

The driver pulled a switchblade from his boot, signaling the other four to hold the boy. He chuckled at the terror in his victim's face as his arms were pinioned by the Rastafarian and the woman in black.

"No. Hey . . . no," Pommier murmured, still wary. He was not a violent man, and he reminded himself that he had seen much worse on expeditions. But this was not Baffin Island or the mountains of Afghanistan, this was an alley in Venice, with the immense sprawl of Los Angeles at their backs. These were not tribesmen losing their slow battle with civilization; these were men and women in gaudy travesties of proper clothing, and the boy they held was not a rival or an enemy, but a forsaken child. He saw the expressions on the faces of four from the black van—such hollow eyes, burning in faces that were masks of loathing.

The driver's knife was in the boy's mouth, the pressure of the blade showing on his distended cheek. The girl in the tank top giggled.

Pommier inched closer wishing he had more than a camera for a weapon. He looked down and saw bits of broken glass, but nothing of a size big enough to use effectively. As he hesitated, he heard a hideous scream that ended on a choking cough.

The driver stepped back holding his bloodied knife aloft; the others released the boy so they could watch his convulsions.

"NO! STOP IT! *STOP!*" Pommier shouted, rushing from the protection of a half flight of rickety stairs. "Get *back!*"

The five turned toward him and regarded him coldly.

Pommier came to a halt, realizing now that he had put himself in jeopardy. The five could turn on him.

Nonchalantly the Rastafarian reached down and picked up the feebly thrashing boy and stuffed him into a dumpster at the side of an old beach hotel that backed onto the alley. As he turned, he gave a hard look to the driver.

This was enough. Pommier took a step back, not wanting to lose sight of the five, but when he almost tripped over the lowest step of the stairs he had hidden behind, he knew he would have to run. Abruptly he sprinted away, heading back toward the street, trusting that there would be someone to assist him or provide a modicum of safety. Surely, he thought as he ran, they would not attack him where witnesses could see.

Introducing the first and only complete hardcover collection of Agatha Christie's mysteries

Now you can enjoy the
greatest mysteries ever written
in a magnificent
Home Library Edition.

Discover Agatha Christie's world of mystery, adventure and intrigue

Agatha Christie's timeless tales of mystery and suspense offer something for every reader—mystery fan or not—young and old alike. And now, you can build a complete hardcover library of her world-famous mysteries by subscribing to <u>The Agatha Christie Mystery Collection</u>.

This exciting Collection is your passport to a world where mystery reigns supreme. Volume after volume, you and your family will enjoy mystery reading at its very best.

You'll meet Agatha Christie's world-famous detectives like Hercule Poirot, Jane Marple, and the likeable Tommy and Tuppence Beresford.

In your readings, you'll visit Egypt, Paris, England and other exciting destinations where murder is always on the itinerary. And wherever you travel, you'll become deeply involved in some of the most ingenious and diabolical plots ever invented ... "cliff-hangers" that only Dame Agatha could create!

It all adds up to mystery reading that's so good ... it's almost criminal. And it's yours every month with <u>The Agatha Christie Mystery Collection.</u>

Solve the greatest mysteries of all time. The Collection contains all of Agatha Christie's classic works including *Murder on the Orient Express, Death on the Nile, And Then There Were None, The ABC Murders* and her ever-popular whodunit, *The Murder of Roger Ackroyd.*

Each handsome hardcover volume is Smythe sewn and printed on high quality acid-free paper so it can withstand even the most murderous treatment. Bound in Sussex-blue simulated leather with gold titling, <u>The Agatha Christie Mystery Collection</u> will make a tasteful addition to your living room, or den.

Ride the Orient Express for 10 days without obligation.
To introduce you to the Collection, we're inviting you to examine the classic mystery, *Murder on the Orient Express*, without risk or obligation. If you're not completely satisfied, just return it within 10 days and owe nothing.

However, if you're like the millions of other readers who love Agatha Christie's thrilling tales of mystery and suspense, keep *Murder on the Orient Express* and pay just $9.95 plus postage and handling.

You will then automatically receive future volumes once a month as they are published on a fully returnable, 10-day free-examination basis. No minimum purchase is required, and you may cancel your subscription at any time.

This unique collection is not sold in stores. It's available only through this special offer. So don't miss out, begin your subscription now. Just mail this card today.

☐ Yes! Please send me *Murder on the Orient Express* for a 10-day free-examination and enter my subscription to <u>The Agatha Christie Mystery Collection</u>. If I keep *Murder on the Orient Express*, I will pay just $9.95 plus postage and handling and receive one additional volume each month on a fully returnable 10-day free-examination basis. There is no minimum number of volumes to buy, and I may cancel my subscription at any time.   07013

☐ I prefer the deluxe edition bound in genuine leather for $24.95 per volume plus shipping and handling, with the same 10-day free-examination.   07054

Name_____

Address_____

City_____ State_____ Zip_____

AR123

**Send No Money...
But Act Today!**

BUSINESS REPLY CARD

FIRST CLASS   PERMIT NO. 2274   HICKSVILLE, N.Y.

Postage will be paid by addressee:

The Agatha Christie
Mystery Collection
Bantam Books
P.O. Box 957
Hicksville, N.Y. 11802

He reached the street; it was empty. Panting as much from fear as from exertion, he started toward the main route through town. He could see the fuzzy glare of neon and even at this hour there were places open—bars or pick-up cafés.

Behind him the pounding of chasing feet grew louder.

Pommier knew that he could not make it. They would catch him. He saw a cross-street ahead and ran for it, hoping that he might be able to evade them if he could not outrun them. He had no illusions about what his fate would be if he attempted to fight them. Not after he had seen what was done to the boy.

The street was empty and dark, but he had sufficient lead to have a few precious seconds. There was an old, battered Mustang parked near another alley that led to the main stret, and Pommier dropped to the pavement and squeezed himself under it. He rolled under the car, where no light spill could reach him, and did his best to lie entirely flat. He opened his mouth wide to breathe so that his panting would not give him away.

The five raced into the street at a steady, practiced run, then faltered. The footfalls slowed to a walk and one of the five began to whistle; the tune was aimless.

Wellington boots stopped no more than two feet from Pommier's head and he had to struggle to keep from gasping. Be still, be still, be still, he told himself, concentrating on the words in his head rather than the boots. A pair of grubby running shoes came up to the Wellingtons and then the Mustang pressed down on Pommier. One of the five was sitting on the trunk.

A match scraped and then dropped, falling in the gutter less than a foot from Pommier's body. One of the five whistled through his teeth. Another match fell.

Now a pair of ancient, down-at-the-heels cowboy boots came along the sidewalk, then army surplus boots. Last a pair of black high heels showed up. One of the five made a clicking sound with his tongue, another snapped his fingers.

Then, as if by common consent, they left, walking back down the side street at a casual pace.

Pommier huddled under the Mustang for a full ten minutes before he attempted to come out of hiding. He knew that the five could be waiting around the corner, ready to ambush him. For that reason, he decided to use the other alley. He did his best to brush the debris off his jacket and slacks and checked quickly to be sure his camera was undamaged. He would have to call the police. He could reach Captain Coglan through the police. But he was in Santa Monica and this was Venice. Did that mean he could not speak to Coglan? And what about the boy? Pommier was not sure the boy was dead, but if he'd been left, unconscious and bleeding in the dumpster, he could succumb to loss of blood and shock before an ambulance had time to arrive.

Reluctantly, Pommier turned down the alley toward the beach once more, determined to find out if the youth had survived. He had that much of an obligation to the child, he knew.

It was with great relief that Pommier found the alley empty and the dumpster apparently undisturbed. Gratefully he let out his breath, not aware until then that he had been holding it for the last dozen yards. Still he went carefully toward the dumpster, not relishing what he knew he must find there.

The dumpster was empty of everything but a stack of blood-stained papers and two window frames.

Pommier stood staring down into the dumpster, trying to reconcile this with what he had seen earlier. One sickening notion occurred to him and it brought bile to the back of his throat: while he had lain under the Mustang, afraid for his life, the five had come back and finished what they had begun with the boy.

There was a soft, cruel laugh behind him.

The five were back, emerging from the shadows where Pommier realized they must have been watching him all along. They formed a rough semicircle around him. Pommier looked around once in the hope that he might find aid. The alley was dark, abandoned but for the five and himself. It was very, very quiet.

How far could he get? Pommier wondered in some calm, remote part of his mind. How far could he get before they caught him and kicked him to death? Who would move first—he or they?

The man in the gang vest strolled up to Pommier, staring hard at his camera. He stopped less than eighteen inches from the lens and bowed to it. The others applauded him. He took a few steps back and assumed a parody of the standard muscle-man pose, then glared at Pommier.

Pommier's hands trembled as he lifted the camera and adjusted the focus for the photograph. All along he had wanted pictures of the five and now he was getting them. He snapped three exposures of the man, thinking that he had no more than fifteen shots left.

The rest of the five applauded and the *Satan's Angel* stepped back, leaving room for one of the others.

The girl in the shorts did a series of little dance steps, lifting her hair the way some of the young glamour queens did in movies. She pouted for the camera.

The Rastafarian blew smoke rings and batted his eyelashes and farted deliberately when he bowed.

The woman in the shiny black clothes unzipped her slacks and masturbated extravagantly, then winked at Pommier when she was finished.

The driver mimed strangling a person so graphically that Pommier began once again to feel quite sick.

There were two exposures left when the Rastafarian came up to Pommier, grabbed the camera and, while Pommier was attempting to recover from the shock of this new intrusion, drove the sole of his Wellington boot hard into Pommier's genitals.

Pommier howled and dropped to his knees, reaching to protect himself and not daring to touch the enormous pain that flooded through him. He coughed and vomited.

The Rastafarian took the last two pictures, then carelessly dropped the camera into the dumpster before joining the other four as they sauntered away toward the place where their van was parked.

Pommier stared after them, hardly seeing anything beyond the agonized red haze in his eyes. He fell heavily onto his side and lay there without moving until the worst of his hurt subsided.

TEN

"Are you all right, miss?" the waitress said for a third time as she chaffed ineffectually at Flax's wrist.

Dazed, Flax blinked up at her. She saw that she had overturned her cup of coffee and that her sandwich was spread about the table in a haphazard manner. Her chagrin showed in her heightened color. It had happened again, this time with no warning at all. "I'm . . . fine," she said.

"Are you sure? Should I call a doctor? The manager, he's pretty worried about you." The waitress looked around. "It wasn't anything you . . . uh . . . ate, was it?"

Flax was able to smile at the suggestion. "No. I . . ." Then she decided to improvise. "You see, I've been volunteering for a graduate project in hypnosis. We were demonstrating posthypnotic suggestion this morning. We were all going to have lunch together, but there was a change of schedules and . . . we didn't. I've got a hunch that for a joke I was told to fall asleep during the meal." Her shaky laugh was almost convincing, and the waitress was pathetically grateful for any explanation that she could offer her manager.

"Hypnosis?" she inquired hopefully. "In the psych department?"

"Well, as part of graduate studies. You must see enough grad students in here to know what they can be like." She had a feeling she should leave the restaurant as soon as possible and attract as little notice as she could. "You've been very kind," she told the waitress. "But if this is the kind of suggestions they've given, I'd better get back to the lab and have a few changes made." She opened her purse and took out a ten dollar bill. "I'd like three back from this, if you please." The bill was just over five dollars and the tip was a generous one. "You've had to put up with a lot from me."

"Gee. Thanks," the waitress said. "That's real nice."

"You've been a great deal of help," Flax said, and tried to apply a touch of lipstick while the waitress went to get the change. She would be remembered, no doubt about that, but she also knew that the waitress would be well intentioned now, rather than simply curious. By the time the waitress returned, Flax's composure was evident.

"You take care, now," the waitress said as Flax hurried out of the restaurant.

Well, Flax said as she stared down the street, where could a nice lady doctor go to have psychic experiences in the middle of Westwood? The library was out, the campus was out, the . . . She grinned. There were three theaters within walking distance, and two of them advertised matinees. In the dark of the theater she would go unnoticed. Feeling more confident than she had since she left the hospital, Flax crossed the street and started toward the nearest theater.

As she took her seat, the screen was filled with supersonic planes chasing over snowfields. She had a momentary lapse as the impression of that photograph of the Eskimo hunter flicked through her mind. Then she sat down and let her thoughts drift. For the time being, she was safer here than she might be at home— Cort was just the type to put some kind of watch on her apartment, and she couldn't have that. If she had another attack, this was as good a place as any. They hadn't been able to do anything for her medically at the hospital, and she was becoming convinced that the only way for her to . . . exorcise herself of this demon was to discover what had happened to her. Then she might know why it was that he . . . haunted her.

Steely-eyed men faced each other across a polished

table on the screen, close-ups making their heads the size of delivery vans. The scrutiny of the camera fascinated Flax, and she had another series of impressions of Pommier taking photographs, and a black van. All those photographs. A hot, dull pain pounded in her temple.

The back door opened and Pommier staggered into his kitchen, closing and locking the door before he started into the hall, his camera clutched to his chest.

"Ah!" Veronique's voice came from the top of the stairs, tight and furious, weak with worry and wrath. "Salut, Jean-Charles! Tu sais depuis combien de temps? . . . Tu te rends compte? Tu te rends compte?"

Pommier limped to the foot of the stairs and held up a hand to her, his stance apologetic. "Stop, ma belle, stop, stop."

"What is this?" she demanded, all her anxiety that she had held in check loosed now. "You drop in?"

Pommier half-pulled himself up the stairs, hanging onto the banister for support. His whole lower body ached abominably and his head throbbed. "I tried to phone you, Niki. I tried."

"J'étais affolée! J'ai téléphoné à tous les hôpiteaux! J'ai failli téléphoner à la police!"

He reached her and paused to calm her. She had every right to be distressed; he knew it. He touched her cheek. "Shush, ma belle. It's all right now. I have only a little work to do and . . ."

"A little work?" she demanded. "Jean-Charles, regardez! You are . . ." She pushed him away, becoming distraught.

"Let me do this, ma belle. It is important, I promise you." He tried to kiss her but was repulsed. He went past her to his study, where he began feverishly to unpack his camera and the rolls of film. "The camera has been damaged. I don't know how badly. I'll have to have it repaired, of that I'm sure."

She followed him to the door. "That camera! Maudit!"

She shoved him aside and came into his office. "And what of this? Hein?" With a sudden, angry movement she grabbed a sheaf of photocopies off Pommier's desk. "Explain them!"

Pommier stopped what he was doing, giving her his full attention. He did not need to see what was on the papers to know she had found the information Captain Coglan had given him. "Well?"

Veronique let her tears run unheeded. "Well? Is that all you wish to say? Tu les connais? Tu sais quelle sorte de gens? Quelle sorte d'animaux? Salaud!" She flung the photocopies down.

"Yes, I know about them," he said loudly, his voice hoarse. Then, more softly, "I know. That's why I went out. I wanted to know what kind of people they are, what they were doing here."

"Mais tu ne m'as pas dit! Why couldn't you tell me?" She wiped her tears away with the flat of her hand.

"I didn't want . . . to worry you," he said, knowing it sounded lame. "When they kept coming to the house, and I found out about that . . ."

"Gutterman? Is that what you mean?" Her eyes were still wet but she no longer paid attention. "Those . . . creatures came here because of him? Grand merci! Do you chase them away like noisy dogs? Tu as essayé de le cacher et tu es sorti et m'as laisse seule!"

"I didn't want to leave you alone," he mumbled, knowing that he had failed her. "I . . . believe me, ma belle, I did not think I would be gone very long. I thought I would take a few photographs and find out why they came here. I did not know it would be"—he gave a bemused laugh—"such a chase."

"And what did it find out for you?" She folded her arms. "You know that there were children killed in this house. The man who did it was insane, that is what the jury said. It happened here. Here!"

"Yes. I know. I *know,* ma belle. And I think that perhaps I know why." He recalled his humiliation and pain, wincing as he felt the ache in his groin flare at the recollection.

"They are monsters, that is why!" Veronique insisted.

"No, no, Niki. It is nothing so simple. You don't understand at all." He stared at the far wall, trying not to permit her to distract him again with her arguments and her nearness. "You remember when we were in Afghanistan? Those shepherd tribesmen in the mountains, the ones who were so suspicious and who permitted no strangers to enter their houses?"

She almost screamed with exasperation. "Yes. Of course I remember. They nearly killed us. What has that to do with—"

"They had shrines, do you remember? The shrines were at places where violent crimes had occurred, and little battles with rival clans. There was nothing remarkable about them except that such battles had taken place and they were considered to be the territories of demons."

Veronique nodded, her expression so patient that it was as if she were indulging a child rather than listening to her husband. "They said so to us, at any rate."

"Yes." Pommier began to gather up his rolls of film. "That's it. That homage to violence. They had to maintain it or forsake their way of life. You know what they did to that boy who came to our camp too often. They cast him out for it, and that made him a ... worthy sacrifice. There was nothing we could have done for him, even if we had been able to get him to a good hospital in time. It was ritual murder; they made sure he knew he was dying, very sure. The suffering was necessary to them, as necessary ... *more* necessary than the death." That terrible event still haunted him, and watching the boy manhandled by the five from the black van had stirred his memory, dredging up this tragic episode. "These ... people are like that. They honor violence to maintain their identity. Or so I think."

"And?" She was growing angry again, knowing that he

had not told her everything and would not do so until he was sure himself of what he had discovered.

"It's this house. The murder has made it a shrine. It attracts them."

"NO!" she shouted, then lunged at him, swearing in the most degraded words she knew. "Not this place. This is *my home!* They cannot have it!"

"Niki..." Pommier protested as she pulled at his hair, then struck him full in the face. He tried to contain her hands, but she broke free, screaming at him, her face wild with fury. "Niki..."

"Cette maison, c'est... *mine!*" she shouted, pounding him on the chest and then the abdomen.

He had been able to handle her until then, but at that attack, he knew he had to stop her. With the last of his strength, he grabbed her arms and pushed her back against the wall. "Stop that! WILL YOU STOP!"

"Mine, mine, mine," she repeated, glaring at him. "They cannot have it!"

"And they won't. They *won't*. I promise you," he said.

She sobbed once and then stopped herself. "Those murders..."

"Yes, those murders." He kept his hold on her arms, but he no longer had to strain to stop her from striking out at him. "Yes, I knew about them. And yes, I did not want to tell you. Because of this. Because of how you love this house. I wanted to know what kind of people could think of a murder as worthy of homage, and make this house a shrine. Do you understand?"

"And you left me here to find out!" she accused him, her voice breaking.

"I've said I did not intend to. Oh, Niki, listen to me, please listen to me. I spent thirty hours following people in a black van who don't live anyplace. Écoute-moi? Do-not-live-*any*place. Don't work anyplace. I'm going to call the government, and the state. There is no license plate on their vehicle. They go from one—"

"Why do you tell me this? Oh, protégé-moi, Dieu, what do they want with us?"

"Remember the Afghans," Pommier insisted. "They're no different. Don't you understand? They're nomads, just as if they lived in the Arctic or the desert or the mountains of Afghanistan. They're nomads, those five people in the black van."

"What?" Veronique said dazedly as she began to release her anger.

"Nomads. Like all of them we've studied. Like every place I've lived for the last fifteen years." He released her arms and stepped back from her. "They have to be."

"But nomads, here?"

"I didn't want to frighten you. I tried to call, but... there was no reason for me to..." He stared down at his hands, suddenly ashamed of himself. "Forgive me, Niki. Forgive me."

"Jean-Charles..." she began, then broke off as if she did not know what to say to him.

"I am tired. I've been up... and I..." He shook his head and kneeled to pick up the rolls of film he had scattered. He was sore to the point of nausea. "None of this may mean anything. I could be completely wrong about the black van. I may have simply assumed..." He could not finish.

Veronique ran her fingers through her hair as if to set it in order, or erase the most obvious reminders of her outburst. "Never mind, Jean-Charles."

He stopped. "But I may have found people who, right here in the middle of Los Angeles, are living *outside*. Do you realize how important that may be? We are not talking about lonely, half-crazed shopping-bag ladies in Manhattan, but something entirely different. These five people do not participate. No exchanges. I never heard them speak. They have no constraints, so they resort to violence at no provocation except their own... amusement. *And they get away with it*. It's as if to the official world, they do not exist, they are invisible." He gathered up the last of the film, his doubts returning. "I don't know. I do not know."

"Jean-Charles," Veronique said, reaching to touch his face. "Look at you. You might as well have spent the time with seal hunters. You are a crazy man, Jean-Charles. You warned me." She helped him get to his feet. "You know you are crazy?"

"Niki . . . ." he said, putting the rolls of film on his desk.

"Have you any idea how worried I was? About you?"

He offered her a grim, contrite smile. "I will not . . ."

She put her fingers against his lips. "Do not make me promises. You will not be able to keep them." She sighed. "You look awful."

"I must," he agreed. "And I smell."

"At least it is only sweat and not dead seal," she said, trying for a lighter tone now that he had shown himself to be less concerned with his films and his nomads. "What a terrible honeymoon."

"I did it then, too, didn't I?" He was not able to hide his chagrin, though he was able to meet her eyes.

"Yes. And in the Sahara, and in Afghanistan. If I had been with you when you were in Australia, it would have happened then, too." She leaned forward and kissed him, very lightly, on the mouth. "There is something more, isn't there?"

"Nothing," he told her, worried that it was not entirely the truth.

"Well?" she asked.

"I don't . . ." He put one hand on her shoulder. "It's nothing."

"How do you mean nothing? What is it?"

He shook his head. "That is it: I do not know. I do not *know what* I will find. But I have a sense that there is something more, that I have not learned enough about them. What is it about the violence? Why do they regard it as . . . holy?"

"That's dangerous, Jean-Charles," she said, her face

showing her concern for him. "You are taking a great risk, if what you suspect..."

"I might be taking a great risk in any case. So might you, simply by living here." He gripped her shoulders with both hands now. "If they are nomads, real nomads, and they do make shrines of... places like this, who knows, perhaps they have a tribal life, with their own rituals. And myths? Perhaps this house is a myth? I don't know. I have guesses, but I don't *know*. I have to know. There must be an explanation for what they are doing. Otherwise..."

"And you will turn the world upside down until you know what it is, n'est-ce pas?" She had seen him this way before, and the pattern was familiar to her, though not entirely welcome. In a day or so, he would have sorted out his thoughts and begun a methodical study of all his theories. "You know you have classes to teach? One is tomorrow at ten? Had you forgotten?"

"Tomorrow?" he asked, alarmed that so much time had got away from him. "So soon?"

"Mon fou... mon petit fou. Yes, tomorrow. While you were out chasing your nomads through Los Angeles, the world kept going. You need sleep, Jean-Charles. You shouldn't let yourself get so tired. That is why you agreed to teach, so that you could get some rest, do you remember?" She put her arms around him. "You should come to bed. Tu dois mi monter?"

He felt the pain in his groin. "When I have slept, ma belle. Right now, I am not much good for anything. You know?" He was grateful he had not told her what had been done to him. Her mood was still precarious and he could not anticipate how she might react to learning about his confrontation with the five in the van.

"A bath, then? So that in the morning, I will want to be near you?" She kissed him again, this time more forcefully. "And a shave, Jean-Charles? It is like brambles now."

He rubbed his chin. "More like berry vines," he

said, letting her go. "You're good to put up with me, ma belle."

"Mais oui," she said, her eyes very round. "Terrible thing that you are." She led him to the door. "Bath first. Then sleep. I will wake you so there will be enough time in the morning. No excuses then."

"No," he said, hoping that the pain and swelling would have subsided enough to permit him to make love. For he wanted that now, and the realization brought with it a stab of desire. He knew this for an old habit with him: once he began his search, he had an increased need for love, for sex, as if he were driven to renew himself in those embraces.

"And tomorrow, you will continue your search?" Veronique asked uneasily, though she knew. "I have read those clippings there. I am afraid of what they say."

Pommier shook his head. "I will develop my photographs and then I will go to the police. The man who gave me those will listen to me, I think."

"After that?" She stood still, watching him intently.

"I won't lie to you, ma belle," Pommier answered seriously. "I don't know what I will do after that. I don't know."

"Must I be satisfied with that?" Her eyes pleaded with him for greater assurances, but he could not give them.

"I'm sorry, Niki." He went after her down the hall. "I will think about it. I won't take needless chances."

"Perhaps," she said, going into the bedroom.

In spite of himself, he went to the window and looked down into the street. The night was misty, so that if the black van was waiting, he did not see it. Slowly he undressed and, wrapped in his robe, he went into the bathroom. Veronique had already begun to fill the tub. "Thank you," he said to her, bending over to kiss her once. "I probably don't deserve this from you."

She laughed a little sadly. "Probably. I should drown you. But I will not. Instead I will wash your back."

Pommier was about to say how much he would enjoy that when he thought of the bruises he could not explain adequately. "Better let me soak a little first. My muscles are in knots."

There was the suggestion of a pout to the curve of her mouth. "Very well. You will call me when you are ready and I will do it." She left the water running and returned to the bedroom.

With a long, worn-out sigh, Pommier tossed his robe aside and got into the water. He leaned back, letting the heat soak into him, and only turned the water off when he heard it gurgle in the overflow. His tensions, which had sustained him, at last started to fade. In a very little time, he was half asleep, his thoughts drifting. He had so many questions about those five. Who were they? Where had they come from? When? How did they manage to live? Were they truly nomads, or were they something else? But what? He was so lost in thought that he did not hear Veronique come back into the bathroom.

"It is just as I thought. You were falling asleep here." She sat on the edge of the tub just as he pulled the washcloth over his abdomen and genitals.

"I guess so," he said drowsily.

"Then you should come to bed. Ça peut attendre. Viens. Monte. Je veux le baiser, Jean-Charles." She started to trail her hand in the water. "It is more comfortable with me. Warmer."

"I know," he said, thinking that he was not quite ready for sleep, or sex. "But there are one or two things that—"

"Non! No more one or two things. In the morning, or after you teach your class, there will be time. J'ai envie de toi. J'ai envie de baiser. Maintenant. I have been so lonely for you. I want to sleep with your arms around

me. Come." Her hand stroked his cheek. "You need not
even shave."

"Oh, yes, I need," he countered, then caught his
lower lip between his teeth. "Is the easel unpacked, do
you remember?"

"The easel? What of it?" She drew back from him.
"Why?"

"I have a couple rolls of film I have to develop. That's
all." He could see the disappointment and underlying
shock in her face, and he tried to soften the blow. "Ma
belle, please. I have seen things I don't understand,
and until I do, I will not be able to rest. Don't you see?
It won't take long, and then . . ."

"And then you will want to go hunt them again, and
when that is done, there will be something else you
have to do. Oh, I understand, Jean-Charles." Her body,
her voice radiated hurt, and she took a few steps back
from him. "Do what you must. And I will do what I
must."

Pommier watched her slam out of the room and his
heart felt leaden with regret. There was no apology he
could make. He cursed himself inwardly, then climbed
out of the bathtub and assessed the damage done to
him in the mirror. It was not as bad as he feared, but he
would not want to try to make love for a few days. The
swelling was not as great as he had thought it was, but
most of the flesh was tender and the bruise he was
developing would be spectacular when it reached full
flower.

He shaved with a straight razor, as had his father
before him, and when he was satisfied, he finished
drying himself thoroughly, then pulled his robe back on
before going in search of the box that contained his
developing chemicals. He told himself that he would
not be long, and that once he got into bed, he would
tell Veronique how sorry he was and show her where he
had been kicked. Then the worst would be behind him
and he would have made some progress toward unravel-

ing the mystery of the black van as well. And even as
he attempted to convince himself, he knew these things
for the lies they were.

In his study he picked up three rolls of film, sternly
warning himself that he would only develop these for
the time being. Later he would do the rest. Then he
abandoned all pretense and grabbed the rest of them.
He had that fine clarity of mind that sometimes comes
with utter fatigue, and he was determined to make the
most of it.

ELEVEN

Behind the door a telephone was ringing. "Goddamn your eyes," Cassie said to Hank Wyler, the manager. "Get it open, won't you?"

"I'm doing my best," he sulked as he worked the lock. "There it goes," he said, stepping back and opening the door to let Cassie and a stoic policeman into the apartment.

Cassie shoved her way down the hall and ran for the phone.

"Look," Wyler said to the cop, "she told me she was a doctor, said that she worked at a hospital. Her credit looked okay. How was I to know that . . ."

"Shut up!" Cassie shouted at him. "She *is* a doctor. So am I." She reached the wall phone in the kitchen first and snatched it off the hook. "Hello? *Hello!*"

" . . . not available to answer your call right now," said Flax's recorded voice on her machine, "but if you care to . . ."

Cassie held out the receiver. "Oh, shit! She's got a machine. I should have remembered. We got to find it!" She pulled the receiver back to her mouth and shouted into it in the hope that she might be heard by the caller, "Hey! Don't hang up! Okay?"

"Try the bedroom," the policeman suggested, having checked the living room. "Has she been here long?" he asked Wyler.

"About six weeks. Real quiet. No complaints. No guests. Well, I guess . . ." he trailed off, looking around at the scantily furnished room.

"Right!" Cassie raced into the bedroom after making

a wrong turn into the bathroom. She dove for the phone just as she heard the beep.

"Hello, Eileen, this is Dick calling back. I've got the information you asked for."

Cassie pounded the pillow of the unmade bed with vexation. "Wait, wait. This isn't Eileen, and..." She took a gulp of air and forced herself to speak more calmly. "She's not here right now. May I take a message for her?"

"Oh," Richard Holder said from Cambridge. "Sorry. She called me earlier about a little research she—"

"You *talked* to her?" Cassie interrupted. "When?"

"Of course. She called me early today to ask about a phrase that she'd run across, and it took me a little longer to find it than I'd hoped, so—"

"Wait a minute; let me get a pencil. Who are you, anyway?" She fumbled with her purse and at last dragged out a ballpoint pen and a little memo pad where she usually made her shopping list. "Now shoot."

"This is Richard Holder. I'm a colleague of her former husband's. We're old friends. She wanted to know about a word in French, and she thought I could help."

"Oh, Christ. Des innois, right?" Cassie said.

"Yes. Okay. Tell her that it is not a place. At least, not one that we could find anywhere. Further, no one in the department that I spoke to seemed to think it had anything to do with anthropological studies."

"Eileen asked you about this?" It seemed unlikely to Cassie that Flax would call all the way across country for answers when she might find them nearer at hand.

"It's my specialty," he said with a mixture of arrogance and irritation. "I've done ethnological studies in Canada and she said her patient is French-Canadian."

"Oh," Cassie answered, more puzzled by the present-tense description of Pommier than the man's attitude; she had encountered that male academic pride often enough in the past.

"One of my grad students found an article, in French,

about nomadic Eskimos, and there is a word that might do: inuat. That's i-n-u-a-t. It's a little farfetched, but if you pronounced that in French, it comes out something like innois. Look, I don't think I should take up your time with this. Have Eileen call me when she has a chance and I'll give her the rest of the information if she thinks it could apply."

Cassie almost gnashed her teeth. "Ah . . . you better go ahead and give me the gist of it. I'll give it to her . . . when I see her. If you don't mind."

"Well . . ." Dick hesitated.

"Look, it could be important, no matter how absurd it seems, so let me have what you've got. It could help her; it really could." That, at least, was the truth, Cassie thought. "I'm ready."

"All right. There's this article, the one I mentioned. It says that the inuat is or are part of the myths of the nomadic Eskimos. The myth is similar to many others: the ieet of the Lapps, the hissi of the Finns, the enuvet in eastern Siberia. These tribes, you understand, live very isolated lives, in almost entirely self-contained groups, and dealings with all outsiders are hedged about with ceremony and rituals. Meetings with other tribes, if they went well, were occasions for feasting and entertainment. When they didn't go so well . . ."

The policeman had come into the bedroom. He nodded toward the suitcase. "She's been packing."

Cassie frowned at him and put her hand over the receiver. "Try the bathroom. See if her things are still there—toiletries, toothbrush, you know."

" . . . then there were fears of the inuat . . . Is something the matter?"

"No, nothing. Go ahead. These inuat?" she prompted.

"Apparently inuat were hostile spirits or malefic ghosts capable of assuming human form. I had one of my students check up on them, just in case. There's a reference in *People of the Polar Desert*, and I'll read you the pertinent part, if you like."

"Yeah," Cassie said, her eyes wide. Had the professor who died gone off the deep end? Did he think he had been possessed by demons? "Sure. Keep going."

"Well, this is the comment. Uh..." he paused, apparently searching for his place in the book. "Here it is. 'The inuat were thought to inhabit places of past calamity; they brought disaster and madness to any humans who made camp with them. This myth was sufficiently strong and persistent that well into the twentieth century trained observers marked how cautiously older Eskimos approached strangers, and avoided many areas of considerable size. Most expressed fear of the inuat and refused to venture into areas they were said to control.' That's... hello?"

"I'm here," Cassie said, scribbling to keep up, her thoughts in turmoil.

"That's all we could find. I don't know if that's what her patient is worried about, but I hope it will do her some good."

"I hope so, too," Cassie said with deep sincerity.

"If she wants to know anything more about them, that French article is about the best one there is. There might be an English translation available through the university, either in Los Angeles or in Berkeley. The title of the article is 'Mythic Traditions of the Nomadic Polar Eskimo,' more or less. The author is the top man in the field; he's teaching out there—maybe Eileen should give him a call."

Cassie felt herself go cold. "What's his name?" she asked, knowing the answer before it came.

"Jean-Charles Pommier. Got that? Should I spell it?"

"No," Cassie said blankly. "No, that's okay."

"All right." He paused. "Anyway, be sure and tell her that she's missed back here. And if she gets tired of all that dolce vita and sunshine, there are a lot of people in Boston and Cambridge who'd be delighted to see her again."

Cassie had to force herself to say something. "Yes. Yes, I'll do that. Thanks."

"Any time. I'll talk to you again, maybe?"

This sudden change of tone, with the faint suggestion of flirtation almost made Cassie laugh. "Sure, why not? 'Bye." The lightness left her as soon as she hung up the phone. She stared at what she had written, murmuring softly to herself, "N'y sont pas, sont des innois. They are not *there*, they are inuat." She heard the policeman open the door of the refrigerator, and it broke her mood. "Crap." She closed her notebook, shoved it and her pen into her purse, then got to her feet. "Crap, crap, double crap. Middle-of-the-night nonsense. The guy was bonkers, is all. Bullshit nonsense." She went toward the kitchen where the policeman and Hank Wyler were opening the cupboards.

"Not very much here, ma'am," the officer said to Cassie in a tone that implied there was something odd about it.

"She didn't spend much time here, just sleeping and relaxing. It's like that when you're a resident." Cassie glanced at her watch. "And speaking of—shit!—I have to be back on duty in half an hour."

"Well, what'd you think?" Wyler asked her plaintively. "I got to know what's going on here."

"You will just as soon as I do," Cassie said. "Look, she hasn't taken any soap or her toothbrush or her Tampax, and there's clothes in the closet, so you can be sure she's coming back. I'm just worried...you see," she said in a hesitant way that was out of character for her, "she's been...uh...exposed to something. It's not contagious," she added quickly, "but sometimes it causes blackouts, and since she doesn't know she's got it...the sooner we can find her and start treatment, the better—you know?"

The policeman's expression said that he didn't believe a word of it. "We'll keep on it," he said. "But it's one of those needle-in-a-haystack things."

"I know, but try, will you?" Cassie said. "And call me if anything happens. *Anything*, okay?" She took lipstick from her purse. "I'm going to put a note on the mirror in her bathroom. If anything's damaged, I'll pay for it," she told Wyler, forestalling any objections he might have.

"I don't . . ."

"You can read it, if you like," Cassie offered, starting into the bathroom. She printed in neat, coral letters: EILEEN, WHERE ARE YOU? PLEASE CALL. URGENT! CASSIE. Then, beneath that in spiky script, *Des innois may be an Eskimo word—if so, not a place, according to caller.*

"Oh, damn, I can't remember his name. You're a dip, Maybeck," she said to herself before she left the bathroom.

The policeman was already out of the apartment and Wyler was holding the door, impatient to be gone.

"It's okay. You go ahead," Cassie said to the men. "I'll lock the door on my way out."

"Sorry," Wyler cut in, "I can't do that. You can't stay here without one of us staying with you."

"Damn it, I'm not going to steal the fucking carpets! Go on, both of you. Go! I will close the door and lock it when I go. All right?" She very nearly slammed the door on them, then went back into the living room as if looking for clues. "Where did you go?" she asked the walls. "Where? And why?" She expected no answer and was not surprised that there were no further revelations. "This is a real loony tune, you know that?" She started back toward the door. "Eileen Flax, if I could find you right now . . . I'd probably wring your ever-loving neck!" With that, she reached for the door and let herself out.

Most of the class members were seniors, but there were a few enterprising juniors among the thirty-six who watched Pommier at the lectern. They are all so young, he thought as he stared at them. And their attitude was almost reverential, except for those few who were determined to find clay feet and questionable accomplishments, he realized, and knew that he had been away from the classroom too long. "It is a pleasure to see you here," he said, hoping to establish some sort of rapport with them. "As the title of the course suggests, we will be dealing primarily with actual field techniques in this class, as compared to the literature and theories of anthropology. As my experience has been with nomadic groups, you will have to keep in mind that most of my opinions and remarks will reflect that experience." It had been a long time since he had lectured regularly, but he knew the way of it, and fell into the style with disquieting ease.

He covered basic preparations in little over thirty minutes, knowing that there would be specific questions later. "You must take care to have *enough* of everything. For example"—he recalled his difficulties chasing the black van—"enough film and at least one spare camera. You will not be able to stop at an all-night drugstore to replace them if something goes wrong. Also, you ought to think about those few items you enjoy. You can get awfully tired reading the same paperback mystery again and again. Strive for maximum variety in minimum space. And remember that many of the peoples you elect to study might have a dim view of your recreations, so select those that are not very conspicuous."

One of the more skeptical seniors raised his hand, the second question of the lecture. "Don't you think, Dr. Pommier," the young man began and Pommier felt himself go on guard. Questions that began that way were often deliberate traps. "Don't you think that it is just possible for an expedition to be serviced regularly with supplies, rather than going in for all that backpacking mentality?"

Pommier nodded and gave the young man a direct stare. "Of course it is possible. And some resupplying is absolutely necessary, as you will discover when you run out of soap. But I have already explained the dangers of disrupting the routine of your expedition and the people you are studying too much. Once that balance is disrupted, it is often impossible to reestablish, and then whatever work you do will be of little value, either to you or the scientific community in general. If that is what you wish, by all means, do it, but don't delude yourself into thinking that you have been given the opportunity to learn something worthwhile." He saw that his blunt answer had made a few of the others uncomfortable and he decided it was necessary to soften the blow if he was to keep their attention. "We all tend to think of those who choose to live what we call a primitive life as being in some way naïve or inferior to those of us living in this so-called civilized world. But think how much we resemble them. You all know persons, I am sure, who hate it if they cannot see their favorite television program, even for a very good reason. This person is actually no different from those less privileged peoples who hate it if their routine of mending nets is altered. I do not mean to make this sound simplistic, but the disruptions are usually over very minor matters, not great or important ones."

This brought about another flurry of questions concerning behavioral patterns, and Pommier did his best to give concise answers, though by now his mind was wandering back to the photographs he had left hanging up in the improvised darkroom he had made in the little dressing room next to the bathroom. He had not seen them yet, as he had worked largely in the dark, as he had so often done on expedition. He would be able to see them at last, and to study them.

"Dr. Pommier?" one of the students asked, jarring him out of his reflections.

"Oh. Sorry. My mind was wandering. When you have been on expeditions as long as I have, there are times they seem to be the whole focus of your life.

This, this room, you, tend to startle me, as if you were not entirely real." He chuckled, giving them permission to be amused. "You will find it out for yourselves. My wife has often accused me of being addicted to expeditions." The last time had been that morning when he finally came to bed. "It may be that she is right."

Flax emerged, blinking, from the theater. Her thoughts were blurred, and she had to resist the urge to return to the campus and search out the anthropology department. But it was late. The streets were dark and the traffic had diminished to almost nothing. She could not read her watch—she was too exhausted to focus her eyes properly—and there were no clocks in plain sight. Flax wandered for three blocks before she remembered where she had parked her VW, all those hours ago. Then she had to make her way over a quarter of a mile in the other direction.

She had never been one to be frightened at night, but this time she hated the darkness, the occasional figures who passed her on the sidewalk or cruised the street in dark cars. And in vans. Once a big Chevy van hurtled by her, and Flax almost screamed at the sight, though she could see it was not a black van, *that* van.

At her car she hesitated. She knew she was afraid, more afraid than she had ever been in her life, perhaps. Yet the fear itself lured her, fascinated her. Seduced her. She was almost dizzy with hunger and exhaustion, but she could not bring herself to go back to her apartment. There was so much to do, she sensed that, and she was convinced that Pommier would not leave her alone until she had accomplished whatever it was he required of her. As she sat behind the wheel she leaned her head back. What was going on? How had this happened to her, whatever it was? Why had she, of all people in the world, been the target? For she was a target of some sort, of that she was sure. Was it simply that she had been present when Pommier died, or was it more complex than that? And what had taken place? Was she haunted? What had he done to her? She covered her mouth with her hand, worried that she might shout or scream or cry. Was it that she had been the last person to touch him while he lived? Was it that her life had been empty and she needed a mystery to fill it, to give it shape and importance again? She was a physician, she should not doubt her own worth. But she had so little to care for, and now, at least there was Pommier. Her eyes filled with tears at her helplessness, at Pommier's ordeal, at her own inner despair.

Three motorcycles grumbled down the street and Flax blinked at them. Then, without thinking, she turned the key in the ignition and started in the direction of Santa Monica. She sensed that at least part of the answer lay there. It had to be there.

TWELVE

Pommier turned into the driveway with an expectant smile on his lips. At last he would have his answers. He parked and got out of the Rabbit, taking the precaution of locking the door before he went into the house.

"Niki?" he called when he came through the kitchen. "Niki? Ma belle?"

There was a note on the table telling him that she had gone shopping and would be back within the hour. Pommier accepted this with a shrug and opened the refrigerator. Now that he was feeling more himself, he was becoming hungry again, and the sight of a wedge of Brie and four green apples made his mouth water. He took the cheese and one of the apples out of the refrigerator, then searched the drawers for a paring knife. He did not mind this last delay, he thought as he unwrapped the Brie, anticipation making pleasure out of every act of preparation.

When he finished with his food, he took another apple from the refrigerator and went upstairs, almost whistling. He had missed his music over the last few days. The incessant drive of punk rock displeased him, and he longed for the ordered and rational strains of the baroque. "Bach," he told the walls of the house, "is a thinking man's composer. He makes sense. His complexity is that of good structure." It was Pommier's most compelling belief that everything made sense once you understood it. For him there were no mysteries, only those matters that were not sufficiently understood. He went into the bathroom and opened the door to the little dressing room. He was feeling very pleased with himself.

There would be just a touch of regret, he knew, when he turned the pertinent photographs over to Coglan. For the last few days, it was as if the five in the van belonged to him; Pommier had felt that way before and knew it was immature and not truly worthy of a man of his standing. He had occasionally dismissed the feeling as being parental, born of care and concern for the people who engendered it. These five, however, did not foster any protectiveness in him, yet his repugnance was tempered by fascination and the desire to know the reason for their behavior. For there had to be a reason. He believed in reason with the fervor of religion, though he would deny it, for such a dogmatic conviction was not—reasonable. He laughed at himself for drawing out the last moment, enjoying that tantalizing hush before the thunder of revelation.

He brought the prints out and looked at them.

At first he thought there had been some mistake with the lighting. He turned on the overhead and mirror sidelights.

The pictures were from the last roll he shot. He recognized the buildings—the old hotel and another faceless brick façade—and the alley with the dumpster. What was not shown was any of the people. Not one of the five from the van was visible.

"It's not possible," Pommier declared as his eyes told him otherwise. He went back into the dressing room and pulled out an armful of prints. The van was on the pictures, always blurred, but there. However, it appeared to be unoccupied, undriven. "It's not possible," he repeated. On impulse he gathered up all the prints and went with them to his study. He dropped them on the rolltop desk, then decided to make himself some coffee before undertaking the frustrating task of examining the photographs to figure out what had gone wrong.

He had reached the bottom of the stairs when he

heard a sound—a soft, low, predatory chuckle—from
the direction of the living room. He turned toward it
and out of the corner of his eye he caught a quick
movement of shiny black. With more care than he
thought the situation warranted, he went into the living
room only to find it empty. All the windows were closed
and locked. The deadbolt was on the front door. A
quick check of the rest of the lower floor revealed that
nothing was open. "It's the pictures," he said, and went
to make his coffee.

While he was waiting for the water to boil, he took
extra care with the filter, then poured himself a bit of
cognac. Ordinarily he did not drink when he worked,
but he reminded himself that he had had a shock and
that it was a good idea for him to calm down before
tackling that mystery. He had about finished the cognac
when the kettle whistled, and so poured the last of it
into his coffee.

Returning to the study, he discovered the light was
on—he thought he had turned it off—and frowned as he
came into the room. He told himself that he was getting
too jumpy, but he could not shake off that disquieting
feeling that he was not alone in the house, or in the
room. He stood still in the middle of the study. "Hello . . . ?" There was no answer, and he reminded himself
that there was no reason for one. He had not fully
recovered from his ordeal of the previous night. A man
with bruised genitals was entitled to be nervous, he
decided. He noticed that one of his photographs had
fallen to the floor.

But it was not one of those he had taken chasing the
van: once again the photograph caught his attention.

There on the ice a single Eskimo stood, the vast,
blank emptiness around him so stark that the frigid
wind seemed to come off the shiny paper. The Eskimo
had been photographed at a distance, so that his isolation was complete.

And yet—there was a sense about him, an uneasiness

that had little to do with hunting. It appeared now, as it had when Pommier had first seen the man and taken his picture, that the lone figure was—he studied the hunter intently—was *trespassing*.

Pommier bent and picked the picture up. It mesmerized him, that lone figure, and he remembered how the old hunter had told him that those who walked the land of the inuat were doomed to join their numbers. It was all foolishness, myths to explain those hunters who disappeared and never left a trace. Or, in the desert, those who died of thirst and exposure and were covered by sand or devoured by scavengers, they, too, were considered the victims of malignant ghosts. He flung that picture away from him, deliberately not watching where it drifted. "It's nonsense; bobard." This last, in French, was the way his father used to dismiss anything he disliked. Taking a handful of the baffling photographs with him, he left his study, rationalizing the move with the thought that there was better light in the living room—there wasn't—and he would be more comfortable.

He drank down his coffee, then shrugged, and had a little more cognac. It warmed him, gave him a touch of the euphoria that he missed in his life. Exhaustion and sex and drink, those were the things that brought about euphoria. And that wonderful moment in study when the mystery is finally explained. He took cognac and photographs into the living room and settled down on the sofa.

Now was the time to be sensible, to think and evaluate critically. He stared at one photograph after the other, eyes narrowed, trying to discover what went wrong. If the camera had been damaged badly when it was dropped, it should mean that the photographs would not turn out at all. Was it that the low-light film was damaged, and the moving figures were too ephemeral for the image to be saved? But there were all the other rolls of film, and they had the same disquieting blankness. He held up one of the photographs so that light from the window fell across it. There was the dumpster, and the old hotel, and across the alley from it the massive brick building with a few high windows. He could just make out on the corner of the building a number. 579. 579. He would have to remember that.

Impulsively he wadded up the prints. "I will have to do them over, with more care." He did not know why he spoke aloud, but hearing the words made him more comfortable. "Yes. Working in the dark was not wise. I must outfit a proper darkroom and do the negatives again. Ça doit s'expliquer. Il le faut. Un film mauvais... ou quelque chose... j'sais pas... sûrement que..." He downed the last of the cognac. "I'm being foolish. Never mind the film. I will examine the negatives and if they are all right..." He rose. "And tomorrow I will telephone Captain Coglan and tell him what I have seen." That much was decided. He went and looked out the window, and the glorious late afternoon. In another hour it would be sunset, and then dusk. Already he could see that subtle shift in color that signaled the ending of another day.

"I have cobwebs in my head," he declared, taking the glass back to the kitchen, but leaving the wadded photographs discarded in the corner. "I ought to clear them." He was not actually aware that he was talking to himself, but he fancied it made the house feel less empty, speaking aloud. He could not believe that the house was not empty.

Cort put his hands on his hips. "I still say we should call the cops. Flax isn't just a run-of-the-mill missing person, she's a neurologist with a major medical problem. What do you think would happen if she had another one of those... episodes of hers while she was driving on the freeway?"

"A fucking disaster, that's what," Cassie said bluntly. "But so you get cops looking for her, what then? You think it would be easy to get them to understand her condition? What if she had one of those things while she was in their care? They wouldn't let us have her until they were satisfied that she..." She stopped. "I did have a cop check out her apartment. So there's something on record, anyway."

"When do you plan to file a missing person report?" Cort asked, taking a long sip of hot tea. They were in his office, the door almost closed, and Cort looked terribly fatigued. "I've got a patient out there in critical condition. We're trying to find out what's leaking and where before it can kill him. I can't spend much time trying to run down Eileen Flax, brain dysfunction or no brain dysfunction. And you can't spare a lot of time."

All these reminders were accurate enough and Cassie had the sense not to dispute them. "But I want to give it another try. If I haven't turned anything up by tomorrow morning, then you can call the cops and make it all official. We can answer silly questions until our eyes cross and then they can try to find out—"

"Tell me," Cort interrupted, "are you *sure* there's no one in Los Angeles she knows well enough to stay with?"

"There's me and there's Jennie McKechnie. And maybe, in a pinch, the Prohaskas in Van Nuys. But I've already phoned them and they haven't heard from Eileen in over a week." Cassie wrapped her arms across her chest. "She's got a brother, but he lives in Atlanta; works for a newspaper or something, a journalist, anyway. There's her ex in Cambridge, but from what I can tell, he hasn't bothered to talk to Eileen since she moved out here. When they split, they *split*. Parents aren't living anymore. She doesn't have any children. I've run out of ideas, Brad. I really have."

"But you still think you can find her?" Cort asked dubiously.

"Look, she called the professor in Cambridge about that inuat stuff. So she's not just drifting around doing nothing. She's . . ." She broke off. "I'm afraid that she's gone somewhere and had another one of those episodes where no one can deal with it. Like a motel or a department store or some other place. If she was in a public place, she might end up at a hospital, and if she did, they'd find her identification soon enough, and we'd know."

"Maybe," Cort corrected her. "That is *if* she had her identification, and *if* she were in any shape to answer questions—you saw what she's like when she's in the middle of one of those things—and *if* they didn't give her anything that might make her condition worse. I still say that we ought to start checking all the hospitals right now. Just in case she can't tell them herself what's going on."

At each of his objections, Cassie winced. "I'm not saying you're wrong," she allowed when Cort was through. "I'm just asking for time enough to look for myself. But you could be right." She sighed and leaned back against the bookcase against one wall. "Oh, shit! I don't know what's best. But I can't sit around waiting for someone to come up with something, sometime. I'll go out of my fucking mind if I do that," she said, her eyes begging Cort to understand.

"Let me call the hospitals, all right? We'll just say that we have reason to think that one of our neurologists was exposed to something . . . the same story you told the cop." Cort pulled a notepad nearer. "And if it turns out that she's been found, we'll bring her back. If we say that we've got the means to treat her here, you know they'll send her back to us. Is that good enough for you, Cassie?"

"It'll have to be. But keep the police out of this until tomorrow. I don't want her to be hounded like a goddamned fugitive." She straightened up. "I go off duty in two hours. I'll get to work on it then."

"And sleep? Or is that a silly question."

"How the fuck do you expect me to sleep with this

hanging over me? I might as well be doing something useful instead of lying there tossing and muttering to myself." She was indignant now, and it relieved Cort to see that she was not caught up in dithering and self-blame.

"You have a point there," he said, finishing his tea. "I'll give Ted a call and tell him what you've decided. Also, David Griffith has asked to be kept abreast of what's going on."

"Jesus," Cassie complained, "I might as well be running a fucking news bureau."

"But you'll do it?" Though he ended it as a question, it was clearly an order.

"Oh, yeah, sure, sure."

Flax drove past the house three times, just to be sure. Then she went back to Santa Monica Boulevard to search for a place that was still open. She would have to go there, and soon. She could sense that whatever it was that compelled her was drawing to a close. But how was she to do it? Could she simply walk up to the door, smile at Veronique, and say, "Hello, there, Niki; you don't know me, but I'm being haunted by your husband"? She would have the door slammed in her face at the very least. And if what she had been experiencing was any indication of what Veronique had been through, an announcement like that would probably distress her more than anything since Pommier's death. There had to be another way, but what? It was close to midnight in the middle of oceanside suburbia. A disruption could well bring the police and then what?

She saw a neon sign that called itself a pub, and she hoped it was true. Flax knew she was in no condition to drink, but a proper pub should offer some kind of food, if only sandwiches. She parked across the street, locked the bug, and went into the building.

The decor was imitation Tudor, with half-timbered

walls and heavy, dark tables. Flax found a place away
from the window and dropped gratefully into the chair.

"What'll it be, luv?" asked a fresh-faced waitress
whose accent sounded a good deal more authentic than
the decor looked.

"Do you have anything to eat at this hour?" Flax said,
looking in vain for a menu.

"Well, we have sandwiches we hot up in the micro-
wave, and there might be a little of the shepherd's pie
left from dinner. Either of those do for you?" She
paused. "I guess you'll be wanting coffee as well, won't
you?"

"Yes, if you please."

"You all right, then?" the waitress asked before going
to fetch the coffee.

"Just tired," Flax answered.

The mug of coffee was large and the smell said that it
was properly prepared. Flax inhaled gratefully.

"Made up your mind?"

"Some of the shepherd's pie, heated up, please,
would be wonderful. And if there's any roast beef left
over, a couple of slices of that would help, too." She had
to get more protein into her system—part of her fatigue
came from lack of it. While the waitress went off to fill
her order, Flax found cream and sugar for her coffee.
She did not often add these, but now she wanted the
flavors. Or was it Pommier who liked his coffee with
cream and sugar? she wondered. Were his tastes rub-
bing off on her? She could only recall his having black
coffee with brandy . . . no, cognac. She would have to
ask Veronique, when she summoned the nerve to speak
to her.

"There you are, ma'am," the waitress said a few
minutes later as she put down a good-sized portion of
shepherd's pie. "There's a little beef left and I'm hotting
that up right now. It'll be a couple more minutes."

"Fine," Flax said, and picked up her fork.

She had taken a few bites when the door to the pub

swung open and two men strolled in. One was tall and lean, with his light-colored hair in a pony tail, the other a shorter, beefier man in denim jeans and jacket. Flax froze, her food suddenly as palatable as cement.

"Hey, barkeep!" the tall one called out, "Get us a couple of those Bass ales, will you?"

"A pleasure, sir," was the courteous answer in an accent that came from the vicinity of Great Russell Street.

"I tell you," the shorter one said to his companion as they both took a seat at the bar, "that Haskell is going to drive us all up the wall by the end of the week. You hear what he said to D'Angelo?"

"Nope; I was loading gear, thank God." He took a long pull on his ale as soon as the bartender handed it to him.

"Called the man an incompetent. D'Angelo! I ask you. There's not a better grip in the business, and Haskell damn well knows it." He paused to drink. "One of these days, D'Angelo's gonna complain, and then there will be shit on the ceiling."

Flax leaned back and resumed her meal. She noticed that her hands were shaking and she chided herself for letting her nerves get the better of her. It was foolish to assume that everyone who had the appearance of those five had to be one of them. And now that she looked at the two men, she saw that they were not really very like the others at all. Most obviously, they spoke . . . their manner was . . . sociable. Yes, Flax thought as she finished her meal and watched them covertly, those two men were part of something, of everything. They were involved in living, in working, they were not rootless or disconnected.

"Will you want dessert, ma'am?" the waitress asked as she brought the beef slices to Flax, along with little pots of mustard and chutney. "We're out of spuds, but the chutney's nice."

"Thanks very much," Flax said automatically. "If you have something simple..."

"Well, it isn't quite simple, but there's a few bits of trifle in the fridge in the back. If we don't use them tonight, the law says we have to throw them out. I'd be happy to bring you one." Her smile was wide and genuine.

"Fine," Flax said. "And a little more coffee, if you will."

"Of course."

It was strange, Flax thought as she cut herself slivers of beef, how easily one loses touch, and how vital that touch could be. She had turned her back on Cambridge with little hesitation and cut the ties that kept her bound to Eric. But now, what was there? Her work, which satisfied her. A few friends, which she had not minded because there was so little time for friendship. But now? What now?

The waitress brought a tall parfait glass filled with trifle. "I'll just get the coffee. Will that be all, then?"

"Fine. Yes. It was very good." She smiled at the waitress, making an effort to be as accessible as the young woman appeared to be. How did she do it, without making herself the target for misunderstanding.

"Ta. Don't mind George and Steve," she added, nodding toward the two men at the bar. "They're movie people, and you know what that lot are like. I saw you watching them earlier. They're loud and they dress that way, but they're no trouble, no trouble at all." She took the money Flax gave her and went to get change.

When Flax had finished her second cup of coffee, she knew she could no longer put off meeting Veronique. With a last, wistful look around the friendly room, she left and crossed the street to her car.

THIRTEEN

Veronique came into the living room and stood watching Pommier. "I'm back."

"Is everything all right?" he asked, getting up from the sofa and coming to take her in his arms. "It's absurd to worry, but the last few days have been so . . ."

"Yes," she said, her arms going around him. "How did it go today? The lecture and the students?"

"Well enough. About what I had expected. A few show promise." He had to think carefully in order to recall the class. He was far more preoccupied with the photographs.

"But it is not as bad as you feared, is it? Jeany?"

He could hear how much she wanted him to tell her it was fine, that he had liked teaching. She was not made for the long, arduous journey and the constant moving that had marked his life for so long. She had gone with him for love and a taste of adventure, but her heart was here, in four walls and a proper garden, with neighbors and a family. He had deprived her of all that, and for the first time, he was shamed. "Not as bad. It will take time to discover if any of them will advance beyond a certain basic competence."

"Did they like you?" Her head came to rest on his shoulder so she would not have to look at him. "Did they?"

"They seemed to. It is also too soon to tell, ma belle." He kissed her. "We will all have to get used to each other. N'est-ce pas?"

"C'est vrai," she murmured. "And the rest?"

"You mean the black van? I haven't seen it," he said, choosing to misunderstand her question.

"But you will not follow it again, will you?"

"I don't know if I'll see it again. I don't want to follow it again," he admitted with an inward shudder. "Don't worry, Niki."

"You will give the photographs to the police?" She waited for his answer.

He felt her arms tighten. "Most of them aren't... much use. I have to develop them again."

"Jean-Charles!" she protested, looking up at him. "Not more of them."

"They... didn't come out," he said. "I shouldn't have tried to develop them last night."

"You were exhausted. You should have seen yourself." She kissed his chin. "I like you better with a shave."

"No more berry patch," he said with a smile. "Tonight, I will be rested." He took his time about kissing her, convincing her with his mouth. She would see his bruises, but these were not as bad as they had been and he doubted she would complain about them too much if he was sensible about them.

"Oh, I am going to like tonight very much," she purred.

"Oui, ma belle. Very much." He nuzzled her neck. "Shall we go out to dinner first, or..."

"Non, non, Jean-Charles. I have already bought a filet mignon. There are mushrooms and endive and asparagus. Let me cook them." She pushed back in his embrace. "I want to make this meal. Comprenez-toi?"

"Yes, I understand. And I am very grateful, Niki."

"I was... not very kind to you last night. You will let me make it all up to you, won't you?"

"I'm looking forward to it," he said with so much sincerity that she grinned at him and made his pulse hammer.

"Moi aussi," she said, and moved away from him. "Now, you are distracting me."

Pommier laughed, a genuine and open laugh. "I won't pretend I'm not flattered to hear it," he said. "What should I do about it?"

She made an airy gesture. "Oh, anything. Plant flowers or go for a walk. Anything, so that I can cook in peace. Otherwise I know you; the meat will be . . . brul . . . what is the word?"

"Burnt. You're probably right." He shrugged, feeling very happy. "I'll take a walk, then. How soon do you want me back?"

"An hour should be long enough. That will permit me to make a special dessert as well." She had a mischievous look now, her vixen's face brightening at the prospect of being able to surprise him.

"You know what dessert I want," he said, reaching out to touch her. Perhaps she was right, he thought, and it was time to live as she wanted to rather than the way they had been living for so long. Was it age? Or had he lost something—courage, an attitude, driving curiosity—that had been propelling him for more than twenty years?

"You're troubled?" she asked as she studied his face.

Pommier shook his head. "No." He looked toward the window. "I guess I should put on a sweater. It's getting dark." There was a trace of fog in the air, as there so often was at day's end near the beach.

"An hour, Jean-Charles," Veronique reminded him as she went back toward the kitchen.

"I'll be back," he promised her, and took a V-necked cardigan from the hall closet. He heard her humming as she set to work in the kitchen. It gave him a jaunty feeling to hear her, and it communicated itself to how he moved.

It was dusk, ripe and soft, cool, salty. He headed south toward Santa Monica Boulevard, whistling a little waltz by Brahms. There were lights in the houses around him winking like lights on a Christmas tree. He lengthened his stride, not quite jogging, as he passed by the library. There were children playing in front of one house, their squealing laughter a delight to Pommier. This was a good life to live, he thought, and hurried on toward the main street.

Here night was banished by excellent streetlighting, and as Pommier turned toward the ocean, he saw it only as a distant and enormous darkness below the last red-gold line of afterglow. Traffic was still fairly heavy but not congested as it often was during the height of commuting hours. The mists were not thick enough to conceal anything yet, but they gave a softness, a blurring of hard lines like a good Impressionist painting. He kept moving, and thought he had found a wonderful place to live. He changed pace to an easy lope, amused at himself for joining the vast company of runners who could be found out in force every morning and afternoon. If he intended to do it often, he would have to purchase the proper uniform for it. A few more blocks and he crossed Ocean Avenue and entered the park that ran between the street and the edge of the bluff. He went right to the rail and stared down the drop to the highway below. No wonder so many people wanted to live up here! They had all the beauty of the ocean before them, and the carpet of the beach, but they were high enough above it, far enough away that none of the flotsam washed up on their doorsteps. He leaned on the rail and gazed out to sea as the last of the light faded from the sky.

A bit later, he began to walk north, not pressing for speed now, but simply enjoying himself. There was a little more fog drifting inland, turning the streetlights into furry balls of brightness. He looked at the leaning and curved trunks of the trees, balletic shapes of darkness in the encroaching night.

One of the trees attracted Pommier's notice, and he stared hard at it, then realized that there was a person leaning against it. Pommier shook his head at the panicky notions that had flooded his mind when he first glimpsed the tree. It *was* time he stopped racketing all over the world. He started forward, then stopped again as the figure by the tree turned.

He was blond, with his long hair drawn back in a pony tail. His eyes, flat with loathing, met Pommier's, and he added an ironic, obscene salute. When he saw the distress in Pommier's face, he turned and walked into the shape and shadow of the tree: he did not emerge.

Pommier could not believe what he had seen, and after a brief hesitation, he hurried to the tree, believing that he would find nothing more than one of the beach locals lounging there.

No one stood behind the tree; no one was walking away from it.

Around the corner of the next street up came a black surfers' van, driving without lights, slowing down as it neared Pommier.

Pommier continued walking, gradually increasing his speed, only to discover that the van was keeping pace with him on the far side of the street. He tried not to look at it, but that was fruitless. He felt it like the clothes he wore, clinging to him, in some unnamable way attached to him ... Without warning he reversed direction and broke into a run.

A pair of figures appeared amid the trees, and Pommier ran straight for them, determined not to be slowed down and trapped as he had allowed himself to be the night before.

"Hey!" shouted one of the two as Pommier slapped into him, grabbing his jacket to spin him around and throw him to the ground. "What's ... ! Jesus, it's some kind of freak! Run, Cathy! He's nuts!" The boy's voice rose higher, cracking at the top in his adolescent panic.

The girl started to sprint off, then faltered, and after an instant, returned and began to batter at Pommier's back with her fists. "No! Please, mister! PLEASE! Leave him alone! *Leave him alone!*"

Gradually Pommier realized what he was doing. He released the boy and stepped back. "I . . . I'm sorry . . ." It was completely inadequate and he knew it, but there was nothing else he could do. Once again he began to run, away from the two teenagers, the black van, back toward the brightness and clutter and crowds of Santa Monica Boulevard.

"You son of a bitch!" the boy yelled after him, anger replacing fear in him. "You goddamned crazy fucking son of a bitch!"

The van was right behind him now, and Pommier put on a burst of speed, wanting only to flee. He was not certain he would dare to cross the street, not with the van so close. Then he saw a service station on the east side of the street, lights glaring brightly. There was an attendant leaning on one of the pumps, a big man, black, in old army fatigues. Running against the light, Pommier made for that urban oasis.

The attendant paid no attention to Pommier, apparently immune to anything that lacked wheels. Pommier stood near the man, only a pump and a *Full Service* sign between them. Finally Pommier cleared his throat.

"You want gas?" the attendant asked. There were Da Nang tags on the cap he wore.

"Gas?" Pommier repeated, incredulously. "Why?"

The attendant spoke as if talking to a person who was hard of hearing. "Did you run out of gas? You got a can for it?"

At last Pommier understood. "Oh. No. I didn't. I was out for a walk. Do you have . . . some soft drinks?" It was the best he could think of at short notice.

"In the office. Costs fifty cents for a can." He looked quizzically at Pommier as if expecting something more. "Is that all?"

"Uh . . . I think so," Pommier said, casting a glance over his shoulder. He could not find the black van but the pricking on the back of his neck told him it was there.

"Be m'guest," the attendant said, indicating the door. "There's coffee, too; that's thirty cents. Perked it an hour ago."

"Thanks," Pommier said as he went into the office. There were four vending machines: one for cigarettes, one for candy, one for soft drinks, and one for nuts and raisins. Next to the last of these there was a table with a twenty-cup percolator bubbling. After a brief hesitation, Pommier took one of the Styrofoam cups and filled it with the thick, dark liquid. It tasted hot and dreadful, but it gave him a few minutes to think. Should he call Coglan? And if he did, what would he say that did not sound paranoid or foolish? He stared out the window, waiting.

Then he saw it, the black van. It pulled into the service station, creeping toward the place where he waited. Outside, the attendant took out a pack of cigarettes and began to smoke. If he saw the van, he gave no indication of it. Pommier stared as the side door opened and the woman in black clothes got out. She blew Pommier a kiss through the glass that almost made him gag on his coffee. The driver turned and looked once directly at Pommier and from somewhere inside the van there was the loud, intrusive beat of punk rock.

"Oh, God," Pommier whispered and turned his back on them. Why hadn't the attendant seen them? Had they paid him? Did he know them? Or . . . Pommier put his hand to his eyes. Or was it like the photographs, nothing there because there was nothing to see? "Am I mad?" Pommier asked the walls of the office in a voice so soft that it was barely audible above the burble of the percolator. There was only the bruise on his groin to convince him that something had happened. That . . . and the van! That, at least, had shown up in his pictures. And yet, the attendant completely ignored them. Pommier walked away from the window, very slowly and deliber-

ately. I will not look at them, he told himself. I will not
look at them.

He forced himself to stand for a good three minutes,
his mind focused on other things, on expeditions he had
been on, on his years in the Royal Navy. When he
could stand it no longer, he turned around.

The van was gone.

Pommier came back to the window, blinking once to
be sure of what he saw. It troubled him that he had not
heard the van drive off: he might have imagined the
whole thing. Cautiously he went out of the office and
walked up to the attendant. "Pardon me?"

"Yeah? Need the men's room key?"

"No," Pommier said. "No, that's not it." He could not
think what to say next. Rather awkwardly, he pointed in
the place the van had been. "Was there a . . . Did you
see . . ."

The attendant waited while Pommier tried to find the
words, but finally said, "Hey, spit it out, man—what is
it?"

Pommier almost spoke again, then looked away. "Rien,
rien."

"What?" the attendant said, making no sense of the
unfamiliar word. "What's that?"

"It's nothing," Pommier said. He put the Styrofoam
cup on the top of the nearest cup and handed the
attendant two quarters. "Thanks for the coffee."

"No trouble," the black man said as he pocketed the
money.

"Later," Pommier told him by way of farewell, then
started out along the street, hoping to make it home.
He checked once, but the van was nowhere in sight—
and might never have been near him at all, he thought
with some bitterness. He began to walk more briskly.

Then dead ahead of him, lights glared on, shining
straight into Pommier's face. He cried out and raised
his arm in protest; as he did, he heard an engine roar
into life.

Pommier turned and ran, trying to evade the inexorable brightness, but the headlights held him pinned, skewered with their beams. Pommier hardly saw where he was going except that it was away. Once he tried to duck out of the lights and almost stepped into the side of a speeding car. He had to run too fast to think or anticipate new strategy. The van chased him, keeping him at the very limit of his strength and speed.

The sound of his steps changed and Pommier faltered, arms windmilling. The fog was growing thicker and he knew that he was headed west. He was afraid of the drop from the bluff, knowing that running him off the bluff would be the sort of thing the five might find amusing. The engine roared and the van raced toward him. Pommier took a few stumbling steps and discovered that he was on a bridge. Behind him he could barely make out the massive shapes of the buildings along Ocean Avenue—blocky skyscrapers, and that huge white building like a Babylonian garden, rising in pyramided terraces back from the street. Was this the pier? He did not have time to question anything more as the sound of punk rock blared over the snarl of the engine.

A break in the railing and the protruding angle of a banister indicated a staircase. As Pommier saw it, the van closed in on him. The noise was shattering. Pommier sprinted for the staircase, leaped the banister at the second bend in the steps, and came down hard on his ankle.

The van rumbled above him, then shrieked to a stop, grunting as it was backed up to make the hairpin turn on the pier. With an ominous churning sound, the van launched itself down toward the boardwalk where Pommier was already trying to find an escape. He ran south, away from Santa Monica toward Venice.

His leg dragged as he ran. "Bon Dieu," Pommier panted. He was afraid he had torn a tendon, or at the least had a bad sprain. Pain lanced up him every time he put his foot down.

At his back came the van, knocking over trashcans and pushing tables and benches aside or breaking them. Loose sand sprayed from its wheels and the engine coughed angrily as it changed gears.

Just when Pommier feared he could run no more, that he must collapse and be destroyed by the van, he saw a narrow alley to his left. With a whimper of gratitude, he ducked into it, hoping that there might be a place where he could take refuge, or elude his pursuers.

Then he looked ahead and saw that the alley was blind. High walls rose up on both sides of him, every foot of them mute testament to decay and neglect. His chest went cold and he dragged air into his lungs with an effort.

One of the buildings had a narrow alcove with a door, perhaps a tradesmen's entrance from more prosperous years. It was unlit, and the weathered door was not promising, but it was the only hint of safety, and Pommier took it. He grabbed the handle, found it would turn, and threw his weight on it as the van came howling down the alley.

With a shuddering groan, the door opened.

There was a brief moment when light caught it, recessed though it was, and illuminated a number of faded paint on the door: 579. Pommier hesitated, the number bringing something to mind, but nothing he could recall.

The van was rumbling up the alley, cutting off all retreat except this door. Pommier slipped inside and closed it again.

"Are you going to need any help?" Ted Oldsman asked Cassie as she pulled on her jacket.

"Probably, but who has time to spare to give it?" Her face creased as she smiled. "Tell you what, though, if it turns out that there's phoning to do, or something that won't take you away from the hospital, I'll let you know, okay?"

"If that's the best you can do," Oldsman said slowly. "I wish I had more time free."

"So do I, Ted. Hell, I wish the whole fucking staff could take the day off and look for Eileen, but that's not gonna happen, is it?" She gave him a wistful look. "I want to know what's going on. I'm scared for Eileen. I keep thinking that we're going to get a call from a cop saying that someone has to come to identify her, and make arrangements for the body. I'm scared shitless that she's been mugged or worse while she was having one of those episodes and is lying in a hidden place, out cold. Hey, she's fragile. She could get killed without knowing it."

"We're all fragile, Cassie," Oldsman reminded her.

"Sure, but not the way Eileen is right now." She walked to the side door. "I'll try to call in at regular intervals. For the time being, I'm going over to UCLA to find out as much as I can about Pommier. It all started with him, so I guess I'll start with him, too." She pushed open the door and waved over her shoulder to Oldsman.

"Hang in there, Cassie!" he called to her.

"Damn right!" she answered, then headed for the parking lot, glancing at her watch as she went.

FOURTEEN

Looking up, Pommier could see the shattered glass of large, old-fashioned skylights. Rubble and glass crunched underfoot when he moved away from the door, and he froze, expecting a new horror to be visited upon him.

Nothing happened.

After a few, breathless minutes passed, Pommier relaxed, beginning to think he might still make good his escape. He made his way cautiously around the room. It had the look of a deserted greenhouse or solarium. Once upon a time, perhaps more than twenty years ago, the room had been sunny and very, very private. Was that before hot tubs? Pommier wondered if this had been one of those very decadent, very discreet places where those with outré tastes had once gone to obtain their pleasures. The high walls would give privacy and the skylights would let in the sun. Was this where some farsighted Madam, of either sex, had once found gold? Pommier smiled at the thought, glad for the distraction his visions of debauchery provided.

Aside from the door through which he had entered, there were two other doors in the room, both leading to the interior of the building, both closed. He did not relish prowling about a derelict building in the dark, but it was preferable to facing the five in the van. There was always the chance that those five knew where he was and were planning to trap him inside the house, to follow him, torment him. Kill him. The last notion hung on Pommier like a bad smell. He knew that the five would kill him without conscience or hesitation, for no greater reason than whim. He shuddered at the thought and looked back at the door to the alley. Had it moved, or was it his imagination? Idiotically he thought that it was time he was getting home. If he were late, he would offend Veronique, and he did not want to do that, not after the shabby way he had been treating her. He went back to the door and leaned on it, making sure it was firmly closed.

"I have a light here if you would like it," said a soft, old, feminine voice behind him.

"Ah!" Pommier exclaimed, turning abruptly, pressing back against the door, hands coming up to protect his face.

"They've shut off the power on this side of the building, I'm afraid," the voice went on, and the single beam of a battery lantern swung in Pommier's direction so that he was unable to see who held it. "It's only a small savings, of course, but in my case, it is also..."

Scuffling steps came up to Pommier. A small white hand extended to touch him and the light wavered away from him. Pommier found himself staring down into the calm, cataract-blind eyes of a white-habited nun.

"... a small sacrifice."

"Sister?" Pommier said in quiet, utter disbelief.

"Yes? I keep the lantern here for visitors. Of late, of course, we have had very few visitors."

Pommier was still staring at her, questions crowding in on him. He was almost willing to think he had imagined her.

"Is there something the matter?" she inquired in that same patient manner he remembered his teachers using when he was young.

"No. No, forgive me. I'm being... rude. Forgive me, please. It is just... well, I didn't think... that..." He gestured at the broken windows, then dropped his hand, knowing that she could not see what he did.

"You'll be forgiven for thinking the building abandoned." There was a trace of amusement in her remark.

"Yes. I'm sorry to say that I thought that." He lapsed

back into some of the attitude of his childhood, when he had deferred to the sisters as automatically as he switched from English to French in his conversation.

"It's a common enough mistake. The location is not . . . what it was."

Pommier thought of the assumptions he had made about the place only a few minutes ago, and kept silent.

"And the handyman we have employed has, like so much of the world, grown lax. It wasn't always like this, of course. But now, with only me here regularly and two other sisters twice a month, the disrepair is a small matter." She indicated the way through the old solarium to the door she had used.

"You're here . . . alone?" Pommier was startled to hear her say so.

"Of my community, yes. Oh, I'll follow the others eventually. For the time being, I'm expected to . . . look after things, as it were. Though I'm not certain that the Order appreciates the humor of it." She laughed, very lightly, almost like a girl and Pommier joined her, though he did not know why. "Gracious, I fear I'm the one being rude. I am Sister Bertril." She held out her hand in his general direction.

"How do you do, sister," Pommier said as he took her hand, merely holding it in his for a moment, as he had been taught to do. "I'm . . ."

"You're Dr. Pommier. Yes."

The comfort that had seduced Pommier into believing he was safe vanished at the sound of his name. "How . . ."

"Won't you join me for tea, doctor?" She smiled at him, but this time Pommier took no satisfaction in seeing it. "If you will come with me?" she said, going toward the farthest door. "I keep only three rooms now, and the chapel. The rest is in a sorry state."

Pommier stared after her as she receded into the darkness, then he went after her, hurrying to catch up. His head throbbed and his mind was in turmoil. How had she known his name? She spoke, and so he did not think she was one of the same creatures as those in the van, but there was something wrong with her. Or was it simply that she was a blind old woman living alone in a deserted building, out of touch with the world? But how had she known his name? That question remained and he had no answer for it.

The lower floor was sagging and neglected, having some of the faded dignity of a mausoleum. The floors had been scrubbed but were aged and cracked. There were a few chairs against the wall, all of them smelling of dust, looking stiff and unused. There was a hall off the front lobby leading to a flight of stairs.

"My quarters are on the second floor, doctor, right next to the . . . kitchen. Dear me, I almost called it a refectory. But that was years ago, of course." She went serenely up the stairs, pale and quiet, almost insubstantial in the dark.

Pommier could find nothing to say as he went after her. The stairs creaked under his weight and after one grab at the banister, he decided it was safer without it.

"I'm afraid I haven't any lemon," Sister Bertril went on as she turned at the top of the stairs. "Though there is sugar. I trust that's satisfactory?"

"Yes," he said, feeling distracted. "Fine."

She went along the dark hall with complete ease and confidence, turning through two swinging doors into a large, commercially outfitted kitchen that had been equipped before the Great Depression. "You know, they used to be so regular about sending groceries, very dependable. The boy came around twice a week with everything we needed, but these days . . . The sisters usually bring me my supplies, not that I need very much, though recently they haven't been as regular . . . or I've got the days muddled again. You can do that, when you're blind. Don't hang back, Dr. Pommier," she said as he stood in the doorway. "Come in here, if you will please."

"All right." He came into the kitchen and stood near the old refrigerator, the kind with the fan unit on top. "You know about them, don't you?"

"Them?" Sister Bertril asked as she busied herself with drawing water and lighting the stove.

"The black van, those people who ride in it." He said it all evenly, as if he were asking a question in class. He was depending on her answer more than he could admit.

Her response, when it came, was oblique. "There are places with secrets, Pommier. Places have pasts, like people. Things... collect in them." She stopped, her head turning as if she heard something.

"What is it?" he asked.

"Nothing. I must have been mistaken." She took a large crockery pot and poured hot water into it. "It must be warmed, or the tea will be bitter."

"The van, sister," Pommier prodded her as gently as he could.

She turned her head toward him, and he had the eerie feeling she could see him with her white eyes. "You've looked too closely, Pommier. Most people are luckier. Most do not pay any attention. They never know what's all around them, never know that a portion of what they see or hear or have dealing with every day, any day... is... not... there."

"No," he breathed.

"But your problem now is not that you know of them. Oh, no. It is that *they* know of *you*." As Pommier heard this he leaned back against the counter behind him, resigning himself to hearing the rest from the little nun. "Listen, Dr. Pommier, and I pray you listen closely. Do not try to fight them; you cannot win. Believe me. Oh, do *believe me*. You are in the gravest danger as long as they can reach you. You must go away from here, far away. Leave your house—that, most of all—and change your job. Go away and hide yourself. If you do, you will still survive this, if they cannot reach you." She broke off again, listening to something that Pommier could not hear. "Dr. Pommier, if you've never run from anything in your life, run from this. You must. I know whereof I speak. They are leading you into another world, their world. And they are ruthless. They will hound you until they find something you are truly afraid of, or for. Once they know that fear, they will win. It's only a matter of time."

Pommier shook his head. "No. They're not . . . real. They can't *do* anything!"

"You say that, after being kicked?"

"I . . ." Pommier began, then looked about in confusion.

"Don't you understand that they brought you here, Pommier?"

It was suddenly very quiet, though Sister Bertril appeared once again to be listening. "Those girls! Oh, dear God . . ." she murmured.

"Girls?" Pommier asked, baffled. "You're not alone?"

"Oh, yes. But there are the girls." She made a curious gesture.

The teapot began to shrill and both Pommier and Sister Bertril jumped at the sound.

"Sister, what is this place? What . . . happened here?"

The little nun turned away from him. "It's inexcusable of me to refuse you something I've offered. But you really must leave. Now." She moved a little farther away from him. "Go, do as I've told you. Far away." Impatiently she picked up a teacup set out on the side of the stove. "Don't pursue this anymore; you will not, you *cannot* win. They're the agents of madness, Dr. Pommier. Madness. They are madness. It's only a matter of time, Jean-Charles, before they find out what they want to know, and you will be lost to them, to their madness."

"Sister . . ." Pommier objected.

"Go." She began to make tea for herself and it was plain that she would pay no more attention to him.

Pommier left the lantern with Sister Bertril; making

his way through the dark building proved to be more
difficult than he had anticipated. Somehow he missed
the stairs to the main floor, or they were farther along
than he thought. He kept one hand on the wall, and
found that there were doors at regular intervals of about
ten feet. Had this been a convent, then, with individual
cells for the nuns? Sister Bertril had mentioned girls—
perhaps this was once a school or an orphanage. The air
was filled with the musty scent of closed-in places, and
occasionally his hand found damp patches on the wall.

"Dr. Pommier," Sister Bertril's voice called after him
as if over an immeasurable distance, "don't go that way,
oh, not that way."

He stopped walking and looked back in the direction
he had come. "Sister?" he said, fairly loudly. When
there was no answer, he shouted. "Sister Bertril!" This
time all he heard was a single, girlish giggle. "What?"
he whispered.

There were more giggles, young, sly sounds, teasing
Pommier.

"Who's there?" He scarcely spoke aloud, but still the
giggles answered him.

Down the corridor he saw movement, and he squinted
at it to bring it into focus. Something came close to
him, brushed past him at shoulder height. A nun? A
girl in a uniform? What? He tried to follow it as it
disappeared in the dark, and suddenly a whole flock of
the dark-draped things fled by him, giggling, giggling.

"Wait!" he shouted, and was met with silence. He
took a few uncertain steps back, not knowing what next
to expect. What could he expect? More of the strange
figures in the shapeless dark garments? He swallowed
hard and started to move again.

A massive, solid shape crashed through the ceiling,
hurtling toward Pommier, missing him by less than a
foot as it crashed into the floor. The corridor echoed
with the impact in concert with Pommier's racing heart.
He was too terrified to make a sound. When he could

move without trembling too badly, he inched away from the object. It looked something like a desk, one of those old railroad-style desks with cubbyholes and drawers. "How the hell . . ." he muttered.

The sound that answered him this time was a low, crooning chuckle, sinister and innocent.

"WHO ARE YOU!" The walls echoed, distorted, and mocked him. "WHO ARE YOU!" He moved away from the desk, afraid of what might threaten him. In a few steps he was running.

He heard scurrying and glanced over his shoulder. To see nothing. But the noise continued, growing louder, as if he were in the middle of a gathering of children trying to tiptoe down the hall.

A bit of dark clothing showed in one of the doors, but was gone before he could reach it.

Another one of the dark figures appeared before him, cutting across his path and ducking into another door before he could grab her. Was it her?

Near a cross hall, a woman stood with her back to him, her nun's habit preternaturally bright in the gloom.

Pommier seized her arm, about to offer an apology.

The nun giggled as she turned, showing her naked breasts. She reached for his hand and began to rub it against her exposed body, laughing softly, low in her throat, her tongue tracing her lips.

This time the giggles were as loud as the roar of an ocean storm.

Appalled, Pommier tore away from the nun and careened into another habited woman. He held out his hand to steady her and saw that the habit clothed a skeleton.

Pommier screamed; bolted.

"Dr. Pommier." Sister Bertril stood before him now, tranquil. "Dr. Pommier," and her voice was deep and masculine. "Go away, Pommier."

"No!" Pommier recoiled from the small, neat nun. He chose the first door he found open and crashed through it. As he felt the platform give way beneath him, he remembered he was on the second floor.

One instant he was suspended in the air, the next he had fallen to the street.

He lifted his head, grateful to be alive, terrified of what might await him.

"Hey, he's come to," said a youthful voice. "Cathy!"

The girl kneeled down beside Pommier. "Can you hear me? Can you talk?"

Pommier shook his head. "Uh cauchemar ... un cauchemar ... a ... dream?"

"Mister ... ?" the boy said, offering his arm to Pommier. "Do you think you can get up?"

"Oh, God, Chris, he's got a nosebleed!" Cathy shrieked as Pommier managed to raise himself off the pavement.

"I ..." He was in the park at the Palisades in Santa Monica. It was dark now and the fog had rolled in. He looked around, at the trees, and for an instant he saw a woman in shiny black clothes move out of the shadow of one into the shadow of another. Vehemently he shook his head.

"Hey, don't do that," the boy protested, his hand on Pommier's shoulder.

The woman in black, if she had existed at all, did not reappear. "It's ... nothing," Pommier said, sniffing once, and tasting blood. He brought one hand to his face.

"You fell pretty hard," the boy said apologetically. "We were roller skating. We didn't see you."

"Roller skating? I don't ... remember ..." He finally managed to sit up. "Have I been unconscious?"

"Yeah," the boy admitted. "About ten minutes. We were getting scared."

"I wanted to call somebody, but Chris said we couldn't go off and leave you, and he wouldn't leave me by myself—you know what it's like after dark." She gave Pommier a hard stare. "You sure you aren't hurt? I mean, you could have a concussion or something."

"I feel as if I had fallen out of a second-story window," he told them, enjoying his own irony.

"Well, you went down kind of hard," Chris said. "I'm sorry about it, mister. If you want me to—"

"Nothing," Pommier cut him short. "I'll be all right." He could feel blood on his upper lip; his slacks were torn at the knee and the right one had a painful laceration where he had skidded on the pavement in his fall.

"You want my name and phone number? My dad will probably have to know if there's anything wrong with you . . ." Chris said, babbling now.

"Help me get up for a start, will you?" So he had been run down by a pair of roller skaters. There had been no black van, no convent, no Sister Bertril. It was all a figment of his imagination. When he was a kid, he had often wondered what that phrase meant, and now he knew. But it had seemed so *real*!

"You're . . . looking pretty strange . . ." Cathy said, a worried frown on her pretty face.

"I feel strange. So would you," Pommier told her. He held out his hand to Chris. "Slowly, please.. I'm still a bit dizzy."

Chris braced himself, hanging onto one of the tree limbs so that he would not be overbalanced on his skates. "I'll try."

It took a little while for Pommier to lever himself to his feet, and once he was upright, he had to steady himself. "Thank you," he said when the dark motes were gone from his vision.

"You sure you don't need a doctor?" Cathy asked. "I could call home and they could arrange for . . ."

Pommier was able to give her a tight smile. "It's all right. I'll be fine. All I need is a little sleep."

Her frown deepened to a scowl. "But still, mister, a guy your age, you know . . ."

At that Pommier chuckled and did not mind the hurt it caused. "I'm not quite that decrepit, young lady."

Cathy flushed deeply. "I didn't mean that, well, not quite. But *you* know."

"Uh . . ." Chris said, visibly screwing up his courage. "I live over on Ashland. My last name's Brodsky. We're in the phone book. If anything happens, just call. I'll tell my dad all about it as soon as I get home."

"Fine. If I need anything, I'll call." Pommier was starting to feel shaky, and he wondered if it might be better to ask for assistance. But who knew how long it would take to arrive, and after that, how long it would be before he could get away. Which would mean disappointing Veronique again. He tried a few steps, gritting his teeth against the pain in his leg.

"How far have you got to go?" Chris asked, growing more worried.

"Five, six blocks," Pommier said vaguely.

"You're not going to make it that way."

"I'll make it." Pommier was determined now. He had endured worse hardships on expedition, he reminded himself. But then he had been prepared for them, and had taken precautions against them, not like here, where he had anticipated no difficulty but what to do to end boredom.

"Look, I'll get you a stick or something. There's a few dead branches around here. That way you can walk a little better." It was almost a plea, and Pommier welcomed the suggestion.

"That I will accept with alacrity," Pommier said. He hobbled to the nearest bench and braced himself against it while Chris proceeded to cast about in the dark.

"Got it," he announced five minutes later, rolling up to Pommier with about four feet of dead branch in his hands. "It's pretty straight and it's steady. I tested it."

Pommier reached out for it. "I appreciate this," he said, and started away from them. He would be a little late for dinner, but Veronique would not quarrel with his reason for being delayed.

"Mister!" Chris called after him. "What's your name, so I can tell my dad."

He hesitated, trying to think of the best way to express it. "Professor Pommier. It's French. Spelled P-o-m-m-i-e-r."

"Yes, sir," shouted the chastened kid. "I'll tell him."

Pommier was too worn out to answer. He waved instead and took a few more steps, leaning on the staff. The pain of the effort made him dizzy, and he looked again for a bench, choosing one strategically near Ocean Avenue and directly under a light. There he slumped down and tried to get up his courage to walk home.

"Hello." The voice came from behind him, a light, teasing voice, young but without the freshness of youth.

"What?" Pommier turned, startled.

"You waiting for someone?" The boy was pretty, deliberately pretty, hardly more than fourteen or fifteen, dressed in very tight white jeans and a net T-shirt.

"Not really," Pommier answered carefully.

"Not even me?" The boy smiled, very brightly, and his tongue flicked over his lips.

"I'm afraid not." Pommier's eyes strayed toward the street. There was a black van turning the corner, and he started at the sight of it. "Oh, God."

The boy followed his eyes. Something about him shrank back, but he gave no other sign of seeing the vehicle.

However, Pommier had noticed that hidden response. "That black van?"

Now the boy pouted. "What about it?"

"You see it?" Pommier asked, feeling a little foolish. "Do *you?*"

"Yes." Pommier was surprised at how much loathing was in that one syllable.

The boy took a few steps back. "You're not one of them, are you? You don't look like them."

"Neither do you," Pommier said.

The boy shrugged and came a little closer. "Then how come you see them, if you aren't one of them?"

Pommier took up the boy's tone at once. "How come you do?"

The boy tried to laugh and failed. "Oh. You know. People like me, we see people like them."

"What do you mean?" Pommier asked, suddenly very intent on the boy.

The van cruised toward the corner and turned away from the cliffs, toward the lights on Santa Monica Boulevard.

"You know," the boy said provocatively. "Hey, mister, if you aren't waiting for me, I got to find someone who is. Know what I mean?"

Pommier nodded fatalistically. "I have . . . twenty dollars." He hoped it was true. He had not checked for his wallet since he had come to. "How much does that get?"

"In talk or . . ."

"In talk," Pommier said with a bit of grim humor. "Even if I were interested in something else, this isn't the best time."

"Oh. You mean your leg and all." The boy came closer. "What happened?"

"I fell."

"People who see . . . that thing don't just fall," the boy said, and came to sit beside Pommier on the bench, slouching so that his jeans pulled tightly across his crotch.

"Why not?"

"Because they just don't. That's not how it happens." He fell silent, then held out his hand. "Hey, man, time is money, know what I mean?"

Pommier reached into his pocket and found his wallet, then opened it, taking out a twenty and a ten. "Half an hour?"

The boy shrugged and pocketed the money. "If that van comes back, I might leave."

"So might I," Pommier said at once. "Tell me what you know about them."

"They're around," was the guarded answer. "If you see them, you know that."

With a slow nod, Pommier set his mind to drawing the boy out. "I've followed them over most of Los Angeles," he volunteered.

"You *what*?" the boy cried, shocked into sitting upright. "Hey, are you *crazy*? Following *them*?"

Pommier looked closely at the boy. "Why shouldn't I?"

"Shit, you let them know you see 'em, they'll come after you. What're you doing *here,* with them after you?" He stuffed his hands into his pockets, looking younger now than when he first approached Pommier.

"Why shouldn't I be here?" Pommier asked.

"God, don't you know *anything*? You been following them, you know what they're like. You know what they do, don't you?"

"I know," Pommier said quietly. "That's why I followed them."

"Oh, shit," the boy said. "You're a fool." He shook his head sadly. "You followed them, and you're here."

"Yes," Pommier said, and waited.

"This is the center of it, you know?" the boy said at last. "You get away from here, and they're not . . . so real. Know what I mean?"

Although Pommier did not entirely understand, he said, "Yes," in the hope it would get him more cooperation from the boy.

"Around here, they can touch you, they can make you see things, they can . . . man, they can *kill* you around here. Out in Encino, they're nothing more than shadows, but not here, not here." He shook his head again.

"It has to do with territory," Pommier murmured.

"Yeah, and this is theirs, you better believe it. This is where they got their temples and their powers."

"Temples?" Pommier asked, anticipating what he would hear.

"You know, that abandoned hotel where all the—" he paused and giggled—"whores got murdered that time. And places on the boardwalk, where some of the crazies and the junkies go. And places like the Gutterman house."

"Ah," Pommier muttered, feeling very angry, as much with himself as with anyone else.

"I guess they're getting stronger, if you can see them," the boy said sadly.

"Why?" Pommier asked, feeling a sympathy for him.

"Well, guys like me, on the street, we're like them, with nowhere to go. You got a home and, well, you're one of those establishment types, aren't you? I heard you tell the skater you're a professor." He pouted, a gesture that did not make him attractive but gave him the look of an unhappy child. "You're not the kind who sees them, or even knows they're there."

Pommier leaned back against the bench, his mind working swiftly. "They're only seen by others who are like them."

"I didn't say that," the boy protested indignantly. "Maybe like them a little, but, shit, man, I wouldn't do what they do."

"And you speak," Pommier said gently. "Thank God for that."

"As long as you're paying," he agreed.

"Then go on. I have a little more time, if they don't come back." Pommier was at once more tired and more renewed than he had been for several days. He needed only a few more bits of information and then he would understand who rode in the black van, and why.

"Well, if we're a bit alive, that's one thing. But . . . I hear that they want to get the ones who can see them. Make them like they are. Convert them, kind of." He wriggled uncomfortably. "If they know you're there, they work on you. Do things to you if they can. Either

you turn out like them, or they kill you. That's what
I've heard about them. I don't know it for a fact," he
added quickly, as if to remove himself from the five as
much as possible. "It's only what I've heard."

Pommier looked carefully at the boy. "How old were
you when you... started living this way? It's called
turning tricks, isn't it?"

The boy shrugged. "Sometimes, that's one way to put
it." He looked around uncomfortably. "A while ago. I
know my job, if that's what you're worried about. And I
never blackmailed anybody."

"No," Pommier said, shaking his head slowly. "How
long were you on the streets before you saw them?"

"Oh, that," the boy said, assuming his worldly air
again. "I don't know, a couple of months, maybe. Three
at the most." He scuffed at the grass. "I was working
over Studio City before I got smart and came out here
where there's more money. And they're strong here.
Real easy to find." He got up and took a few steps away
from Pommier. "Hey, look, I'm sorry, but I got a living
to make, know what I mean? And if they're after you, I
don't want 'em to know you've been talking to me. I got
to go. And you better go, too."

"Thank you," Pommier said sincerely. "I hope... I
hope they stay away from you."

"No more'n I do," the boy said, then began to jog
away from Pommier, going north along the winding
path among the trees.

In the fog the walk to his house seemed longer than
he thought it would be; the staff eased his discomfort so
that he could turn his mind to what the boy had told
him. He did not have energy enough to brood on the
disquieting fears that now assailed him, remnants of
Sister Bertril and all the horrors of his first years
studying surrounded by nuns. That had made his early
years nightmarish, and even now he could recall the
fear that possessed him whenever he had to confront
one of those imposing white-clad women who instruct-

ed him. He should have thought of that earlier. But he had been too disoriented and too . . . afraid.

Finally he could make out the front of his house, less than a block away. His spirits began to lift.

The driver, tattooed and pony-tailed, stepped out from behind a fence.

Pommier came to a halt. He could feel himself begin to shake—not from fatigue or shock but from cold, relentless dread. Not now, he begged of no one in particular. Not so close. Not now.

The driver moved, one, two steps closer.

Resolutely Pommier took a few more faltering, uneven strides, trying to give the driver a wide berth on the sidewalk without actually going himself into the street. Though the driver watched him with steady, predatory patience, he did not move. Pommier started away from him, wishing that he was not limping, that he could simply stride away from the silent man, untouched by the hostility that radiated from him like a dark halo. Pommier had gone almost half a block when the driver came lightly up behind him.

Pommier stopped again, and turned to face the other man. His voice was restrained, almost conversational. "Stay away from me."

The driver came closer. There was the sound of punk rock drifting with the fog now. The driver laughed once, a loud harsh sound, like someone choking.

Pommier swung the staff up, holding it across his chest defensively. "I said stay away."

The driver grinned.

Pommier could not ignore his hurt, but he shut it away in the face of this greater threat. He lurched forward, lashing out with the staff; his arm shuddered as the wood struck the driver full in the face.

The driver stumbled, half falling, his hand clasped to his face. Blood welled out around his fingers and seeped down his hands.

Pommier started after him, then stopped. He brought the staff up again, waiting for what might happen next.

The driver reeled into the street, staggering against the side of a parked car, then turned back to look at Pommier. Though the distance was more than five yards, Pommier could see that the man was smirking.

Fury roiled through Pommier's veins, and he no longer cared that his face was cut, his leg was bleeding— he wanted only to give back some of the ghastliness he had endured at the hands—and feet—of the five. He advanced on the driver, and when he was close enough, he brought the staff down on him again. On the shoulder! The head! The head!

The driver collapsed, folding up into a huddle at Pommier's feet. He no longer strove to protect himself from the blows, but lay limp and shapeless. He did not make a sound.

Revulsion and disgust filled Pommier: revulsion for the act and disgust with himself for having committed it. He flung the staff away from him, and it bounced and rolled into the gutter. Sick at heart, Pommier limped away, heading for the one refuge he knew was left to him—not the house, but Veronique.

FIFTEEN

Slowly Flax brought her head up from the steering wheel and assessed the damage. There was a lump on her forehead where it had struck the windshield; her lower lip was already swelling from striking the steering wheel. Her teeth hurt. Trembling, she reached down to start her stalled bug. God, what had happened! There had been something, a dog, perhaps, running right in front of her car and she had slammed on the brakes. The car had all but stood on its nose stopping, and she had slammed forward.... She parked the car a few feet from where it had stalled, across the street from the Pommier house.

She turned off the engine and set the handbrake, making each task an act in itself until she felt steadier. It was bad enough having the jitters from... all the lapses, but now this! Her hands closed to fists so that she would not start crying. How long had she been stalled in the street, she wondered, had she had another vision? Dream? psychic contact? psychotic fugue? What was it? She would soon find out, when she finally walked across the street and met the woman who lived in the house. The woman was alone, Flax told herself. She was alone because she had just become a widow and she was new in the neighborhood, and foreign; no time to make friends.

Her vision slid from focus, blurred. What was that she saw? A man running, favoring one leg? Vertigo got hold of her; she joined her hands at the top of her steering wheel and let herself go.

*   *   *

"Jean-Charles!" Veronique burst out when she saw him on the doorstep. "What has become of you!"

He gave her half a smile. "It was stupid, Niki. I was down at the park, just on the Palisades?"

"Oui, oui, j'ai connaissance." She reached out and hurried him inside the door. "You went there on your walk?"

"Yes." He limped to the sofa.

"This is not more of . . ." There was a warning edge in the way she asked.

"No," he said, a fraction too quickly. "Nothing . . . like that." He wanted to look out the window, to discover what had happened to the driver. How could he have acted that way? *Their* way? "No," he repeated, his hand to his brow. "It was a silly accident. I was not looking where I was going and two teenagers on roller skates ran into me."

Veronique's expression changed from outrage to relief to rueful amusement. "You? Were run over by *roller skates*? YOU?" She started to laugh, there being no other way for her to express the emotions that Pommier could see at war in her. "Roller skaters! Bon Dieu!"

"I bloodied my nose and scraped my knee," he said, like a child dutifully reporting playground injuries.

"Do they hurt?" she asked when she was able to stop laughing. "Of course they do," she went on, not bothering to let him deny it. "Here I was prepared to be angry for being late, and you come home this way." A chuckle escaped her, but she kept it from turning again to laughter. "Come to the kitchen. I'll clean you up."

Pommier followed her meekly enough, grateful that she had not been too irate or too worried about him. He had seen the quiet, pitying look in her eyes of late, and it troubled him that she should feel that way about him, if only for an instant. He could feel his knee stiffening as he moved. He would have to soak it and put liniment on it, but later, later.

"They were fierce, these roller skaters?" Veronique teased him as she dabbed at his face with a cloth.

"They were scared. I think they were afraid I'd been badly hurt—a skull fracture at the least." He winced as she pressed his lip with force.

"No! You will not make a joke of that. You could have been hurt!" She put down the cloth.

"I *was* hurt," he reminded her. "But not seriously, ma belle. I came home under my own power." He bit his lip once.

"It was painful?"

"Painful enough," he said. "Where is this fabulous meal you promised me? That kept me moving."

"You! You're impossible, Jeany," she said, her pout turning to a smile that lit her russet-brown eyes, giving her face a brighter vitality than it had had for the last few days.

"I'm hungry," he corrected her, and kissed her lightly on the nose. "I do not say it often, ma belle, but I love you."

Her face softened. "I know, I know it." She turned to the stove, embarrassed at this sudden, much-desired confession. "The vegetables are a little overcooked, but it is not serious."

"Wonderful," Pommier said, who would not have cared if they had been reduced to carbon. "When do we eat?" He was grateful that she was easily satisfied with his explanations. He could not tell her that he wanted food, wanted her, because they were indisputably real, undeniably present. He already knew that he had to make love to her as soon as dinner was over, to ground himself to the world in her treasured body.

"I made two sauces for the meat," she said, starting to carry platters and plates to the dining room. "No, don't help. You might drop something."

"I have not become an invalid," he said. The weight of a dish in his hands would be welcome.

Veronique merely laughed.

The dinner was probably excellent. Pommier ate with enormous appetite, taking larger helpings of everything and swallowing most of his food with wine. Ordinarily the discomfort of being too full would have irritated him, but now it seemed to him that it was yet more proof that he had not succumbed to whatever those five people in the black van represented. Between bites, he kept up a flow of conversation that had Veronique visibly enchanted, responding to him flirtatiously, as she had when he had begun his tentative courtship, uncertain of her emotions and his own. It delighted him to see her find excuses to touch him—his hand, once the corner of his mouth. He wanted her to take great pleasure in him, so that he would feel how *real* she was.

Unbidden, he recalled the solid way his staff had battered the driver of the black van, and his face clouded.

"Jeany?" Veronique said, her hand going out to his. "Is something the matter?"

"C'est rien," he answered, forcing all those dreadful impressions from his mind and concentrating on her. "The salad now?"

She served the salad last, in the French manner, and had Camembert and apples for dessert accompanied by a deliriously sweet moscato amabile that had been grown in California but sang like the Italian sunshine.

Pommier could feel the wine go to his head and for once he truly loved it, not caring that his thinking was no longer precise. Ordinarily he found that too much sensory stimulus distracted him, interfering with his thoughts and the acuity of his mind. He had assumed that one of the reasons he married late was that, until he met Veronique, he had never been quite able to suspend that analytical side of his nature long enough to accept the emotionality needed for a continuing in- volvement with another person. When he was young he had viewed this as an accomplishment, a triumph of reason and intellect over the irrationality of emotional entangle-ments. Now that he had grown older he knew that he had permitted a vital aspect of life to escape him, and it saddened him.

"You're philosophical now?" Veronique interrupted his reflections. "What is on your mind?"

"You," he said softly.

"Thus you are so solemn?" she inquired, the corners of her mouth twitching upward but with a lack of certainty.

"Yes. What I feel is not trivial. And it is solemn. You are for me my life and my soul, ma belle. Nothing less."

Her eyes grew large at this, and there was a shine in them. "Jean-Charles," she whispered. "You are . . . very good."

He leaned over the corner of the table and touched her face, so gently that it might have been an errant breeze that caressed her. There were so many things he did not notice about her, and it shamed him to think he had overlooked them. There was an irregularity to her features, for instance, that only served to make her more attractive. Her right brow was fractionally higher than the left and slanted at a more quizzical angle. Her nose was not quite straight, her mouth turned up in the left corner more than in the right. Such little things, and each one of them treasured because it was part of her and all that he loved in her.

"Jean-Charles . . . ?"

"Come," he said, taking her hand as he got up from the table.

"But . . ." She looked around at the plates and dishes and glasses and silverware.

"They will be here in the morning," he told her, a bit more insistently. "I hope that . . ."

"What?" she asked when he fell silent.

He banished the dark thoughts that flooded in on him. "Nothing—only that you will let me help you clean them up, since I am the one who will not let you do so now."

"How absurd you are," She laughed, capitulating. "Lead the way. I will follow."

He had intended to make love slowly, sensually, but as soon as he had removed her clothes, he fell on her in a frenzy that startled them both. He could not get enough of her, the feel of her, the taste of her, of her warmth, her receptivity, her love. He went into her deeply and repeatedly, unwilling to have less of her because his testicles still ached. His need, his demand for her was greater than any hindrance he could imagine. She was reality. She was life. He urged her to respond to him, to use him for her own pleasure, to awaken him to more passion, greater need. He heard her cry out, her body arching up to his, her release more complete than he had ever known before. His own followed almost at once, shuddering through him with a force that left him breathless and replete, his arms locked around her, his face pressed into her red hair, his legs wrapped with hers, sweat slicked over them both.

Only gradually did they draw apart, and no farther than comfort required. Pommier kept her close to him, holding her securely. Negligently he stroked her hair as she went from contentment to sleep murmuring his name. He was too sore to sleep easily, but that was not unwelcome. It, too, was another proof of his reality and it pleased him to test his knee and feel it send hot painful fingers up his thigh. "You haven't got me," he told the walls of their bedroom. "You haven't got me and you never will get me."

Just as he dozed at last, he thought he heard a low, malignant giggle.

Morning came suddenly, as if their sleep had been no more than a nap of ten or fifteen minutes. One instant Pommier was asleep, the next he was awake, Veronique still held close to him, the various hurts he had suffered in the last few days sufficiently remote to make the morning wonderful.

"Look at you," he whispered to Veronique, kissing her ear as he spoke.

"Um." She was not awake and would not be awake for a little while longer.

Pommier sighed. Then he rolled onto his back and stared up at the ceiling. All of the previous evening flooded over him, anguish and tenderness, fulfillment and revulsion. He did not want to have to face all he had done, not yet, not while Veronique was so near. But if he did not make sure, then perhaps she would discover what he had done before he had the chance to tell her, to ease her mind.

He got out of bed and reached for his robe, tying the sash as he went to the window. If he had done anything... irreparable to the driver of the van, he would find out now, in the warm morning light. Reluctantly he lifted the corner of the curtain and looked down into the street.

The branch he had used was still there lying across the street in the gutter, but no trace of the driver, not a single smear of dried blood. Pommier leaned his head against the windowpane, giddy with relief. He imagined it. He must have. He must have had a mild concussion and not known it. The worst that was wrong with him was that he had had a mental lapse, something brought on by change and fatigue. That was it. It explained the photographs, it explained the dream he had had while he was out cold. It was disturbing but acceptable, a rational answer for a rational world. He ignored the question of the attack and the enormous bruise it had left on his lower abdomen. He had fallen, that was all, and dreamed it, as he had dreamed about the convent. That was all. *That was all*.

He heard Veronique turn on the bed, yawning, adorably, he was sure. The rustle of the rumpled sheets brought a residual thrill to him, softened by his joy.

"Jean-Charles?" she called, her voice still husky with sleep.

"Um?"

"What are you looking at?"

Flax spun around from her place by the window, pulling up the blanket defensively. She stared around the room—Pommier's living room. There was a white-cased pillow at one end of the sofa.

"Well?" Veronique asked from the door to the dining room. "What *are* you looking at?"

"I . . ." Flax began, making her way back to the sofa slowly, groping as if she moved in the dark rather than the first flush of morning.

Veronique came a little farther into the room. Her robe covered a sensible cotton nightgown and there were dark circles under her eyes, as if she had not slept very well.

"How did I get here?" Flax asked, staring up at Veronique.

"It puzzles me, too." Veronique came into the living room and chose one of the chairs to sit in. "You came here last night. You knocked on the door and said that . . . Jean-Charles had sent you." She faltered. "You came in, and then . . . I don't know what is happening to you. You seem . . . ill."

"It's not that," Flax objected, having no idea how she might be able to explain herself. "I didn't mean to intrude, but . . ."

Veronique sighed. "But you seem to know a great deal about my . . . husband. More than I can account for."

Flax, recalling what had overwhelmed her last night, suddenly flushed darkly. It had been bad enough to experience Pommier's intense love secondhand, as it were, but to have to face the woman herself was unspeakably awkward for her. "It's . . . ah . . . difficult for . . ."

"What is it?" Veronique asked in alarm, uncertain what Flax's dramatic shift in demeanor indicated.

"It's . . . I'm . . . embarrassed. I don't know . . ." She looked away from Veronique, wishing she could be swallowed whole by the floor.

"Ah," Veronique said sadly. "You *do* know everything."

"Did I say . . . anything that distressed you?" Flax could not imagine she would blurt out all the intimate details of Pommier and Veronique's marriage, but she had no idea of what she did or said when in the throes of one of the strange visitations that had plagued her days and nights.

"I don't know what you said," Veronique answered carefully, guessing some of the reason for Flax's discomfort. "I did not hear you. You slept on the couch; I was upstairs."

"Oh." She felt deeply relieved. That at least would be spared her. "I should have known that."

"Should you?" Veronique asked. "I wish I knew how."

"So do I," Flax admitted, drawing the blanket even more tightly around her.

"But what is it?" Veronique persisted, determined to get to the bottom of the mystery.

"I don't know. I don't know *what's* happening! I don't know *why* it's happening. It doesn't make any sense. I didn't know him, not at all. I only saw him that once, and—" She stopped abruptly. Hard as it was for Veronique to hear what Flax had said so far, the rest could be too painful.

Veronique gave a fleeting, wistful smile. "I know. You were the one with my husband when he died, weren't you?"

"Yes," Flax muttered, hating to say even that.

"Then you know that I am Veronique Pommier," she said, speaking more to herself than to Flax.

"Yes! Yes, I know your name. Niki, I know your

name, I know . . . oh, God, and I've *seen* . . ." Suddenly
she sobbed. "I'm sorry. I've seen too much . . ."

"Seen?" Veronique repeated.

"Maybe not seen, not in the usual sense, with my
eyes, but . . . still seen—too much about you." She began to cry, not wildly or noisily but with a steadiness
that was more alarming than histrionics would have
been.

Veronique half-rose from her chair. "Hey-hey, no.
Don't . . . don't. Remets-toi. Stop, please. Reste. You're
very tired." She made up her mind, crossing the room
to Flax's side.

Flax stared at her, helpless to respond.

"You're just tired," Veronique said. "Écoutez, why
don't we go out today? Go . . . what do they call it?
sightseeing? We could act like tourists. Ça serait joli,
n'est-ce pas?" She ruffled Pommier's hair lightly. "What
do you think, Jeany? Should we do that?"

They ended up on the observation platform of the
tallest building in Los Angeles, staring out over the
hundred-mile sprawl.

"Well?" Pommier asked, bowing to her as if presenting
her the view as a bouquet.

"Ou là, it goes on forever. It is enormous!" She
clapped her hands delightedly.

"NO!" Flax screamed, thrusting Veronique away from
her. "Please, please, no! I don't want to, not now!
Please, stay away from me. I don't want to go!"

Veronique, hurt and upset, moved back from Flax.
"Go where? What is it? What have I done?"

Flax was trembling, her hands clapped over her
mouth, her eyes huge in her despair. "No, not you,"
she was able to say at last. "It was . . . then. He
wanted . . . wants something from me. He was trying to

tell me. Something! Oh, God! And I can't understand.
He screamed his whole memory into my head . . . oh,
please, I'm not making this up. And I don't understand
why. Or how. I *still* don't know what he wants. They're
driving him mad and I don't know what he wants!"

She sat down on the sofa beside Flax and put her
hand on Flax's arm. "Who? Who is doing this? Are you
talking about . . . Jean-Charles?" It was so hard to say
his name and miss him when she said it.

Flax rubbed her face, smearing her tears. "He
thinks . . . he thinks that they're innois . . . inuat. Do you
know what it means?"

"Inuat," Veronique said, aghast at the word. "It's
Eskimo, what we might call revenant, a malefic ghost,
but . . . the inuat are hunters. It's a legend. Jean-Charles
doesn't . . . didn't believe in legends." She saw Flax shake
her head, growing more frightened at Veronique's at-
tempts to calm her. "Still . . . he thought it strange that
the same legend should be found in so many places.
Eskimos, Bedouins, Afghani hill tribes, Australian ab-
origines, Lapps, they all have similar legends." She was
speaking automatically, recalling all the times she had
heard her husband begin a lecture on the subject.
"How do you know of this?"

Flax did not answer; her eyes were fixed on some
point very far from that pleasant room that should have
been cozy and wasn't.

SIXTEEN

It was windy on the observation tower, and fairly crowded. A large and boisterous family with strong Iowa accents pointed out the Hollywood sign to one another, marveling at it loudly. Beyond them a guided tour group of Japanese listened respectfully to a fresh-faced Japanese-American who was running through her standard routine for them. A Chicano couple leaned on the high, sturdy rail and held hands, gazing at each other instead of the view. Three young men in trendy clothes lounged in the sun, aching to be noticed, or mistaken for someone famous. A short, scruffy-looking middle-aged man in a denim suit was just beyond them, arguing with a building official about using the observation platform to film a commercial for cigarettes. Pommier and Veronique were on the rail just beyond a group of schoolteachers, all wearing name badges and buttons that identified them as union supporters.

"I was so frightened for you last night," Veronique said into the warm silence that had grown between them.

"How do you mean?" Pommier asked, knowing how terrified he had been.

"When you came in . . . you were shaking. And there was that blood on your face. I thought . . . it was like the other time." She put her hand through the crook of his arm, pressing close to him.

Pommier stared out at the city through narrowed eyes; he did not speak for some time, and when he did, he sounded strangely unlike himself. "Did you ever have a dream . . . a waking dream and found out you didn't know when it started? Or how it started?" He glanced around once, then fixed his eyes on the horizon. "We're very far from home, you know. All of us. Not just these"—he indicated the others on the observation platform—"but everyone. We've wandered, so very far from home." His voice was quieter now, and more intense. "There are deserts of sand, deserts of ice. This is a desert of glass and pavement."

"Jeany," Veronique said, troubled. "Stop. Please."

He tried to shake off the fatalism that gripped him, and the loneliness. "It's nothing, ma belle. Not important. I was tired. Very tired, that's all. I let myself get worn down. Then I was more stupid and went two days without sleep. It made me a little . . . irritable." He looked down at his loosely joined hands. "C'est fini. Tout fini."

"What?" Veronique asked, openly pleading with him to tell her.

Pommier pretended he had not noticed her anxiety. "Well. It's just as well, no doubt. We should talk about our new life, our bourgeois life in this enormous, civilized place."

Veronique made an effort to smile. "If you wish, Jean-Charles. First you must buy sunglasses."

He snapped his fingers, shamming lightness of spirit. "You're right. Neither of us has them. And goggles will not do, will they?"

"No," she murmured.

It was a little more awkward now. "There were things we had talked about, you know? A few plans. A family, perhaps. Would you still want to get pregnant?"

Veronique blinked at him. "I . . . haven't thought about it for a while. We'll have time enough to talk about it. Later."

"Oui. Oui. This is not the time or the place. Later." He kissed her on the forehead. "I haven't thought about it for some time, either. I think I should have. But there has been so much to do." His apologetic smile did not last. "I don't suppose I'll be able to finish, now."

"Jean-Charles?" Veronique said.

"Oh, pay no mind, ma belle. Last night . . . made so much clear to me. About you. About myself." He let his breath out slowly and turned away from the view. "I treasure you, Niki. I always will."

For an answer to this, Veronique leaned forward and put her arms around his waist. "Oh, mon amour."

He helped her snuggle closer. "You know, if any of these people are watching us, they'll be scandalized." He looked around the crowd, preparing to fondle Veronique brazenly, but wanting to be sure they were not noticed. One of the three trendy nobodies was staring in their direction but his glazed eyes said that he saw nothing. There was another knot of people on the other side of the platform; Pommier looked them over quickly.

And froze.

One of the group by the stairs to the lower level was a man with a blond pony tail.

Pommier stared hard, trying to see him clearly in the crowd, to be certain that he was not mistaken, hoping that he was.

"What is it?" Veronique whispered, trying to follow his eyes.

His jaw was tight. "Nothing. I thought . . . I was wrong." Please, please, please, he pleaded inwardly, be wrong, let me be wrong. He deliberately looked away to stare at the Japanese tourists. His smile was like a death mask.

A tall girl, one of the Iowans, ran by, laughing. She was leggy in jeans and a loose shirt. Her blond hair was caught up in a pony tail.

Pommier laughed a little wildly. "That girl . . ." he said, knowing that he would have to tell Veronique something. "There's an aggressive young man in my class, not unlike her."

"Were you afraid it was him?" Veronique asked, puzzled.

"I *did* overreact, didn't I?" He tweaked a wisp of her hair. "I told you I was tired. I still am. If I'd had to argue with him again, well..."

"Only on campus," she said. "The rest of the time, no arguments."

Again he laughed, leaning back on the rail to steady himself. He turned to the person on his left to offer a social apology.

The driver looked at him, smiling a feral smile—all teeth under famished eyes.

Pommier was too shocked to say anything. He took Veronique by the shoulders and pushed her back from him, looking at the driver of the black van. "Oh, no. No. No. Not you." He reached for the rail and was appalled to see that it was not as high as he had supposed.

The driver of the black van put on sunglasses and stared out over Los Angeles; he paid no attention to Pommier.

"Who is that?" Veronique demanded in an undertone so as not to be rude.

"C'est un touriste. Un touriste." He forced himself to ignore the driver and put his mind on other things. The scenery was spectacular. There were other people. And, oh, God, one of them was a Rastafarian. He was not sure that it was the same Rastafarian who rode in the black van, but... There was Veronique. He wanted to keep her close to him and at the same time he knew that he put her in the gravest danger. What would happen to her if those terrible five got their hands on her? The thought very nearly made him physically ill. He had to put it out of his mind. It was essential that he put it all behind him.

"You're frightened, Jean-Charles. What is it?" Veronique said.

He faltered, not wanting to expose her to greater

risks. "Ah... you brought the camera, didn't you? I
think the... the height has gotten to me. May I see the
camera? If I take a picture, I may be better. Donnez-
moi l'appareil, Niki," he said, holding out his hand for
the camera, then turning abruptly and with a tremen-
dous effort, reaching for the driver—why was there
nothing wrong with his head, his face?—to lift him—
don't look, don't think about what you're doing, Jean-
Charles, he ordered himself—lift him and push him
over the rail, off the platform of the building.

The driver hung suspended, his hands joined behind
Pommier's neck, pulling, pulling to drag him down.

Deliberately, insistently, one finger at a time, Pommier
broke the hold the driver had on him, watching as the
driver fell away from him, watching the driver blow
him a kiss before he struck the side of the building,
bounced, and continued to hurtle toward the pavement
so far below.

How he hated to turn around. It would be bad
enough to see the accusations and disgust in the eyes of
the crowd on the observation platform, but there would
be the betrayal in Veronique's eyes, disgust and dismay
that he did not think he could bear. Very slowly he
made himself face her.

Nothing had changed on the platform. The tourists
still stared and photographed and exclaimed. There
were no policemen rushing to restrain and arrest him,
no one accused him. He put his hand to his brow and
shook his head as if to clear water from his eyes and
ears. "Niki...?"

Veronique had pulled her pocket camera out of her
purse and was still holding it out. "Are you better now?
Jeany? Qu'est-ce qu'il y a? You look pale. Come away
from the edge, Jeany. It must be that you have vertigo."

He blinked rapidly several times. Nothing changed.
"I... I am feeling... a trifle queasy," he admitted and
suppressed the desire to howl with laughter. He had
just thrown a man off the platform and no one, not even

his wife, had noticed. It was not surprising he would be feeling odd. What was wrong with the rest of them? he wondered.

"Come, Jean-Charles," Veronique said, offering her hand to him. "Perhaps we should go down."

"Yes. Down." He let her lead him to the elevator bank on the level immediately below them.

Flax held her arms tightly across her abdomen. "Oh, God. It gets so much worse," she said.

Veronique sat up at her end of the sofa. "You have . . . recovered?"

"I hope so. It was terrible." She knew she sounded sick, which was how she felt. "God! What he went through." Slowly she uncurled and looked at Veronique. "I've got to use the bathroom."

"I'll show you . . ." Veronique offered.

"I know where it is." Flax reminded her. Her bones seemed brittle and old as she walked up the stairs. How familiar it was, and how that distressed her! She got to the bathroom, used the john, then went to wash her face. She stared in amazed disbelief at the reflection in the mirror. Flax had always been trim, but now she was gaunt, her eyes ringed and sunken, her cheeks pale with the skin stretched taut over her bones. She looked as if she had lost fifteen pounds overnight, all through stress. As she rinsed away the soap she had used, she heard a sound behind her. In the mirror she could see Veronique come a few steps into the bathroom, looking at her.

Flax met her eyes in the mirror. "He loved you, Niki. He loves you more than anything in the world." She was not aware of her shift of tenses, but there was a change in Veronique's expression that warned her she had gone too far.

As Veronique handed her a towel the telephone started to ring.

"Are you going to answer it?" Flax asked when she made no move to respond.

"There is no one I wish to speak to. It's been ringing on and off all day." She folded her arms. "If you want to answer it, go ahead."

Flax finished wiping her face. "I think I'd better," she confessed, and went into the study.

Again there was the same eerie familiarity in the room, the same sense of belonging. Flax did not pause to examine the sensation more closely, but hurried to pick up the telephone. "Hello? Pommier residence."

"Oh, thank God! You *are* there!"

"Cassie?" Flax asked, not trusting the voice.

"Who else? Eileen, what's been going on? Are you all right?"

Flax caught her lower lip between her teeth before she answered. "I think so. It's not important."

Cassie, giddy with relief, paid little attention to Flax's enigmatic response. "Where the fuck have you *been*? We've been going out of our frigging minds. We've had the police out at your apartment. I thought you might have been mugged or murdered, the shape you were in!"

"You went to my apartment?" Flax asked with a shake of her head. "But why?"

"Because you were fucking *missing*! You were sick and missing. Hey, and while I was there," she went babbling on, "there was some guy who called you from Boston, said that you'd called him . . ."

"Dick Holder?" Flax guessed, hoping that was who it had been.

"I think that was the name. Sexy voice, anyway. He did a number about spooks who aren't really there and are considered bad influences. It scared the shit out of me, if you want the truth. But the kicker came at the end of it. He said that the biggest honcho in the field was that Pommier guy." She began to slow down.

"What was that all about? Why did you ask him about that innois word?"

"I don't know. I had to start somewhere. That seemed as good a place as any." She paused. "We'll talk about it."

Cassie cut in on her at once. "I got the address. It's in Santa Monica, isn't it?"

"Yes, but . . . you don't have to come, Cassie. I can arrange to—"

"Bullshit. You'll say that you'll meet me somewhere, go off on another one of those things you go off on, and bingo! I'll have to start all over again. Oh, no, none of that. I'll be there in about twenty minutes." The line went dead.

Flax hung up slowly, unease coiling up in her like a poisonous reptile. "Niki, what did he do then?"

Veronique was standing in the hall behind her. "I don't understand."

"On the platform—what did he do?"

Ted Oldsman was adding his notes to a chart at the nursing station when Cassie came jauntily up to him, her purse swinging to show her satisfaction. "Hey, Oldsman!" she called out.

"Shush," Oldsman admonished her. "Remember the patients."

Cassie ignored him. *"I found her!"*

"You what?" He looked up sharply. "Flax?"

"None other." Her walk, her smile, the tone of her voice ranged from saucy to smug. "She's all right. She sounded okay."

"But where?" Oldsman demanded. "After all the places . . ."

"You'll never guess," she taunted him.

Oldsman stared at her. "You're kidding!"

"Dead bang on! She was at that fucking Pommier's house. I just got off the phone with her." Suddenly her confidence deserted her. "Ted, I was getting so scared for her. I was afraid that we'd get a call from the morgue and have to go identify her. Shit, I couldn't do that."

"Yeah. I know what you mean. I was having a few of those qualms myself." He put his arm around her shoulder. "You've been doing a great job, if you tracked her down."

"Right," she said, striving to get some of her old outrageous manner back. "Well, I'm going over to pick her up now. I'll be back in about an hour, I'd imagine. With Eileen. Tell Cort and Griffith and the rest of them for me, will you?"

"Glad to," he said. "I wish I could come with you."

"You're on duty. And I've got a couple hours yet to go on my off-duty time; I'm going to put it to good use." She was gone in the next instant, a happy smile seeming to hang in the air behind her.

"What did he do?" Flax repeated to Veronique.

Veronique gave a perplexed frown. "You don't know?"

"I . . . no, not really. I don't know what happened and what he *thinks* happened. I never know what is real and what isn't. I don't think that he did, either. That was what frightened him." She looked around the study. "He loved this room."

"Did he?" Veronique said, wanting to be distracted. "I was not certain."

Inexorably Flax brought them back to her question. "All right. You were on the roof, that platform, and you say he looked pale. You had had your arm around him and he moved you away from him. He asked you for the camera, and then . . . what happened then, Niki?"

Veronique put her hands to her eyes, though she did not weep—instead, she tried to picture the whole episode clearly and without illusion. "He bent over the rail, his hands behind his head. I thought he was trying not to be sick. It is a high rail, perhaps four feet? But I was worried for him. I thought that he still might overbalance or there would be . . ." She stopped. "He stared down for a time and then he turned back to me. He looked so . . . the word . . . beseeching? As if he were begging my forgiveness. I thought it would break my heart." She stared down at her hands, saying in a stifled voice, "When this began, I thought it was that there was, you know, another woman. I am much younger, and I was always afraid that he would find someone who was more accomplished or experienced, who could share more with him. I was his student when we met. He used to joke with me, when we first became lovers, about Héloise and Abelard, because she was much younger than he, and had first been his student. I did not want to think of that. It ended so badly. I suppose this has, too."

"Oh, Niki," Flax said in kindness and sorrow. "He loved you . . . enough to give up his life and soul for you."

At that Veronique began to cry in high, strangled sobs that shook her body. "Non, non. Il fait bien. Reste." She pushed Flax away from her, too trapped in the intimacy of her grief. It was some little time before she could speak again; as she wiped the tears from her face, she went on in as sensible a tone as she could. "Ah . . . after that, we left the . . . platform quickly. He . . . ah . . . took me to a hotel. I forget the name. It is near Wilshire. He told me to . . . stay there, with the door locked . . . until he returned for me." She paused, fighting off more sobs. "He never . . . that was the night . . . he died that night." She got up and walked around the study. "When I came back here the next day, I found two suitcases. One was on the bed in . . ."

"The bedroom, yes."

"And the other . . ."

Flax got up and went out of the room, stopping at the head of the stairs. "And the other was here . . . wasn't it?" She did not know if she wanted to be right about it or not.

"It was there," Veronique confirmed tonelessly.

Almost to herself, Flax said, "Oh, God, I'm frightened."

"Oui," Veronique said softly. "Moi aussi."

SEVENTEEN

Cassie drove a disreputable ten-year-old Mustang convertible, on which she ruthlessly kept the top down except in actual rainstorms. She had come along the freeway and then driven into Santa Monica. She resented the time she spent holding to thirty or thirty-five instead of sixty. She didn't like stoplights. She didn't like cross traffic. She hated left turns. She pulled up at the stoplight above the pier on Ocean Avenue, thinking that she had about ten or twelve blocks to go. She looked around impatiently, trying to guess how long she would have to wait. There was a girl on the curb, one of those ubiquitous teenage blondes, in a skimpy tank top and running shorts, with a few buckets of flowers she was selling in dozen bunches. Cassie almost smiled.

That was encouragement enough for the girl, who started toward Cassie's Mustang, holding out a bunch to her.

The last thing Cassie wanted to do now was get into a scene with a beach freak. "No, thanks," she said, trying to wave the girl back. "I really don't want any."

The girl came up to the side of the Mustang, holding three bunches in front of her like ceremonial implements. She had a vacant smile on her face.

"Hey, no. Come on. I really don't want any." Cassie knew that the light was going to change any second, and she wanted to get to Flax.

There was another figure on the sidewalk next to the flowers; a tall woman in her thirties in shiny, narrow black pants and a black jacket.

"Looks like someone might take your flowers," Cassie

suggested, a little desperately. "Hey, go the fuck away. I mean it. I don't want any flowers, so go bug someone else."

The blonde leaned on the side of the car.

"Now look, sweetheart, I said that I don't want any and that's . . ."

The passenger door was yanked open.

"What the . . . what kind of shit is . . ." Cassie began, her annoyance turning to fear.

The Rastafarian calmly started to get into the car, only his eyes showing expression, which was of loathing.

"You! Get out! *Get the fuck out of my car!*"

Ahead the light changed. Cassie stomped on the accelerator, veering around the car ahead of her in the hope of dislodging the Rastafarian. Without success.

In a panic, Cassie floored it, the old Mustang leaping ahead—straight into the path of an oncoming semi.

The Mustang struck the cab of the truck, the impact so great that the little car bounded into the air, flipping once before it fell. And exploded.

The house was horribly quiet. Only the quiet conversation of the two women as they came down the stairs disturbed it, and that grudgingly. There were no echoes.

"Do you remember what time he dropped you at the hotel?" Flax asked.

"That afternoon."

She shook her head. "No. What *time*. The hour."

"Around four-thirty. Why?"

Flax did not answer at once. "And what time is it now?"

"I don't understand; why does—"

This time Flax spoke a bit more sharply. "Niki, what time is it?"

She looked at her watch. "Just after five-fifteen. But what does . . ."

Flax crossed her arms, holding her elbows as if the

bones would afford her protection. "It happened here. Here. At this time." She listened, as if waiting for the house to tell her something. "Niki . . . I don't think we should be here."

Pommier rushed in the door, his breath coming in huge gasps. He had not dared to park in the driveway, and he did not want to be seen on the street. "Who knows who is watching," he muttered as he rushed up the stairs. "We must leave. We must, we must," he went on as he entered the bedroom. "Just enough for a few days. The rest . . ." Dorothy Praeger could send the rest to them, wherever they went. They had to have a few clothes, their personal things. He had some material in the study, and the rest could be left. It would have to be left. His hands shook as he pulled open the closet and fumbled with the clothes hanging there. Nightwear. Shoes. Slippers? Two changes of clothes, maybe three at the most, for each of them. There were drawers with underwear and socks. He ransacked them, grabbing whatever came to hand. Brushes on the dresser. Take those. A bottle of Veronique's perfume—leave that. He stuffed these all anyhow into the larger of their two suitcases. In the bathroom there were toothbrushes and other items. His straight razor—he had to have that. A bottle of vitamins. Aspirin. He snatched up things indiscriminately in his haste to get out. He dropped the aspirin bottle and it shattered, sending glass and little white pills scattering over the floor. He cursed, using French terms Veronique did not know he understood or used. He wrestled the suitcase closed and left it on the bed, then grabbed the smaller one and went to his study.

Files left on his desk were packed, and three cameras. A few books went into the suitcase, and a stack of papers from his students. A dozen of the peculiar photographs of the black van went in next, along with the Eskimo hunter. There were stacks of lecture notes, and these he took with less enthusiasm. A few other oddments were tossed in—special pens, a good flashlight, his old first aid kit—and then the suitcase was closed. Pommier took it to the head of the stairs, then put it down. He heard a sound, insinuating and low, coming from the front of the house. It was a laugh.

"Now!" Flax screamed, grabbing Niki by the shoulders. "We've got to get out of here now. I can't stand this. What happened to Jean-Charles began here."

Veronique made a sudden gesture, as if to push away her thoughts, or Flax. "I don't want—"

"Listen, Niki. I don't know why, but we shouldn't be here anymore. Not either of us." She saw the hesitation in Veronique's eyes. "Believe me! However it happened that he died, it started here, and . . . it's starting again."

"I don't understand," Veronique said, even as she started for the bedroom. "I have the suitcases at the hotel. But there are a few other things."

"Yes. Jeany didn't get your makeup, or that box of tampons in the cupboard in the bathroom." Flax said it automatically as she hastened after Veronique.

"Tu sais ou sont tous les affaires." This, more than anything else, brought home to Veronique how complete Flax's link with her dead husband was.

"C'est ma maison; je vis ici," Flax snapped back, then blinked. "Oh, God," she whispered, and turned to face Veronique. "I'm sorry, Niki."

Veronique stared hard at her. "Pourquois cette—"

"Niki," Flax interrupted her. "Don't you see? I don't speak French. I took it in high school, and that's all."

"Oh," Veronique said in a small voice. "Jean-Charles . . . ?"

"I don't know. Please, don't linger. Take what you need. We've got to go now!" She grabbed up a coat and sweater from the closet. "Hurry. Please hurry."

"What about your friend? Will she take us away from here?" Veronique asked, trying to regain some part of her composure as she gathered up the last of her things.

"I don't know. I thought she would be here before now." For the first time Flax wondered what had happened to Cassie. "Maybe she *can't* help us," she suggested with a frown, not knowing precisely what she meant by that, but not liking the way she felt as she said it.

"Why?" Veronique asked, attempting to close the little case she carried.

"She . . . can't get through . . ." Flax said vaguely, heading for the stairs.

"What was that!" Veronique burst out at an unfamiliar sound.

"A . . . motorcycle . . ." Flax answered, feeling herself slipping away from where she was. No! she protested inwardly. Not now! She went to the window at the end of the hall and looked out. There were cars on the street, which did not surprise her, but made her apprehensive, nonetheless. And across the street was a motorcycle, parked, its rider still mounted on it, a faceless apparition in black leather, glossy helmet covering his head, the visor down. From nowhere came the thought that this was the modern equivalent of the old knights, lacking their war-horses and mounted on cycles instead. They were as anonymous as a figure in armor, and only the heraldry of gangs and jackets differentiated one from another. This figure had nothing to identify him but the enormous Harley he rode. Flax shook her head, refusing to be sucked into another distraction, yet she could not entirely banish the notion that the black-sheathed figure was . . . guarding something—them, the house, something.

"I can't find the keys!" Veronique said behind Flax. "I've looked everywhere."

Another motorcycle pulled up, keeping its distance from the first.

"Just take what you must. Take what you must and go!" Flax strove to shut out the confusion that grew in her mind. *"You can't ever come back here! Don't you understand?"* she shrieked. "No!"

"Oh..." Veronique began to protest, but without conviction.

There was a sound near the front of the house, a purr of engines.

"There's a little time. You can still survive this," Flax promised desperately. "It's not us they want, not yet. It's still the house."

The two women started for the stairs, Veronique clutching the overnight case she had filled as if she were a child. Halfway down the stairs, the case opened and spilled half its contents. Veronique stopped, trying to pick up a few of the items.

Flax grabbed her by the arm. "Not now. *Leave it, Niki! Go!!"*

There were shadows in the living room, shadows that had no business being there. Veronique pointed to the most angular of the lot, and as they watched, suddenly silent, the shadow moved and became a figure. "Who are they? How long have they been here? Lorsque le temps..."

Flax ventured to the window in time to see the driver and the Rastafarian get out of the black van, followed by the blond teenager and the woman in black. All that was lacking was the *Satan's Angel*, and Flax thought he must have been the shadow she had seen.

Outside other vehicles were gathering, drawing together in ominous silence.

"Who *are* they?" Veronique shouted. "Why are they here?"

"*You* see them?" Flax said as they stood near the window and watched the others approach the front door.

"Of course," Veronique answered, startled at the question. "Shouldn't I?"

Flax bit her lip. "I don't know." Carefully she moved away from the window, doing nothing sudden. She reached the telephone and lifted the receiver, pressing the "O" button, and forcing herself to speak softly. "Operator, please put me in contact with the Santa Monica Police Department, Captain Coglan, if he's available. This is an emergency. The address is..." There was a snap on the line and the phone went dead. Flax looked at Veronique. "They've cut the line."

"And the police?" Veronique was looking distraught. "Will they come?"

"If the operator calls Captain Coglan, they might. Jean-Charles spoke to him. He might assume..." It was the most slender hope, but it was the only one she could offer.

There were more noises around the house, soft, furtive sounds, all without words, not even the few overheard mutterings that marked most gatherings, no matter how covert.

"How many are there?" Veronique whispered.

"I don't know," Flax answered. Her eyes traveled around the room. "Are all the doors and windows locked?"

"I think so," Veronique said. "But..."

"We'll check them. Together. Don't make any noise, okay?" Flax was resisting the urge to scream, and could see from Veronique's eyes that she was at the end of her strength. "The front first."

"Oui. C'est bien." She went woodenly to the door and made sure the deadbolt was secure. Flax followed after her. The dining room windows were all locked, and both the lock and bolt on the back door were in place.

Flax and Veronique had just secured the lock on the inside door to the garage when the blows started. They were gentle at first, a quiet, insistent rhythm that was less of an intrusion than the sound of a television set.

"What are they doing?" Veronique whispered, her face set in hard lines from fear.

"They're . . . at the doors, I think," Flax said, trying to stay calm in the face of this new, greater threat. "They're . . . trying to get in."

"No!" Veronique stifled her cry with her hand. "No, no."

Flax put her arm around Veronique, in the familiar and protective way that Pommier had done in the past. "We're going to go back upstairs. All right?"

The noise was growing louder, more abrasive, turning to a steady drumming that made the walls boom with sound.

"They'll get in, they'll get in," Veronique said, moving toward the stairs with Flax. "If they find us."

"Not if we get into the attic," Flax told her firmly, finding herself once again in peril of drifting into Pommier's life. "Hurry, Niki. Please."

They were halfway up the stairs when the back door gave way.

Flax screamed and Veronique cursed. They raced the last steps as they heard windows breaking behind them.

"The end of the hall. We'll need a chair," Veronique said. "We've got to reach the pull-down ladder." She did her best to ignore the sounds behind her, dreading the first sight of those malignant, silent figures. There was a crash from the dining room. A blare of punk rock erupted with the sound of breaking crockery.

"The study. There's a chair . . ." Flax said, still caught in the drift away from this time, this place.

"I'll get it. Wait. I need your help." She kept her voice low, but there was a shout in them, and Flax brought her head up sharply in response to that shout.

"I'll try, Niki." She slumped against the wall, trying not to see too much. The ferocity of the breaking and other damage below was appalling, worse because she

could not see what was going on. The silence was from
the five from the black van and the rest of the freaks
who hunted with them. Inuat? The word came unbidden. She did not want to think about it.

"I have the chair," Veronique said as she dragged it
from the study. "I think it's high enough. Keep watch."
She positioned the chair under the narrow entrance,
then carefully climbed onto the seat.

"Niki," Flax murmured, "I don't think I can hang on
much longer."

"You must!" Veronique cried as she worked the catch
on the folding steps.

There was the sound of a large appliance overturning
in the kitchen.

"What was it?" Veronique demanded, almost losing
her balance on the chair.

"Probably the refrigerator," Flax answered. "It's easier to overturn than the stove."

The latch worked and the ladder folded down.
Veronique jumped off the chair and started to climb.

Flax was moving slowly, hardly able to keep her
thoughts clear. She got up and dragged the chair back
to the study, finding it difficult to focus on anything but
the sounds of destruction coming from the floor below
her.

A figure in a motorcycle helmet and black leather
appeared at the top of the stairs, then stood still.

"Oh, God," Flax muttered, and started to back toward the folding steps.

"Hurry!" Veronique urged from her place on the
ladder. "Allez, allez!"

Flax reached the ladder, never taking her eyes off the
still figure in black. She gained the first of the steps,
and Veronique reached down to seize her arm. Her
mind swirled, changing images of chaos appearing and
fading before her eyes as she half-climbed, half-fell up
the stairs. The last thing she saw as the ladder was
hauled up and secured was the motorcyclist starting to

chop away at the top of the main stairs with a heavy motorcycle chain.

"Has Cassie got back yet?" Ted Oldsman asked Brad Cort when they met in the cafeteria a little more than an hour after Cassie had left the hospital.

"I haven't seen her," Cort answered.

"Maybe she took Eileen home first," Oldsman said, then took a bite of the sweet roll he had just bought. "These things are bad for your health."

"So they are," Cort concurred, his black face showing little of the apprehension he felt. "You'd think," he said carefully a bit later, "that Cassie, being Cassie, would have called by now."

"Yeah," Oldsman admitted reluctantly. "I guess."

"There might be a call at the desk," he suggested, drinking a bit more of the bouillon he favored.

"I checked there not more than ten minutes ago," Oldsman said with a touch of worry. "Nothing then. There was no answer at Eileen's apartment then, either, just the machine."

"Maybe Flax had another one of those..." Cort began, then interrupted himself. "If that had happened, she would have called."

"True," Oldsman agreed. "Well, I guess we have to wait a little longer."

"Could be," Cort said. "But I don't like the smell of it. I keep thinking of the way Flax would just blank out. What if she did that in the car on the freeway? Cassie couldn't handle that and drive at the same time."

"She's got sense enough to pull over," Oldsman reminded Cort, needing a little reassurance for himself.

"Then why am I so worried about her? Tell me that," Cort said, looking hard at Oldsman. "Ever since you told me she left, I've had this sick feeling... you know the kind I mean, Ted. I keep thinking that something is wrong."

"Should we call the cops?" Oldsman said this reluctantly, as if the call would be an admission of defeat in itself.

"Not quite yet, I don't think," Cort said. "If she isn't here in half an hour, or if she hasn't called in, I suppose we'd better put in a call for her." He wadded up the paper napkin in his lap. "I don't like it. Ted?"

Oldsman's face had changed from merely concerned to something more intense. "I hope nothing's happened to them. I hope you're just suffering from nerves. I'd hate to see anything go wrong with . . . either of them."

"But Cassie in particular?" Cort asked with a knowing lift to his brows.

He did not answer directly. "Hey, I know she's outrageous and she likes shocking everyone on the staff, but she's a good kid, a good doctor. I can't imagine what it'd be like around here without her."

Cort said nothing; he finished the bouillon. "Does she know you care that much about her?"

"It's nothing like . . ." Oldsman began at a bluster, then he shook his head. "No. All we ever did was joke around. She gave me a big lecture on sexual politics when she first came here, and I don't know how to get around all that. I'm eleven years older than she is, and she knows about the divorce and Peg and the kids and the whole mess. What could I say to her, anyway? Forget all that? I won't be a turkey this time? And would she believe me?" He ate the last of the roll and got up.

"Maybe you should tell her," Cort said thoughtfully. "Sometimes that's all it takes."

Oldsman laughed once, but the sound was sad. "For the time being I'll settle for getting her back here in one piece and safe. That's all that matters right now. The rest . . ."

"You might tell her that, too," Cort suggested, then took his trash to the nearest container for it. "Call me as soon as you hear something."

"I will," Oldsman promised. "Hell, if there's no news, I might go out looking for her myself."

"And be gone when she gets back," Cort reminded him. "Stay here. So she'll know where to find you if she needs you. Because she's counting on you, Ted. You might not believe it, but I've seen it." It was all the encouragement he could offer, and to his own ears it sounded pretty thin, but he saw Oldsman's face brighten a little.

"You're right; I better stay here. The waiting's a bitch, though. You know?" He patted Cort on the shoulder by way of thanks, and went back on duty, pausing only long enough to ask if there had been any messages for him.

EIGHTEEN

Pommier saw the shadows through the window and knew that the five were coming. He dropped the suitcase at the top of the stairs and went quickly down to the main floor. There was almost no sound in the house, and when the refrigerator clocked on, Pommier nearly yelped in shock. "C'est rien," he muttered to himself, as he had done as a child when the wind blew the branches of the old fir tree against the window of his bedroom late at night. "Ça va bien."

A stealthy sound in the dining room claimed his attention, and he crept toward it. He could vaguely make out the shape of either the driver or the *Satan's Angel* fiddling with the window in an attempt to break the latch.

Had this been a day earlier, he might have been tempted to take them on, but he knew well enough now that they could not be beaten in direct combat. He would have to be more subtle, outmaneuver them in any way he could. He went quickly back toward the living room.

Remote tappings warned him that one of the five had got onto the roof. The hackles on his neck rose. There was a window open on the second floor—he was almost sure of it. Once they found it, they would get into the house.

Suddenly the doorbell began to chime, loudly and insistently; the noise was made worse as someone began to pound on the door in accompaniment to the bell.

They're trying to cover something, Pommier thought. They're using all that noise as a diversion so they can get in without my knowing. And if they were getting in, he was getting out. There was one safe route of escape now—through the inner door to the garage and out onto the street. From there he could make his way to the neighbors or to a phone booth where he could call Coglan. He was a fool not to have called him before, but with nothing convincing to offer the policeman, Pommier had been embarrassed to take up his time. Now he knew that had been a grave mistake.

The garage door opened quietly. Pommier went through into the darkness, not daring to turn on the light for fear it might warn the five. He knew that the trickiest part would be to get out onto the street. When the door swung upward, even a fraction of an inch, it might be seen. He reached the door and hesitated. What he would do—he would have to roll under it. That way he need only lift it up a foot or so. He took four deliberate, deep breaths, and then reached for the release. As the door started to swing up, he dropped to the floor and rolled down the concrete, getting to his feet at once and reaching to close the door before it rose any higher.

Only to find the Rastafarian standing at the foot of the driveway watching him.

Pommier stood completely still, despair clutching at him, draining him of his good sense.

The Rastafarian took a step forward.

That was enough. Pommier bolted, sprinting for the fence at the side of the house. He would see if his neighbors would help him. He grabbed the top of the fence with one arm and vaulted over it, then came down too hard on his sore leg. It collapsed under him and he grimaced as the pain went through him. He could feel the scab pull open and blood seep through his slacks.

But there was no time. He lurched to his feet and limped to the back door of the house. He knocked briskly, then waited, casting uneasy glances back toward his house as the seconds dragged into minutes. He saw the woman in shiny black lean out of an upstairs window and point toward him; he moved away from the door and sought the protection of the shadows along the side of the house.

It was apparent that no one was home. The next house along had dogs in the yard and so Pommier tried the front door. He could hear the sound of news on the television, but no one answered his knock. Were they deaf? Did they want to be left alone? Pommier wanted to break their windows or force the lock on their door, anything to get out of range of those five from the black van.

He dared not linger. The next house had four children in it, and Pommier hesitated to go near it, recalling what had happened in his own house not so long ago. He could not endure the thought of bringing so much risk to the children, and so he went along to the house after.

This time a woman answered the door. "What is it?" she asked.

"Ah ... I'm Jean-Charles Pommier. I live up the street from you."

From her expression she did not believe a word of it. "Yeah?"

"I ... was repairing a window on the second floor," he improvised to account for how he must look. "I fell off the ladder and dropped my keys. Do you think I might telephone the police for assistance?"

The woman looked him over thoroughly and with a little disgust. "You can't come in."

"Then will you be kind enough to telephone them for me? I do ... want to get back into my house." He glanced uneasily up the street to see if the black van was in sight, and saw that it was coming slowly toward him. "Look, please ... call the police. It's ..."

"I don't know who you are, mister," the woman said unhappily, "but I don't want you hanging around here, okay?"

Pommier tried to think of a convincing argument to offer her, but none came to mind. "I would appreciate it if you would call the police. Ask for Captain Coglan. Tell him it's about the Gutterman . . ."

"Gutterman," the woman scoffed, and slammed the door.

It was a few seconds before Pommier could bring himself to move again. He knew he dared not take any more time trying to persuade residents of the neighborhood to call the police on his behalf, but he toyed briefly with the notion of causing a commotion that would result in the police arriving. The only trouble with that was that he was fairly certain now that the five would not allow him to get away with such a maneuver. He would have to find a way to fight them on his own. It was a frightening idea, one that he did not know if he could carry through.

He was moving again, staying on the street, trying to keep far enough ahead of the black van to have a chance to make a break from them when and if the chance presented itself. If only he knew why they pursued him so single-mindedly, then he might be able to come to terms with them. The thought was dismissed as soon as it became coherent. Whatever the five wanted, it had nothing to do with bargains or accommodations. They were determined to win, and nothing else mattered to them. But win what? His life? They might have killed him any time before now. His soul? Pommier would have been able to laugh at the idea a few days ago, but now he was not so sure. He prided himself on his rationality and intellectual pragmatism, but that had led him into his current danger, and offered him no solution. Was it his soul? What did they want with it? Why did they want it? He did not like the answers he considered.

He was less than two blocks from Ocean Avenue when he heard the van come snarling up behind him and he ran, stumbling, toward an alley to escape. The

darkness was tempting, as seductive as the lure of those
unexplored parts of the world. But this time he knew
that he must not permit the fascination to gain control
of him, because that way led back to Sister Bertril and
madness.

The black van followed after him, not coming fast
enough to run him down, but not giving him a chance
to lag. There was only the sound of the engine and the
tires; for once no persistent punk rock accompanied it.

Pommier found a narrow break through two buildings
and he took it, confident that though the van could go
around the end of the street, it could not follow him
through that narrow walkway, and that would give him
a little time, which he needed desperately. Once on
Ocean Avenue, he had only to walk down to Montana
or Santa Monica and find a phone booth. He would not
cross to the park, he would not get any nearer the
ocean, for he thought that the strength of the five was
greatest when they were near the beach. He hurried
across the street and ducked into the parking lot of a
large apartment building, which he knew went all the
way through to Ocean.

He was halfway across the parking lot, grateful for the
closely parked cars and the low level of light, when he
heard the black van come into the garage behind him,
driving at a reckless speed. Pommier stepped between
a shiny new BMW and a splendid old Jag XKE. Pommier
watched the van prowl up and down the aisles, tires
shrieking every time it turned. The BMW and the XKE
could hardly be part of the same horrid reality the van
and its passengers represented. When he thought he
was safe, he slipped across the aisle to a Scirocco and a
year-old Volvo. The black van tore down the aisle
toward him, and he knew he had been seen.

Caution was no longer as important as getting away
from the van. Pommier broke cover and ran for the
Ocean Avenue entrance.

The van could not leave the garage the way Pommier

did without shredding its tires on the toothed guard in the floor, and once again hid to reverse its direction. Pommier again welcomed the respite, but knew that it was fleeting. The van would stalk him inexorably until it reached him.

On the street again, Pommier kept deliberately to the east side of the road, away from the strip of grass and trees of the Palisades park. He had had enough of that place. But he could not resist an occasional uneasy glance in its direction.

Two kids on roller skates slipped down the walk in the park. Pommier watched them as he walked, wondering if they were the same teenagers as the ones who had run him down. Chris and what was her name? Cathy? Katy? Something like that. He welcomed this distraction, because it eased the apprehension that still threatened to paralyze him, leaving him at the mercy of the occupants of the black van.

Pommier had almost reached Montana when the black van came screeching around the corner, heading in his direction. Pommier continued to walk, doing his best to ignore the threat, because he was reasonably certain that the van would not come up on the sidewalk to reach him. As long as he did not step into the street—*any* street—he reckoned he was in as little danger as he would ever be. With that realization he reached the corner and hesitated, not willing to step off the curb.

The van made a U-turn farther up Ocean and came back, keeping abreast of Pommier, hovering on the opposite side of the street while Pommier tried to decide what was best to do.

A bus pulled up at the corner across the street, heading north up Ocean, bringing home the last of the evening commuters. More than a dozen people got off, and about half that number started to cross the street.

It was risky, Pommier knew that even as he did it, but there was nothing else he could bring himself to do.

As the commuters stepped into the intersection on the far side of the street, he began to cross from his.

He had reached little more than halfway when he saw that one of those he had mistaken for a commuter was the woman in shiny black. She passed Pommier and gave him a hard, wide smile.

Pommier froze, and lost precious seconds, so that he was once again alone on the street.

The black van came alive, whipping across six lanes of traffic, racing directly toward Pommier. Brakes squealed around it, and horns blasted the air; punk rock brayed out of the black van with new ferocity. Pommier stood his ground, not willing to retreat again. "Tuez-moi, tuez-moi," he taunted them. "If you can."

He fell back as the van grazed his side, striking just hard enough to send him flying. As he struggled to get to his feet, he was almost struck again by an oncoming Pontiac. He made a last, unthinking lunge at the curb and crawled onto it.

At the end of the block the black van pulled to the side of the street, hovering, waiting. Pommier could feel the vile weight of eyes on him, eyes that sought him as prey.

He knew he had been hurt, that if he did not have help fairly soon, he would be lost. It was ridiculous, he told himself as he struggled to get to his feet; he was in the middle of a large city, and he was being hunted as casually as a solitary wanderer in the jungle. He might have expected this kind of hazard out on expedition, but here? He was used to acting on his own, working without much assistance or support—his profession required it. But this—this was absurd. It was laughable. Except that he was getting killed.

As he attempted a few, faltering steps, the black van moved away from its parking place, turning around and coming slowly down the street.

This time Pommier made no pretense of ignoring it. He turned toward it, glaring at it. His voice was husky and when he tried to raise it, it became strident. "What are you doing this for? Why are you doing it? What have I done?" He did not expect an answer, but this time the silence of the five infuriated him. *"Je t'ai pose une question!"* he shouted, and almost fell.

A woman walking her dog started toward him, then gave a distressed motion and changed direction.

Pommier touched his face and looked at his hand. Even in the small amount of light from the street fixtures, he could see that there was more blood than he had thought smeared across his palm. He knew that his clothes were disheveled and torn. He was not surprised that no one stopped for him. He could hardly walk in a straight line, his speech was uneven, and he was doubtful if he could speak at all without slurring his words through his bruised lips.

He stumbled and fell, landing in a service driveway, out of the glare of the light. His scream was little more than a squeak, not enough to attract attention. He drew his knees up to his chest, feeling the damage that had been done with new misery. He did not want to move again. He wanted to lie in the shadows, let his mind drift away, forget the whole despicable mess. His eye was swelling, his legs ached, his ribs were agonizingly sore. The sensitivity of his abdomen warned him that he might have serious internal injuries. Let it go, he thought. Just forget it. C'est parfait ici. Ça suffit. For some time he lay, making no effort to move or protect himself.

Then a fear-filled cry brought his head up.

"Jeany! Jeany, aide-moi! Aide-moi!" Veronique screamed.

Pommier forced himself to rise, shaking his head. "Niki?" he said uncertainly. "What is ..."

Then he saw her across the street in the park. The Rastafarian held one of her arms, the woman in shiny black the other. The driver was reaching for her.

"NO!" Pommier shrieked. "No! No!" He could hear

their taunting laughter and the sound of tearing cloth. This enraged him even more than the terrified whimper he heard Veronique make. Moments before he thought nothing could bring him out of the mortal lethargy that had taken hold of him, but now he knew otherwise. He could not bring himself to lie back, even in his own congealing blood, while Veronique was being assaulted by such loathsome creatures as the five from the van.

"*Jeany!*" This time her cry was infinitely worse, filled with the loss of hope and capitulation of spirit that went through Pommier like acid.

He staggered across the street toward the figures in the park, his body consumed with pain, his heart urging him to be faster. As he reached the grass, he saw the five drag Veronique away, going down the swath of green to the south, toward the pier and the chaos of Venice beyond.

Desperately he followed them, seeing only enough of what they were doing to keep him moving, though he could tell in that distant, cool part of his mind that he was making his injuries much worse.

At the walkway over to the pier, the five lingered to permit Pommier to get close enough to see the shreds they had made of Veronique's clothes, and the first bruises they had put on her body. The man in the *Satan's Angels* jacket bowed deeply to Pommier before they once again dragged Veronique away; she had stopped screaming and was past sobbing. Hardly any sound came from her now but an occasional deep, shuddering moan as the abuse she suffered grew more unendurable.

On the pier, where the shops were shut up for the night, the five began a systematic battering of Veronique as Pommier shambled toward them. When he was near enough, the driver plunged a knife deep into her abdomen, standing back as the blood gushed out.

Pommier fell to his knees, reaching out for her. "Je vous en supplie," he grated. "Don't. Don't."

Casually the driver stepped back as Veronique fell, her open eyes turning upward in her livid face. At a signal from the woman in black, they picked up the body and tossed it over the side of the pier. Then, with quiet chuckles, the five turned and strolled off, down toward the boardwalk and the silent, sun-raddled buildings that fronted on it.

Pommier crawled to the edge of the pier and stared down, but it was too dark to see anything. He dragged himself upright and, using the railing to support him, he found the stairs that led downward. "Niki. Niki. Ma belle. Niki," he repeated as he felt himself weaken. He had to find her body. He could not bear to think that she would be washed out to sea. Unless he washed out with her. Either way, it only mattered now that they were together.

"Shh. Ça va, ça va bien, Jean-Charles. Va bien, Jean-Charles, Jeany." Veronique's voice was soothing, calming, no longer the soul-rending scream it had been.

Flax opened her eyes and looked up at Veronique. They were huddled together on the attic floor. The house was silent. "What . . . ?"

Veronique wiped Flax's hair off her brow. "You are back."

Flax nodded. "It was . . ."

"Was it what happened to Jean-Charles?" Veronique asked when Flax could not go on.

Flax nodded, turning away. The impressions were still raw in her mind and she did not think she could describe what she had seen without breaking down.

"Tell me," Veronique begged.

"Later," Flax said. "Not yet. I can't." She looked around, her attention coming to focus on the house. "Are they . . . ?"

"They're gone. They left sometime ago." She drew

her knees up to her chest and dropped her chin on them. "Do you think it's safe?"

"I'm not sure. They could be waiting." She thought of all the horrors she had seen those five perpetrate in the last two days. "Let's stay here awhile."

"As you wish," Veronique said. She remained still, looking at Flax from time to time, letting the minutes drag by. "It has been silent quite awhile."

"They don't talk, Niki. They could be waiting. They could be sitting under the folding stairs, waiting for us to come down."

"Ah."

Some little time later a door slammed and there was a scamper and thud of many feet outside the house. Engines came to life, tires shrieked, gears clashed. Gradually the noise faded.

"What do you think?" Veronique asked when the last mutter had faded and there was only the distant background hum of regular traffic.

"If we're going to do it, we'd better do it now," Flax said, taking a deep breath. "Let's open the trapdoor. Before I lose my nerve." This last was added with a failed attempt at a smile and laughter.

"What about lights?" Veronique asked. "It's late."

Neither of them had matches. "We'll just have to be very careful," Flax said, trying to dismiss their worries. "Does it look clear down there?"

Veronique peered through the slot where the stairs started to drop. "Nothing in the hall up here. It doesn't look damaged."

"Maybe they didn't bother much with this floor," Flax suggested as they lowered the ladder and began the precarious descent.

The second floor appeared to be mostly untouched. Files had been destroyed in the study and there were a few minor items missing from the bedroom, but otherwise the rooms were in reasonably good order.

"Maybe it won't be too bad," Veronique said, making the statement a question with her doubts.

The first sign of trouble was at the top of the stairway. It was now apparent why there had been so little damage to the upper floor—the stairs had been destroyed and there was a two-foor gap between the top of the stairs and the next tread.

"Oh, God," Flax whispered, remembering the cyclist with the chain.

"How do we get across?" Veronique asked, staring with no comprehension at the destruction before her.

"A chair, something that will reach across. Get the chair from the study," Flax said, making an effort to think.

They both went to get the chair, and then spent almost ten minutes trying to jockey it into position. In the end they lost control of it and it fell through into the closet with a crash that rocked the entire place.

Both women stood trembling, afraid of what the noise might bring.

"No one came," Veronique said with amazement in her tone.

"I guess they're really gone," Flax agreed.

"Well, then we must try to reach the end of the banister and... reach across," Veronique said, looking in dismay at the splintered stub of wood more than eighteen inches away. Ordinarily the distance would not frighten her, but now, with the closet gaping like a hungry mouth and nothing to reach for if she did not make the jump properly, she felt as if she would be trying to cross the Grand Canyon in a single stride.

"Take my hand," Flax said. "Then if anything happens, you can—"

"Merci," Veronique said, not letting Flax go on. "And I will help you."

In the front hall they found that all the lighting fixtures had been brought in and smashed in a tangled pile of brass and china and crystal and glass. Under it all were the remains of Veronique's overnight bag with human feces in it.

Nothing on the main floor remained unbroken or unmarked. The chairs were ripped, eviscerated, broken. The carpet had been pulled up and stained. Where the draperies had hung there were now broken windows and burned rags. Paint had been used on all the walls, showing crude and obscene drawings supplemented with a wide variety of profane and sexual slogans.

The dining room was worse—everything was destroyed and that destruction was so wanton that Veronique, who had been able to hold herself in check, began to weep steadily at what she saw. "I am sorry," she tried to say several times before she actually got the words out.

"Hush, hush," Flax said, putting her arm around Veronique's shoulder. "Come on. We must get out of here."

Flax's VW was still across the street, untouched. The two women moved toward it like survivors of a bombing in fear of fresh assaults. Flax found her key and opened the door. "I'll have to get gas . . ."

"I have some money," Veronique offered. "Jean-Charles gave me all we had. He thought we . . . might need it." She started to cry again, but mastered herself. As Flax let her into the passenger's seat, Veronique stared hard at her. "Tell me. You must tell me what you saw."

There had been enough time for Flax to prepare an answer for Veronique, for she deserved an answer, and one that she could live with. "They found something he was afraid of. The thing he was most afraid of." She looked out the window, afraid to meet Veronique's eyes. "He thought . . . they'd killed you."

"Oh, my dear God," Veronique whispered, and her dry eyes were immeasurably worse than tears would have been. "Jeany. Jeany."

Flax could think of nothing more to say. She started the bug and put it into gear, turning east, away from the ocean.

"Is it over?" Veronique asked when they had gone several miles in silence.

"Christ, I hope so," Flax answered, knowing it was no answer at all.

EPILOGUE

When sunrise came, Flax was sleeping on the back seat and Veronique was driving. She wakened Flax as the first rays touched the desert. "Look."

Flax sat up, bleary-eyed. "What time is it?"

"Dawn. Who cares what the clocks say." Veronique had lapsed into a curiously serene grief. "We will be in Nevada soon."

Flax took over driving. "I wish the old bug could go a little faster," she complained. "It'll get us there, but not as fast as I'd like."

"N'importe," Veronique responded. She pointed toward the horizon. "Can you see?"

"The sun?" Flax asked.

"No; trees." Veronique sighed. "I thought I was dreaming, but there are trees."

Flax stared and nodded as the distant outcropping became plainer to them. "Trees. Out here." She smiled a little. "I've missed trees."

Veronique was about to answer when the roar of a motorcycle engine deafened them both.

A big Harley came up beside them, then passed, holding to a position ahead of them by about fifty yards. The rider was dressed entirely in black leather, with a black helmet and visor on his head.

"Oh, no," Flax moaned. "Look."

There was nothing Veronique could say. She stared at the Harley, her hands gripping each other so tightly that her knuckles stood out white against her skin.

For the next five miles the motorcycle held his distance between them, serving as a terrifying outrider for the Volkswagen, a shadow that preceded them toward the rising sun.

"Maybe that's not the same one," Flax suggested in a voice a little above a whisper as they began to ascend a gentle rise.

"Of course not. Oh, non, c'est ridicu..." She pressed her hand to her mouth. "Je...I can't see him very well."

"It's the heat off the road," Flax said, trying to follow the Harley's progress without losing her concentration on the road.

"Yes. How stupid of me," Veronique murmured; she could not tear her gaze away from the black figure.

A mile went by, two, five; the Harley stayed with them, a patch of wavering darkness in the glare of morning.

"He'll turn off...somewhere," Flax faltered. "He's keeping...to the speed limit." It sounded more false to her own ears than to Veronique's.

"Yes. He's...cautious. The police must...watch the road in planes." She clung to that explanation though neither of them believed it. "Ah, qui? Pourquois?"

At the crest of the next rise, the Harley startled them both by swinging off the the side of the road and coming to a gravel-spraying halt. The rider stood, straddling the machine, watching the Volkswagen approach.

"Oh, God," Flax murmured.

"We will not slow down," Veronique vowed, her hands changing to fists in her lap.

Yet as they neared the cyclist, Flax let their speed drop; both women stared hard at the figure that waited like a smudge beside the road. At their approach, the cyclist removed his helmet and directed his cold-burning eyes at the women in loneliness and desperate hunger.

Veronique and Flax gazed back in appalled recognition at Jean-Charles Pommier.

Then he turned away from them, focusing on the

road again, as it stretched out across the desolation toward the west.

"*Jeany!*" Veronique screamed, grabbing toward the steering wheel. "Stop! We must stop! It is Jean-Charles! C'est..."

"No!" Flax insisted, struggling to keep control of the little automobile. "We can't stop. Let go, Niki! We have to go on!" Her whole body felt clammy; sweat stood in a cold sheen on her forehead.

"But it's Jeany! Jeany! Jeany!" Veronique protested wildly, her eyes so wet that she could not see the road.

Flax swallowed against the acrid taste at the back of her throat. "No," she insisted quietly, forcing herself not to look into her rear-view mirror. "No, Niki. Not anymore."

The bug swayed, wavered, then corrected and continued on toward Nevada as the cyclist in black leather once again started the Harley and began the long ride back to the place he belonged, where he could feed.

They stopped to sleep in Taos, thinking that they had put enough distance between them and the coast to afford to relax at last. In order to forget the worst of their ordeal, they spent part of the afternoon looking around the town, and it was Veronique who stumbled upon the photographic gallery.

One photograph caught her attention.

There on an outcropping of rock a single Hopi stood, the vast blank emptiness around him so stark that the hot wind seemed to come off the paper. The Hopi had been photographed at a distance, so that his isolation was almost complete.

And yet—there was something about him, an uneasiness that had little to do with his hunting. It appeared that the lone figure was—she studied the Hopi hunter intently—was *trespassing*.

A novel of terror from the bestselling author of
THE GOD PROJECT

NATHANIEL

by John Saul

Some thought him no more than legend, a folktale
created by the townsfolk of Prairie Bend to frighten
their children on cold winter nights. Others believed
him a restless spirit, returned to avenge the past.
But for eleven-year-old Michael Hall, Nathaniel is
the voice that calls him across the prairie night, the
voice that beckons him to follow . . . and do the
unthinkable.

NATHANIEL will be available July 1, 1984, wherever
Bantam Books are sold, or you may use the handy
coupon below for ordering.

Bantam Books, Inc., Dept. JS2, 414 East Golf Road,
Des Plaines, Ill. 60016

Please send me _____ copies of NATHANIEL (24172-9) at $3.95
each. I am enclosing $_____ (please add $1.25 to cover postage
and handling. Send check or money order only—no cash or
C.O.D.'s please).

Mr/Ms _____

Address_____

City/State _____ Zip _____

JS2—5/84

Please allow four to six weeks for delivery. This offer expires 11/84.
Price and availability subject to change without notice.